Samoan Clipper

A Nick Grant Adventure
By Jamie Dodson

Samoan Clipper
A Nick Grant Adventure
by Jamie Dodson

Contents

To the Reader:

I have based my novel around the true story of American efforts to link its Pacific outposts with a dedicated air service. Decades before the space race, the United States was in a contest with Imperial Japan to control the Pacific. As the world edged closer to World War Two, Pan American Airlines was expanding service across the Pacific with flying boats. Seen as an encroachment, Japan decided to take direct covert action to insure its failure. It was a time of intrigue and adventure.

As the *Samoan Clipper* flying boat surveyed routes to American's closest Pacific Allies, Australia and New Zealand, Japan attempted to disrupt and sabotage the effort. Aircraft of the day did not have the "legs" of modern jets and needed re-fueling stations along the route. Japan's effort focused on denying island refueling stops. One of the main efforts was in American Samoa – where I've set the majority of Nick's adventures.

I have had the opportunity to visit American Samoa four times over the years. I found the people and culture amazing. I encourage those who love to travel to hop a flight and explore this utterly amazing tropical island. Among other things, American Samoa hosts the southernmost US National Park.

Dedication:

Many people helped me write *Samoan Clipper,* the fifth in the Nick Grant Adventure Series. Some sweated through multiple iterations of the manual script, others provided invaluable technical and historical information. Family and close friends provided encouragement. In particular, I'd like to thank:

- Members of the Southside Scribblers Writer's Critique Group, Huntsville, Alabama. Over many iterations they provided great feedback and tough criticism.

- Members of the Coffee Tree Fiction Writers Group. Their support and enthusiasm kept me writing in my darkest hours.

- Pan Am Historical Foundation (www.panam.org) for the use of many of their photos, graphics, and historical files.

- Ron Cole of www. roncole.net for the wonderful aviation art that graces the cover. Ron has faithfully reproduced all of the Pan American flying clippers from Trimotor to Boeing 747.

- The late aviation artist Ian Marshall for use of his wonderful watercolors from *Flying Boats, the J Class Yachts of Aviation.* His artwork graces several chapter headers.

- Roger Pugliese of Black Sheep Entertainment. Thanks for all the Hollywood introductions. We'll make a movie yet!

- Homer Hickam, Walter Boyd, Michael Dobson, Ralph Peters, Annie Laura Smith, Rev. Evan G. Butterbrodt, C. M. Fleming, and the many other authors who took time out of their busy schedules to read and comment on my work.

- Finally, to my family near and far for their endless enthusiasm and tireless efforts to help prepare Nick's latest adventure.

And now I hope you enjoy *SAMOAN CLIPPER, A Nick Grant Adventure*, Book Five.

Prologue

Early Morning, November 16th, 1936
Toshio Miyazaki Residence
Yokohama, Japan

Commander Toshio Miyazaki dipped the sponge into the steaming water, raised it to his forehead and squeezed. The scalding water cascaded over his face and neck adding to the dense cloud of steam rising from his garden bath. Miyazaki rested his arms on the bath's cedar planks and gazed up into the cloudless night sky. The luxury was something few possessed. After his latest success, his commanding officer had provided the funds to build this magnificent garden bath. It was big enough for a family of four, but Miyazaki never quite found the time to pursue a wife, let alone a family. One day perhaps that might come. Nevertheless, only after his time with the Black Dragons.

As instructed by Imperial Naval Intelligence, Miyazaki had delivered the stolen blueprints for the H-1, Howard Hughes' advanced racing airplane. The schematics would save Japan years of research and development time, not to mention expense. Miyazaki's recent efforts would make the Emperor's air forces superior to those of the Americans and the British. Miyazaki had also managed to steal a metal strut at the Hughes' California factory. Even now Japanese metallurgists were analyzing the strut. The metal was strong, flexible, and incredibly light.

Still, for all his success, Miyazaki felt deep disappointment and bitterness. They had been so close, so very close, to loading the actual H-1 onto a ship headed for Yokohama. That was before Nick Grant's plane appeared out of nowhere.

Miyazaki's men promptly shot the plane down, but Grant and his accomplices survived and made it to the island. Despite Miyazaki's efforts, Grant destroyed the H-1 before he could load it aboard a ship headed for Yokohama. Incensed, Miyazaki gave chase with armed sailors. They finally cornered Grant's saboteurs against a cliff face. "Grant!" Miyazaki had screamed. "Now you will pay."

Then suddenly four mounted cowboys opened fire from atop the cliff. Miyazaki had fallen into a clever trap. He watched aghast as the withering fire cut down his men. "Back!" he yelled. "Get back to the ship!" The survivors retreated, dragging the dead and wounded with them. They had lost many Black Dragons and sailors to Grant that day.

As his ship departed for Japan, the smoldering wreck of the H-1 continued to burn on the beach. Defeated, Miyazaki stood on the fantail, seething, and scanned the beach. In the day's last light, he saw Grant standing on the beach with a *katana* held high over his head, taunting him. Miyazaki was sure it was his family katana. The one Grant had taken off his lifeless body after their last encounter.

Blind rage surged through him and set his soul on fire. Miyazaki leapt up from the hot tub and screamed into the star-studded night sky. "You will pay someday, Nick Grant! You will pay!"

Chapter One

9:15 a.m., Saturday November 14th, 1936
Alameda Airport,
Alameda, California

    Leilani Porta leaned out of the open cockpit and met the mechanic's eyes. She yelled, "Contact!"

    Dressed in greasy coveralls, Tony Devlin replied, "Contact!" Then Tony pulled the propeller down with all his might and stepped back sharply. The engine responded with a loud bang and caught as a dense cloud of oil-infused exhaust engulfed the ancient biplane.

    Nick Grant, seated in the rear of the Curtis JD-4 *'Jenny'* cockpit, coughed, and tried to wave the noxious smoke away from his face. The engine backfired once more but soon picked up speed. As it did, the prop blast cleared the air sufficiently that Nick could once again see. He tapped Leilani on the shoulder and yelled, "Ready?"

    Leilani looked back, her long brown hair hidden by a leather flying cap. She tugged her goggles down over her eyes, rendering her all but unrecognizable. She smiled, flashed a thumbs-up, and tucked the loose end of a white silk scarf into her leather jacket.

    Tony moved warily around the whirling prop as the engine smoothed out and picked up more speed. He pulled the wheel chocks free and held them up. Leilani nodded her thanks and advanced the throttle. The ancient trainer, a Great War relic, lurched forward.

The sudden move slammed Nick's head into the once padded head rest. "Ouch!"

Leilani looked back and yelled over the engine's roar, "Did you say something?"

"Easy on the throttle."

Leilani said, "What?"

"Never mind," Nick shouted, sending another spasm of pain through his skull. Leilani waived and returned to the task of taxiing the biplane out to the end of the runway. Nick checked his instrument panel and noted with satisfaction that the engine temperature gauge was slowly rising into the optimum range. Most aviators considered the OX-5 engine to be unreliable, but his old boss, Mac, had rebuilt the V-8 and it had proved more reliable than most. Mac bought the war surplus Jenny for $20 fifteen years ago. And it still flew – most days.

At the end of the grass strip, Leilani turned the Jenny around and did an engine run-up. Nick watched his instruments and listened closely for any tell-tail sound of trouble. So far, the engine seemed to be behaving. He skimmed his instruments one last time and looked up to see Leilani looking at him.

She yelled. "Are you ready?"

Nick flashed a thumbs-up. She smiled, turned back, and advanced the throttle to wide open. The Jenny slowly picked up speed as it bumped down the rutted dirt runway. The control stick between Nick's legs moved gently back and forth as Leilani felt for life in the controls. As the tail wheel lifted, Nick felt his own rudder pedals move as Leilani worked her pedals to compensate for the engine's torque. They hit a deep rut, bounced up into the air and stayed there. Slowly the Jenny climbed into the clear skies over the San Francisco Bay. It was a beautiful day for flying with an aviatrix and Leilani was one beautiful aviatrix.

At 500 feet AGL – or above ground level, Leilani executed a coordinated turn, banking the biplane back towards land and continuing the climb to the agreed 2,000 feet AGL. They never flew this old crate out over the bay. If the engine quit, they would have to swim home. Nick was not up for another ocean ditching for a long, long time, if ever.

As the Jenny continued its slow climb, Leilani lined up with the Southern Pacific Railroad tracks heading south towards San Jose. Nick had taught her to fly IFR and it was handy when flying between

10

cities. When Nick first mentioned the technique, Leilani had asked, "What does IFR stand for?"

Nick replied, "It means I follow railroads – IFR. It's hard to get lost as long as the weather cooperates."

Leilani's reaction was swift. She punched Nick on the shoulder. "Nick Grant that is the stupidest thing I've heard you say. You're pulling my leg. Isn't that why we have a compass?"

"Well, yes," Nick conceded. "A compass is essential, but the railroad tracks are a lot more reliable than a 20-year-old compass."

So far, the check ride was going great. After they landed, he would sign off on Leilani's pilot's log and her next flight would be her first solo. He turned his attention to the instruments and noticed that the altimeter needle moved up and down, indicating about a 100-foot oscillation. He watched for a few moments, then tapped the glass to confirm that the instrument wasn't acting up. Concerned, he looked at Leilani.

She was hunched over, staring at the instruments. Not good. A pilot had to maintain situational awareness. He tapped her on the shoulder and motioned to ease back on the throttle, so they could talk. Once the engine was at idle the Jenny started to slowly lose altitude. Nick began. "You need to scan the instruments, but most of the time you should be looking outside the cockpit. We've discussed this before."

"How am I supposed to keep my altitude looking outside the cockpit?"

"Staring at the altimeter isn't helping. We call that chasing the needle. Find a spot on the horizon and use it to judge your altitude. That way you can also make sure your heading isn't drifting. More importantly, you are less likely to run into something — like another airplane."

"Okay, I'll try that." She advanced the throttle, increasing power, and they started to climb back to 2,000 feet AGL.

Leilani fixed her gaze on the horizon and the oscillation eased considerably. Nick relaxed and took in the view. To the west the bay stretched out below. He could see Mills Airfield across the bay and –

BANG!

The Jenny shook violently as oil started to spew from the engine, coating first Leilani then Nick. He grabbed his scarf and wiped the oil from his goggles. "Leilani, kill the power!"

She cut the ignition and pulled the throttle all the way back. With another bang and a shudder, the engine screeched with a very loud metal-on-metal sound. It was tearing itself apart. Then it seized. It stopped so violently that half of one of the wooden props sheared off and dropped from sight. Suddenly, it was very silent, and the only sound was the wind singing in the guy wires. Somewhere below they heard a train whistle.

Nick grabbed the control stick. "Give me the aircraft!"

"No, I got this!"

"Leilani, this is not the time to argue. I've got the experience and the best chance of getting us back on the ground in one piece."

"Nick, a student pilot must demonstrate an engine-out landing. No time like the present."

"Sure, but in training the engine is at idle. If you run into trouble, we throttle up the engine and go around. There's no going around this time."

"I can do this Nick. Let me try."

Nick knew he should insist and forcibly take control, if necessary. But this was his girl. Besides, she'd shown a flair for flying since her first lesson. "Okay, you can take it until final. Then I'm taking it back. Deal?"

"Maybe ..."

"No! Leilani, not maybe. Agree or give me back control right now."

"Okay – okay, already."

While they discussed control, Leilani turned around and headed back towards Alameda Airport. Nick pulled out a map and studied it. "We're losing altitude too fast – we'll never make it back. The Jenny glides well but it's just too far. We've got to head for Oakland Airport, just past Oakland Street."

Leilani nodded as they continued to sink. "I see it!"

Nick leaned over and looked between the wings. The engine still threw off a lot of black smoke but at least the oil had stopped gushing out and there was no fire. Ahead he saw the broad flat field that served as Oakland Airport. To the west of the terminal, and four large hangers, two clearly marked runways crossed in the middle. He glanced at his altimeter, 450 feet. It was going to be close. They might wind up in the salt marsh that bordered the southern end of Oakland Airport. Well, at least the saltwater would squelch any post-crash fire. *I hate crashing.*

"Leilani, head for the runway on the right. Line up and let me have it."

Trailing smoke, they crossed above the salt marsh at less than 200 feet.

Leilani silently lined up.

150 feet.

"Okay, Leilani, good job, now let me have it."

Silence.

Nick glanced over the side. He could see individual sea gulls flapping in the marsh. Then he picked out discarded tires and other trash. He didn't need the altimeter to judge this height. They were low. Somewhere ahead a siren came to life. Nick followed the sound to see a bright red fire truck pull away from the airport fire station.

Nick grabbed the stick and tried to waggle it side-to-side in the universal sign to cede control. The stick would not move. Leilani had a death grip on the control and refused to yield. His choice was clear, and he didn't like it one bit. He could try to overpower her or let her land. He decided on the latter. A fight for control now could land them in the salt marsh or worse.

They passed over Oakland Avenue. Nick looked down to see their wheels barely clear the airport fence. Leilani held the glide until the wheels touched down. Then she released the controls and slumped back.

Nick grabbed the stick and used the rudder pedals to guide the rapidly decelerating Jenny toward the terminal building. They came to a stop about 100 feet away just as the fire truck arrived. Firemen leapt off and ran towards them with axes and portable fire extinguishers in hand. On top of the truck, another fireman was furiously pumping a red handle. He stopped, pointed a bronze nozzle at the Jenny, and fired. Copious amounts of a slimy white foam coated the biplane, Leilani, and Nick. They unstrapped, jumped down and ran toward the fire truck.

When they were a safe distance away, they turned to see that the fireman had buried the Jenny under what looked like a mountain of foam.

Nick frowned. "Tony's not going to like that." He glanced at the Jenny, then Leilani, and chuckled. "You are covered from head to toe in foam." He cocked an eyebrow "You look like you just walked in from a snowstorm."

She took a step toward him and swiped her hand across his forehead. She held up her foam-covered hand. "And you look like

13

someone kicked you out into one." She giggled and threw herself into his arms.

He hugged her back. "Nice landing. But don't you ever do that again."

She looked up, her green eyes twinkling with mischief. "Whatever are you talking about?"

"You know darn well. Why didn't you give me the landing?"

"You never asked."

"What? I know you heard me. Besides, what about the stick wobble?"

"Oh, was that you? I thought it was turbulence."

"Leilani!"

She reached up and kissed him on the lips. "God, that stuff tastes horrible. So, do I get credit for a dead stick landing?"

"Leilani!"

Nick was about to give her a piece of his mind when two firemen trotted up, one carrying a fire extinguisher the other an axe. Axe man asked, "You two hurt?"

Nick looked over Leilani's shoulder and sighed. "No, thank goodness." He gently pushed Leilani away but held onto her arms. "We could have been hurt or worse. You're good, but you must follow the instructor's instructions – *my* instructions."

Leilani pulled free of Nick's grasp. "You don't own me, Nick Grant."

"Your right, I don't. But if you can't listen to me – to follow my instructions while in the cockpit – you'll have to find someone else to teach you how to fly."

"Okay, okay already." She hugged Nick and looked up at him. "I'll be good if you sign off on my logbook?"

"No, Leilani. Once Tony cleans up the Jenny, we'll go up again and, if you listen, you can shoot a few dead stick landings. Then and only then will I sign off on your dead stick."

She turned her back on Nick and kicked the dirt a few times. "Humph."

Nick folded his arms. "So, do we have a deal?"

Leilani turned back and glared at Nick. "Deal."

Chapter Two

6:15p.m., Saturday Evening, November 15th, 1936
Grant Home,
Alameda California,

Nick finished knotting the tie and checked his handiwork in the bathroom mirror. Satisfied, he walked into the kitchen. "Hmm, something sure smells good."

Dora Morris turned from the stove and wiped her hands on her apron. She was a tall woman of about sixty, with white hair worn in a bun. "Oh hello, Nick, I didn't hear you come in. I take it you're hungry, lad?"

Nick loved her West Country accent. It reminded him of his parents'. As it happened, Mrs. Morris was from the same English county as his mother. The thought made him realize how much he missed his mum. The family was still down in Rio and would be for the foreseeable future. At least until Pan American found another station manager for Rio. His growling stomach brought his mind back to the kitchen. His stomach had been loud enough that Mrs. Morris heard from ten feet away. "I thought so. Sit down at the kitchen table and I'll serve you. It's shepherd's pie – your favorite."

"Tempting, Mrs. Morris, but I've got a dinner date."

Mrs. Morris raised her eyebrows. "Oh, so my food isn't good enough for you?" She took a pie from the oven and set it on the open windowsill to cool.

"Mrs. Morris, you know better. I love your food – it's just like my mother's. I want to spend some alone time with Leilani, that's all." Nick glanced at the windowsill. "Say, is that gooseberry pie I smell?"

"It might be but it's only for the dinner crowd."

"Will you save me a piece?"

"Shame, Nick," she said with a hint of a smile, "Doubt there will be any left. You know how much the aircrews love my pies…"

The kitchen door opened, and Walter Morris walked in from the garden holding two cabbages. "Here you go, love."

Mrs. Morris took the proffered vegetables and tried to turn away, but Mr. Morris had other ideas. He swept his wife up in his arms. "Oh, you lovely lass, come dancing with me this very night. We'll win first prize."

"Oh, go on — you old goat. Don't be daft. That's for the young, like Nick and Leilani." She kissed his cheek, deftly disentangled herself, and popped one cabbage into a large pot of boiling water.

Mr. Morris noticed Nick and looked him up and down with a keen eye. "Well, don't you look spiffy? You're off for dinner and dancing with Leilani, I'd wager."

Before Nick could answer, Mrs. Morris reached over and smoothed out a non-existent wrinkle on Nick's suit coat. "You look so handsome. Leilani won't be able to keep her hands off of you."

Mr. Morris crossed his arms and tried to look indignant. "Mrs. Morris, where is your sense of propriety? Leilani is a respectable girl." He turned to Nick and winked. "So, Nick, when are you going to bring that lovely young lady over again? I demand a rematch."

Nick shook his head, "I don't know, Mr. Morris, that girl is one heck of a chess player."

Mrs. Morris said, "Off you go, young man. You don't want to keep the young lady waiting. She's pretty and she'll be batting off all the boys."

As the screen door slammed behind Nick, he heard Mrs. Morris say. "They are such a sweet couple."

Mr. Morris replied. "They are, love. But they are so young and have many trials ahead."

"So true. I hope that they can stick together. Leilani is a firebrand, but if anyone can handle her, it's Nick."

*   *   *

6:51p.m., Saturday November 15th, 1936
University of California, Berkeley, California
College Hall Woman's Dormitory,

      Leilani Porta slipped on her overcoat and joined the other girls as they made their way downstairs toward the street door. On the landing, she saw Mrs. Malice standing next to the exit, inspecting the girls as they headed out for their dates. A short stocky spinster in her late fifties, Malice and Leilani had never quite seen eye-to-eye. Leilani braced herself for the coming confrontation.

      "Remember girls, I lock the door at 10:00 and you must be in by then. Don't expect me to get out of bed to let in late girls. If you're late, you can sleep on the porch for all I care."

      Several of the girls chorused, "Yes, Mrs. Malice," as they filed out the door.

      Leilani nodded and almost made it past the old battle axe when she heard, "Leilani, please step aside."

      Leilani's shoulders slumped at the prospect of another tongue lashing. "Yes, Mrs. Malice."

      When the other girls had left, Malice turned to face Leilani. "Where do you think you're going dressed like that?"

      Puzzled, Leilani gazed down at her modest blouse, below-the-knee skirt, and saddle shoes. "What?"

      Mrs. Malice tossed her head in an overly dramatic move. "Well, I never! You are going out on a date with a young man and you are not wearing hose. And, young lady, your skirt is way too short. I don't know what passes for propriety with you *natives* on that island of yours, but it won't work here at Berkeley."

      Leilani paused and gathered her thoughts. She had no desire to raise the house mother's ire again, but she had had enough of the woman's racist rants. "Mrs. Malice, there are no natives on Oahu. There are locals of many races including members of the Hawaiian race. They are all American citizens who, like you, pay taxes, vote, and worship in the manner of their choosing. Most Hawaiians would be deeply offended being referred to as 'natives.'"

      Mrs. Malice drew back and placed a hand on the top of her substantial bosom as a look of shock washed across her reddening

17

face. "How dare you speak to me in that manor. You go upstairs this instant and put-on hose or you're not leaving."

Leilani steamed. This was not the first time this horrible woman had picked on her. "Other girls wear skirts and dresses shorter than mine. Besides, I don't need hose. I'm sure you've noticed that my legs are naturally the color of hose."

Sputtering with anger, Mrs. Malice replied, "Going out without hose is undignified and un-lady-like. Your date will see your bare legs."

"Oh, don't worry about that, Nick has seen a lot more of me — in my bathing suit. I hate garters and nylon hose. They are uncomfortable and ridiculous – clearly some man invented those hateful things."

Mrs. Malice's eyes hardened. "I'd expect nothing less from a half-breed!"

Leilani took a step forward, glared down at the hateful woman and whispered, "Listen you prejudiced old bat. If you ever call me half-breed again, I will strip you naked and toss your butt out on the street. My mother is of royal Hawaiian blood and my father is from a distinguished Portuguese family. What's more, I'm a human being even if I'm only a *half-breed* in your eyes."

Mrs. Malice looked at Leilani as expressions of shock and fear fought to dominate her pasty white face. Malice drew back to slap Leilani. But Leilani was faster. She caught the woman's wrist mid-strike and twisted – just as Nancy Tanaka had taught her.

Malice howled, "Ow, let go of me!"

Leilani dropped the hand. "Now get out of my way. I've got a date."

The stunned Mrs. Malice stepped aside rubbing her hand. "We'll just see about this. Hawaiian princess, indeed – you're just an uncouth mulatto unfit for polite white society."

Leilani tensed at the insult. No one had ever called her such a hateful name. She considered punching Malice before her martial arts discipline took over. She exhaled to calm herself and pushed through the door. However, her anger still got the best of her. She slammed the doors so hard the glass panel shattered. Great, she thought, one more charge for the old bat to use against her.

Outside, Nick was leaning on the hood of his battered pickup truck. When he heard the crash, he jumped up and walked to meet her. "What's up, beautiful? You looked rattled." He gazed at the dorm entrance. "What happened to the door?"

Ignoring his question, she wrapped her arms around him, and hugged hard. He hugged her back. She looked up at him, tears streaming down her cheeks. "Do you have a spare bedroom at your house?"

"What? Yes. Leilani, what's going on?"

"I think I'm about to be kicked out of my dorm."

"Oh, no." Nick glanced at the porch covered with shattered glass. "For the door?"

She laid her head on his chest. "No, well yes, oh I don't know." She tugged Nick's arm. "Come on, let's go. I need to blow off some steam at the Dojo. Then I'll tell you — maybe."

Nick scratched his head, "Okay, doll. Whatever you say."

Chapter Three

0945 hours, Monday, 17 November 1936
Naval Intelligence Headquarters
Yokohama, Japan

Miyazaki watched as the aid rapped on the admiral's office door. He heard the admiral bark. "Enter."

The admiral's aide-de-camp opened the door and bowed deeply. "Admiral, your ten-hundred hours appointment has arrived."

"Show him in, Nagasaki."

The aid bowed and stepped back. Commander Miyazaki entered, bowed, stood to attention, and snapped out a crisp salute. "Commander Miyazaki reporting as ordered, Admiral."

The Admiral smiled. "Toshio, come in." He motioned Miyazaki to a chair in front of his desk. "Nagasaki, bring tea and close the door."

Nagasaki bowed and left.

The admiral removed his glasses and looked at Miyazaki. "You are well?"

"Yes, Admiral."

"It is good to see you in such fine health. Your latest mission was a remarkable success."

Miyazaki started to speak but the admiral held up a hand. "Toshio, you do not need to say a word. You accomplished the mission you were given. We have the H-1's technical specifications, and the metal you brought back is yielding its secret as we speak."

"But the H-1, Admiral — "

"Enough!" The admiral sighed, "Toshio, take a seat." He picked up a pack of Lucky Strikes and offered the pack to Miyazaki.

Miyazaki shook his head, "I cannot, my master. It ruins my wind. I must remain swift if we are to best the Americans."

The admiral took one from the pack, lit it, and took a long drag. He exhaled, blew the smoke at the ceiling, and looked at the burning end. "You are right, of course. But I no longer need to be swift. The only exercise I get these days is climbing the stairs to my office. It was different when your father and I were young. We could run like the wind."

"Quite so, Admiral."

"However, I digress. I have had some interesting news from our California agents."

Miyazaki raised his eyebrows. "What is it, Admiral?"

"It seems that the Americans are not satisfied with their Trans-Pacific *China Clipper* route. They insist on pushing another air route into our area of interest. Pan American Airways is exploring a new route to link Australia, New Zealand, and the South Pacific."

Miyazaki sat impassive. "I am surprised that the British will allow them landing rights."

"The British refused Australian landing rights, but Pan American Airways convince — New Zealand to accept mail and passenger service. But the New Zealanders have stipulated that service must begin by the end of the year — or the deal is off."

Miyazaki nodded. "The Pan American plan could hamper our plans for the Greater East-Asian Co-Prosperity Sphere. We must have access to Australia's and New Zealand's resources to succeed."

"Exactly right, Toshio. Australia for iron ore, magnesium and other key elements — including uranium, and New Zealand for their abundant harvests."

"Admiral, none of the Pan American Clippers have sufficient range to reach New Zealand from Hawaii. They must secure refueling stations as they did for the *China Clipper* route."

"Just so, and that is where you come in." The admiral picked up his desk phone. "Nagasaki, show our guest in."

The door opened, the aide bowed, and then stepped aside. Miyazaki stood but the Admiral remained seated. A short squat man of about thirty walked in. He wore a suit coat and tie, but instead of trousers, he wore a flower print cloth that wrapped around his waist and fell below his knees. He wore what Miyazaki would call *zories* – open-toed sandals – where any sane individual wore shoes against the snow. He stopped in front of the admiral's desk and looked over to Miyazaki. They both stared at each other like two male dogs sizing each other up before the fight.

The admiral switched to English. "Commander Miyazaki, may I introduce Mr. Ta'isi Olaf Johnson. Mr. Johnson, this is Commander Miyazaki."

Warily they eyed each other then, reluctantly, reached over and shook hands.

The admiral gestured to the chairs in front of his desk. "Sit down, both of you."

They sat but still eyed each other warily. To Miyazaki, Johnson looked like a very short Viking with a deep tan. His face was the color of mahogany, but his eyes were green, and his hair was a white blond. His muscles pulled the coat material tight across his chest and arms. From Miyazaki's vantage point, he could see that the arms were as thick as trees. Johnson could be a worthy opponent.

The admiral turned to Johnson. "Please relay to the Commander what you told me earlier."

Johnson began. "The US Navy has given Pan American Airways permission to refuel at Kingman Reef and the Pago Pago Naval Station for the New Zealand route extension."

Miyazaki spoke. "Where exactly is Pago Pago?"

Johnson frowned, as if the answer was obvious. "It is what you Japanese call American Samoa. Pago Pago Bay is suitable for flying boat operations but only just. The approach from the west makes sense. The wind blows from the southeast — and there is a thousand-foot ridge to clear in the west and north. But it is not Pioa, which is east of the harbor and higher still. Some now call it the Rain Maker. The pilot must clear the peak and then dive into a steep valley that many cables crisscross. At the bottom of the valley the pilot must pull up sharply and splash down extremely close to the shore. If not, the flying boat will end up on the reefs at the bay entrance and be destroyed."

The admiral added, "Our navy flew a new Kawanishi H6K flying boat into the bay and the pilot reported that it was unsuited for flying boat operations."

Miyazaki frowned. "I am surprised the Americans allowed us access. I mean, they know we stole their Sikorsky S-42 plans, and the H6K is a close copy."

The admiral replied, "Our pilot declared an emergency and the Americans relented. However, two armed sailors appeared at the H6K when it docked with three engines turning. No one could deplane from the flying boat. Once it appeared that we had finished repairs, the Americans insisted the H6K depart."

Johnson continued in his accented English. "Take off is also difficult. Again, those entrance reefs pose a significant risk to a flying boat and crew."

Miyazaki sat back and smiled. "I think I see the admiral's plan. We sabotage the survey clipper and Pan American cancels the project. Then the air route would not prove troublesome to our plans. So, tell me Mr. Johnson, what is in it for you?"

"I am a member of the Mau Resistance Movement. We want independence from the world's imperial powers. First it was the Germans, then after the Great War, the British and Americans split Samoa. The Brits administer Western Samoa and the Americans Eastern Samoa. Neither power allows anyone with a drop of Samoan blood to belong to the government or have a say in its affairs."

The admiral nodded. "We have given assurances to Mr. Johnson that Japan has no territorial ambition in Samoa. We ask only for landing and port facility access."

Miyazaki smiled. "Then, Mr. Johnson, pray tell how we can mutually assist each other."

There was a knock and the admiral called out, "Enter."

The aide entered with a traditional tea service and placed it on a side table. He filled three earthenware cups and offered one to each.

As the admiral stood, Miyazaki and Johnson leapt to their feet. The admiral raised his cup. "Gentlemen, let us toast to success of our mission and that the Samoan people gain their independence."

They raised their cups and said, "Hai!"

Johnson offered the next toast. "May the Americans go down in flames."

They raised their cups again and yelled, "Hai!"

As the hot tea burned down Miyazaki's throat, it warmed his whole body. He raised his cup. "I propose a follow-on toast. May Nick Grant *also* go down in flames."

"Hai!" they chorused and drained the remaining tea from their cups.

Chapter Four

Pre-dawn, November 18th, 1936
Christie Ranch, Santa Cruz Island,
Channel Islands, California

Ring... Ring... Ring!
Brian O'Malley rolled over in his sleep. *What was that noise?*
It sounded like a rodeo starting bell gone mad.
Ring... Ring... Ring!
He opened his eyes and surveyed the dark bunk house.
Nobody moved. "Shorty! Answer the dang phone."
Ring... Ring... Ring!
Shorty pulled his pillow up to cover his ears. "You get it.
You was the one who had to have it."
"Shorty, it's a foot from your head."
"Nope. Darn thing rings all the time. Must have rung three
times last month." With that, Shorty pulled the pillow over his head
and rolled towards the wall.
"Dang nab it!" Brian slid his feet into his slippers and
stepped out onto the cold stone floor. The phone continued its
insistent ringing. "All right, all right. I'm coming." He picked up the
handset, leaned in and spoke into the wall-mounted speaker.
"Christie Ranch, O'Malley speaking."
"Hello, Brian. Did I wake you?"

"Oh hello, Mister Hughes. No, sir. Well, maybe a few minutes early, but we was fixing to git up at five anyway. What can I do for you?"

"Got you in mind for a job. Tell me, you ever been on a ship?"

Brian scratched his head and thought a moment. "Unless you count that cattle barge from the mainland — no. Why do you ask?"

"The US Government has asked me to head up a project on a US territory that involves cattle. You think you and the boys might be up for that?"

Brian nodded. "Anything, Mr. Hughes. Me and the boys owe you. Why, wasn't for you and Nick, we'd be punching cows somewhere far off. Like Argentina, where they don't speak no English."

Hughes chuckled. "Well, you better hear the details before you commit. But there is some good news."

"What's that, Mr. Hughes?"

"They speak English where I want to send you."

*   *   *

Noon, November 28th, 1936
Aboard the S.S. Aladdin, Birth 23, Long Beach Harbor
Long Beach, California

Brian eased Sarge into the horse stall below the foredeck. "Come on, Sarge. It ain't so bad. At least you're off that swinging harness."

The good-natured horse had been through a lot with Brian. However, hoisting him up from the dock, out over the harbor and then down into the hold had left Sarge wide-eyed with fear. Brian felt a vibration travel up his cowboy boots and resonate in his teeth. The ship rocked gently and then listed slightly. They were underway. Sarge turned his head and looked accusingly at Brian.

"What? You silly old horse." He took a carrot out of his vest pocket and held it up to Sarge. The horse sniffed the offering, looked at Brian again, and then snatched the carrot. Brian gently pushed the horse's rump until he could close the stall gate. Sarge put his head into the feed trough and started to munch. "Good boy. I'll be back directly."

He checked to see that the other horses were secure and then climbed the ladder to the deck. As the *Aladdin* picked up speed, the

26

breeze across the foredeck increased. After the stuffy hold, it was good to be in the open air. He moved to the right — *the Starboard side*, he reminded himself — and walked past the ship's bridge, towering 30 feet above. As he reached the back – *or stern*– he spied three cowboys leaning over the rail, watching as the steamer eased out of Long Beach Harbor. It occurred to him that Shorty Mack, Buck Thomas and Leslie Pearl must look crazy out of place among all the sailors and the few other passengers. Come to think of it *he* felt crazy out of place. "Howdy, boys. You doing alright?"

Shorty pushed his sweat stained Stetson back on his head. "I still don't understand why a movie mogul and famous aviator would get mixed up with a bunch of dairy cows and breeding bulls. And why on Earth would any sane man want to start a dairy ranch in Samoa?" He spit tobacco juice over the rail. "And where on God's green Earth is Samoa anyway?"

Brian leaned on the rail. "Does sound pretty nuts, but here's the thing. We wouldn't have no job a'tol if it weren't for Nick Grant and Mr. Hughes. Then there's the pay to consider."

Leslie flicked his cigarette butt into the ocean. "Shorty, I don't care how crazy it is. The man is paying us almost five years' wages, plus room and board, for what amounts to less than a year's work."

Buck said. "Maybe. Who knows how long it's gonna take to train up those natives to be real cowboys?"

Brian shook his head. At 19 he still felt a little odd as foreman of the men much older than him. But that's the way Hughes wanted it when he bought the Christie Ranch last summer. "Now Buck, you heard Mr. Hughes. We're not supposed to call them boys natives. They's American citizens just like us. We call 'em 'locals' or use their names. But never natives."

The ship's horn blasted unexpectedly, startling the four cowboys. Brian laughed. "We'd better get used to that and lots more things for the foreseeable future."

Leslie looked up at the ship's funnel and shook his head. "Twenty-two days on this rust bucket feeding cattle and horses and mucking out their stalls. Charming."

Shorty snorted, "Charming? Nothing about being a cowpoke is charming. I can tell you've been hanging around your mother again."

Leslie tensed, "Leave it, Shorty."

Shorty smirked. "Tell me again how the son of an *opere* star winds up a penniless cowboy."

Leslie straightened up and leaned over his much shorter friend. "Shut it, Shorty!"

Brian stepped between his two friends. "Fellas, it's a long trip on a small ship. I think we're all a little tense since that shoot 'em up with those *ninjas* back on Santa Cruz."

They were quiet for a few minutes as the California coastline started to drop below the horizon. Buck continued to stare out at the empty ocean and said, "I ain't never shot at a man before. Hard to tell how many I got. We was all firing and reloading so fast I sort a lost track."

Brian picked a piece of hay off his jeans and nodded. "Don't believe that any of us can say for sure. But they was about to kill Nick, Leilani — and Nancy."

Shorty leaned over and poked Brian's ribs.

"Ow, what you do that for, Shorty?"

Shorty just grinned. "You're sweet on her ain't you?"

"Who?"

"Nancy."

Brian replied, "No."

"You figure she'd step out with you?" Shorty quipped.

Brian cocked his head. "I ain't asked her. But sure, why not?"

"I hear them Asian girls only go out with their own kind."

Brian smiled and eased back his Stetson. "See, there's where you're mistaken, my friend. I have it on good authority that she was seeing a white guy. Another FBI agent – some German extract named Zimmer or Zimmerman. Something like that."

Leslie leaned in, "On good authority? And who told you that?"

Brian replied, "Why, Nick Grant, course."

The three cowboys chuckled, and Shorty handed Buck a five-dollar bill. "You was right, Buck. He's sweet on her."

"Aw, come on guys. Give a guy a break, will ya?"

"No way, boss man!" The three chorused and laughed deep and long.

Chapter Five

Nick reached over and squeezed Leilani's hand. "I wish I could come in with you."

They sat on a bench outside the president's office. Leilani nodded. "It would be nice, but I'm not allowed any advocates. Though, in truth, I'd rather have a lawyer. Do I look alright?"

Her crisp white blouse, matching navy-blue skirt and blazer, and her pillbox hat seemed appropriate for a meeting with the president. Nick smiled, "You look great. Try not to worry -you'll do fine, Leilani."

Before she could reply, the double doors leading to the president's office opened. A solemn looking man of about fifty in a black suit and vest stepped out. He looked more like a fugitive from a funeral parlor than a secretary to a college president.

"Miss Porta, the president will see you now. Please follow me."

Leilani stood and sighed. She ran her gloved hands over her skirt, smoothing imaginary wrinkles, and shot a worried look at Nick. "Wish me luck."

"Sure, good luck. You've faced Black Dragons and *ninjas* and lived." He winked. "Piece of cake."

29

"Hmmm," the black suited man intoned impatiently and then motioned Leilani inside. He closed the doors after her, turned, and stood facing Nick as if on guard.

*   *   *

The first thing Leilani noticed was the light streaming in through the floor-to-ceiling windows. They formed the far wall and the president's desk was situated against the center. The room was much larger than she had imagined. A large oriental rug occupied the floor in front of the desk, between a leather couch on one wall and a large oak table on the other. Awards and pictures of famous alumni covered the dark wood paneling. Centered behind the table, under a picture of a smiling famous pilot, Jimmy Doolittle, sat Dr. Robert Sproul, the President of the University. To his left sat a professor she did not know, and to his right sat Mrs. Malice.

The president said, "Over here, Miss Porta."

She approached the table and stopped in front of President Sproul. He wore his academic robes, as did the other man. Leilani noted that Mrs. Malice did not wear a robe, just a plain gray suit and skirt. The men showed great interest in the papers spread out on the table. Malice was not reading. She was glowering at Leilani with hate in her eyes.

Leilani stood with her hands folded in front and waited for what seemed like hours as her accursed garter belt straps dug into her thighs. She wanted to adjust them – or better yet, rip them off. But she couldn't. Instead, she began to do a mental *kendo* calming exercise. She hoped it would distract her from the annoying things.

After what seemed an eternity, Dr. Sproul looked up from his papers. "Miss Porta, this is Professor Stein, head of the Department of Jurisprudence. You know Mrs. Malice. She has brought some serious charges against you, including assault."

Leilani interrupted. "Wait a minute, President Sproul, I grabbed her wrist when she attempted to slap me."

Evidently, students did not interrupt Sproul, and he looked annoyed. "That is as may be. "He consulted a paper on the table. "You are a resident of the Hawaiian Territory it would seem."

"Yes, sir."

Professor Stein added, "Young lady, under California law, communicating a threat is assault."

30

Leilani replied. "Did she mention that she called me a half-breed and a mulatto?"

The two men glanced at Malice but said nothing.

Sproul continued. "Did you threaten Mrs. Malice?"

"No, I never threaten. I merely stated that if she referred to me again in those racist and hateful terms, I would strip her naked and toss her into the street."

Professor Stein, who was sipping from a glass of water, almost choked. He put the glass down and Sproul patted him on the back. "Easy, Bernie. You're too hard to replace. Lawyers don't like university pay."

Leilani thought that she saw a flicker of a smile on Sproul's face before his professional demeanor returned. "Miss Porta, we have rules and regulations at UCB. If someone uses racist or inappropriate language, we have channels to report such abuse."

"Yes, sir, but I'm a student and she's staff. Would you accept my word over hers?"

Sproul looked uncomfortable but said nothing.

Leilani continued. "It's just that it's everywhere. I'm sick and tired of being treated like a second-class citizen. Mrs. Malice may be the most vocal I've encountered. She seldom missed an opportunity to call me out for things she let slide with other girls. She has repeatedly referred to my people as natives."

Red faced and sputtering, Malice started to rise from the table. Sproul put out a hand and eased her back to her seat. She looked like she was about to blow a cork. Seated again, she spat out, "Well, I've never been treated in such a manner by a half-bree–" Malice stopped mid-sentence, seemingly aware that her words were not in her best interest.

Leilani seethed at the injustice. "My people are American citizens!"

Sproul raised his voice. "Enough, ladies! Mrs. Malice, I will remind you that the UCB campus is open to people of all races."

Not for the first time Leilani wondered why she was so intent on coming to the mainland. The insults and 'native' comments were just endless. Hanna had warned her that mainland people were very conscious of skin color and race. Hanna was lighter skinned than Leilani but still experienced instances of senseless racism.

She wanted to scream but caught herself. She took four deep breaths, and with each exhale she calmed down. In her mind's eye, she concentrated on Nick's face and regained control. For the first time she realized what it might mean to be with him. She loved him so much but wondered -would she hold him back?

Stein glanced at Sproul and nodded. Stein took off his glasses and rubbed the bridge of his nose. "Miss Porta, as a Jew, I have known prejudice all of my life. However, violence never solves anything." He leaned over and whispered something in Sproul's ear.

Sproul looked at Leilani. "Miss Porta, please wait outside while we decide if you have a future at the university."

"Yes, sir." Leilani turned on her heel and left the room, still seething.

Outside, Nick leapt to his feet as she emerged. "How did it go?"

She silently grabbed his hand and pulled him back on the bench.

Nick squeezed her hand. "So, tell me?"

"Did you know that communicating a threat is assault in California?"

Nick shook his head. "No. In that case, boy, am I in trouble."

"You can call people horrible names and discriminate against them. But if you raise your voice in defense, you can get expelled or worse."

They waited in silence for a while. Nick decided to try to distract Leilani from the proceedings. "It's been a tough day. Do want to postpone your belt test this evening?"

Leilani seemed a million miles away and answered in a dreamy voice. "No, Nancy and I have been sparring daily. She's showed me so much. I've also been practicing my *katas* at the DoJo. Yes, I'm ready."

"You've come so far since August. It took me almost six months to test for my Green Belt. But you got there in half the time. Nancy says that you are very driven, and I agree."

Leilani took off her hat and placed it in her lap. "I need to be good. As good as Nancy when we tackle Miyazaki again."

Nick nodded. "My involvement with Miyazaki has put your family in danger. I'm sorry."

Leilani reached over and took Nick's other hand. "No, Nick, that's not completely true. My dad was working a sting operation with Army Intelligence against Miyazaki. If you hadn't recognized Miyazaki, I don't know what would have become of us. I had no idea until that awful day that the man we thought was Mr. Moto was actually Miyazaki."

Nick lowered his voice. "I still find it hard to believe that Army Intelligence and Navy Intelligence were both working operations against Miyazaki and neither bothered to tell the other."

"It does boggle the mind. Thankfully, the Military Police arrived in time and my family escaped serious injury."

Nick smiled at her. "You were great even before Mr. Nieshi's martial training. You swing a mean tire iron."

That brought a smile to her lips. "Yes, that was quite the night." She leaned against his shoulder. "We make a pretty good team, fly-boy. You still want to be with your Hawaiian princess?"

He reached an arm around her. "Yes, more than ever." He kissed her head. "Leilani, you're the one, if you'll have me."

The president's doors opened, and the secretary motioned for Leilani. She put on her hat, stood, and then tugged at a garter belt strap through her skirt.

Nick looked away, embarrassed, unsure. "What are you doing?"

"Ugh, I hate these darn things. Never mind." She straightened and walked erect through the doors. Once again, the secretary closed the doors and stood guard.

*   *   *

The president looked over the top of his reading glasses. "Miss Porta, did you at any time put a hand on Mrs. Malice?"

"Yes, sir. I deflected Mrs. Malice's attempt to slap my face."

Malice interjected and held up her black and blue forearm. "That's a lie. She grabbed my arm and twisted."

Leilani looked directly into Sproul's eyes and held his gaze. "Yes, I did twist her arm as I blocked the slap. If she hadn't resisted, she would not have been bruised." The seconds seemed to slow down to a crawl, but eventually Sproul looked at his papers. "Mrs. Malice, did you attempt to slap Miss Porta?"

"Not exactly."

Sproul sighed, "Not exactly? What exactly did you do?"

Malice sputtered, "Well, ah – she was being rude."

Sproul shook his head. "Mrs. Malice, I officially caution you. Had you struck Miss Porta I would have had no choice but to suspend you. Do you understand?"

He turned to Leilani. "Young lady, other than the blocked slap, did you lay a hand on Mrs. Malice?"

"No, sir." It wasn't technically a lie, she told herself, not one she would have to own up to in confession. While she had hip-checked the old battle-axe out of her way, she didn't actually 'lay a hand on her.'

Sproul nodded, looked at Stein and Malice, and addressed Leilani. "Miss Leilani Porta, you are hereby placed on probation for the remainder of the academic semester for unladylike behavior. You are expelled from College Hall immediately. You will return to College Hall, turn in your linen, return your room key, and remove all your belongings at once. Is that clear?"

Leilani was stunned. "But where will I live? Finals are next week, where will I study?"

Mrs. Malice looked up and smiled. "You should have thought about that before you acted in such a disgraceful manner."

Leilani closed her eyes and let the magnitude of their decision sink in. "I'm not going to run home crying, if that's what you think. I'm much stronger than that. By the might of King Kamehameha, whose blood runs through my veins, this will not best me."

She turned on her heel and walked calmly through the doors. Outside, Nick stood, and just as they were about to leave, the secretary put up his hand. "Hold on, Miss Porta, you've got some paperwork to sign."

"Will this never end?" She stepped over to his desk where papers awaiting her signature lay. She glanced at the secretary. "I suppose that you think this is all very amusing."

He glanced up from his desk. "Not in the least, Miss Porta."

Nick stood beside her. "What happened?"

Leilani ignored Nick. "What and where do I sign?"

The secretary handed her a pen and pointed. "Here and here. For the record, I've been agitating to remove Mrs. Malice for years. She always finds some poor freshman to harass. Last year it was a poor Negro girl from Oakland. That girl was sweet, and she deserved better."

Nick's brow furrowed. "What happened to her?"

"Mrs. Malice trumped up some charge and the girl was expelled halfway through the first semester."

Leilani finished signing and handed the pen back. "If Mrs. Malice is so much trouble, why does the university keep her?"

"Ah, that's an interesting question. You see, she is the spinster sister of Mrs. Sigmund Stern."

Leilani handed the paperwork to the secretary. "Who's that?"

"The late Mrs. Stern put up the funds for College House — the girls' dormitory. Sadly, continued funding is contingent upon Mrs. Malice's employment. It is *quid pro quo.*"

Chapter Six

4:30 p.m. Monday, November 30th, 1936
Alameda Japanese American Club and Dojo
Alameda, California

Nick looked up the newly painted sign hanging outside Mr. Nieshi's Dojo. The bright red Kanji letters on the white background were sandwiched between a painted 48-star US flag on the left and a Japanese flag on the right. GOD BLESS AMERICA in large gold letters famed in white adorned the store front window. Through the glass they saw Nancy Tanaka in front of a group of Japanese American six-year-olds intently focused on her. They straightened their crisp white *Gis*, tightened their white belts, and then as one they bowed to Nancy. She tugged on the ends of her black belt and returned the bow.

Then like a wave of white cotton, the group of boys and girls surged forward and gave Nancy a group hug. At first Nancy looked stern, but then she laughed and scooped up several in a hug. Putting them down, she said, "Off you go now, little ones. We will see you again tomorrow."

As they ran into the arms of their waiting parents, Nancy picked up a towel and mopped sweat from her neck and then patted her face. She looked through the glass and, noticing Nick and

Leilani, waved them in. Once they were inside, she asked, "How did it go, Leilani?"

Leilani sighed, "It could have been worse. I was tossed out of the dorm, but I can finish out the semester."

Nick eyed Nancy. "I wanted to bust the President in the nose but what good what would that do? And the old bat, Mrs. Malice. It seems she's gone after freshmen girls before. It's just so unfair."

Nancy hugged Leilani. "I'm so sorry. But where are all your possessions?"

Leilani broke the embrace and pointed across the street to Nick's old truck. "Nick said we could store them in his garage. Nancy, is there any way I could stay with you? I hate to ask but it's only for a few days."

"Oh, I'm so sorry. We're hosting a newly arrived family, my cousin, her husband, and their baby. They will be with us until they find a place that will accept Japanese tenants."

Leilani hung her head. "Why did I ever leave Oahu?"

Nick took her hand. "Look, you can stay in Jude's room until you return home. Like you said, it's only a few days. Besides, Jude won't be needing it as long as she's in Brazil."

"That's very thoughtful, Nick, but my parents would never approve. My mother would faint if she knew I was staying under the same roof as my boyfriend. My father really likes you, Nick, but I'm afraid he'd try to kill you if he ever found out. Have you ever seen a Portuguese temper?"

"Other than yours, no."

"Very funny, Grant, but I'm serious."

"Leilani, I've stayed at your home any number of times – so has John Borger, come to think of it."

Leilani shook her head. "That's different. My parents were home and you slept in the garden house."

Nick took a breath and continued, "Look, I'm sorry, your Highness, but we don't have a garden house. Your parents need never know. Hey, they don't know that my family is living overseas. All I have to do is convince Mr. and Mrs. Morris. Piece of cake."

Nancy said, "We can discuss this later. Why don't you two go change into your practice gi. Leilani, you need to warm up if you want to advance to the next belt."

*   *   *

Nick tied the brown cotton belt around his sweat stained gi, closed the locker door, and checked himself in the mirror. The knot was centered, and the ends hung down equally. He noted that his dark blond hair was getting long and needed a trim. The summer highlights were history and his tan had long since faded. A least his height had stabilized. Good, he thought, at six-foot, three inches he didn't want to grow anymore. He was already the tallest boy in the freshman class—except for the basketball team.

Satisfied, he emerged from the men's locker room and saw Mr. Nieshi waiting for him on the hardwood floor. Nick approached his sensei, came to attention, and bowed deeply. He said in Japanese, "Greetings, Master Nieshi. "

Nieshi bowed and answered in kind, "Greetings, honored student Grant."

Continuing in Japanese, Nieshi asked, "How go your academic studies, Mr. Grant?"

It was always a little disconcerting to be so formal with Mr. Nieshi. When they were tearing down engines or repairing the clippers at the Pan American Airways hangar, there was little formality. But here in the Dojo their relationship was very formal. Nick bowed his head slightly in respect and answered in his best Japanese. "My studies go well, Master Nieshi. Math and science are easy enough, but rhetoric and foreign language are difficult."

"Just so, Mr. Grant, but you were warned how difficult my language can be. There are many more subtleties than in English. Still, your pronunciation is reasonable enough for a first-year student."

Nick bowed. "You are too kind, my sensei."

Nieshi said, "Now please demonstrate *Bassai Dai kata*."

Nick assumed *Heian Shodan*. He cupped his left hand in his right, held them at a forty-five-degree angle away from his body, his shoulders relaxed. "Hieee!" He drove forward, raising his right leg, and slammed his right fist up to block an imaginary strike to his head. "Hai!" He continued through the well-practiced *kata*, fighting imaginary opponents as Nieshi watched intently. Nick struck and blocked as he spun and kicked. Several minutes later, he ended in a downward block. Returning to *Heian Shodan* — or peaceful warrior – he bowed.

Nieshi nodded. "Your footwork is sloppy, and your timing was off. Are you here in the Dojo, Mr. Grant? Or is your *Ki* elsewhere?"

"It is here, now, Master Nieshi."

"Good. Please demonstrate *Bassai Dai kata* again. This time with your *Ki* in the Dojo."

Elsewhere in the Dojo, Nancy was working one-on-one with Leilani. "Your *katas* look good, Leilani. But your kicks are still a little over-extended."

"I know, Nancy. I don't have the reach. The men sparring partners outreach me every time. If I don't reach, how can I land a strike?"

"Remember, wait for your opponent to come to you. Block and then strike when *they* are over-extended. You are wise to strike with your legs when you can. They are equal in strength to many men. Compared to men, women's arms are weak. Yes, we can strengthen them with weights, but we can seldom match the arm strength of the men."

"Okay, Nancy, I will try to remember that."

Nancy glanced over at the testing. "It looks like Nick has finished his lesson. Are you ready?"

Leilani exhaled and nodded. "Sure, what else could go wrong today?"

Nancy turned on her. "You are the master of your world. If you want this badly enough you must focus on your *Ki*. Block out everything else."

Leilani straightened her *Keikogi* – or *gi* -and tightened her belt. "I'm ready."

Ninety minutes later, Mr. Nieshi dismissed Nick and Leilani. After they showered and changed to street clothes, they met Nancy in the foyer. The girls' hair was still wet, and their faces glowed from the exercise.

Leilani ran up to Nick and hugged him. "I did it, Nick. I got my Green Belt!"

Nick looked downcast. "That's great, Leilani."

Leilani frowned. "What's wrong?"

"I failed my preliminary. I can't test for my Black Belt until I pass the preliminary."

"Oh, Nick, I'm so sorry. What did Mr. Nieshi say to you?"

Nick sighed, "Basically, that my head was not in the game."

Nancy put her hand on Nick's shoulder. "I saw a few of your moves and you seemed distracted. Is everything okay?"

Nick looked at his watch. "Not really, I was thinking about Leilani staying under my roof. I'm worried that the Portas will find out and then forbid me to see Leilani ever again."

Nancy shook her head. "That's not going to happen. They might be mad for a while, but they love you, Nick. It's going to be fine."

Nick brightened. "You really think so?"

"Yes, I do. Sorry to run but I've got to get home and help out with my cousin's baby girl. She's so cute! Good luck with Mrs. Morris. I'll see you guys at class tomorrow."

The 1927 Ford truck let out a rusty screech as Nick yanked the passenger door open. Leilani sat on the threadbare seat in silence as Nick joined her in the cab. He depressed the clutch, hit the starter switch, and the engine caught. Nick shifted the truck into gear and started off. "Hey, maybe it will be alright. Your parents will never know, and Mrs. Morris will understand. If I know her, she'll watch over you like a mother hen."

Leilani put her head in her hands. "I miss Hawaii."

Chapter Seven

6:30 PM, Monday, November 30th, 1936
Grant Home
Alameda, California

Nick pulled the truck into the garage and stepped out. Leilani met him at the tailgate. He gazed at a desk lamp, some blankets, a small suitcase, and a very large steamer trunk. "What do you want to take up to Jude's room?"

"Just the trunk and the suitcase."

Nick opened the gate and placed the suitcase on the garage floor. He reached over and tugged on the trunk. It did not move. At least the dorm had a cart to move the darn thing. Several young men hanging around waiting for their dates helped lift it into the truck. Too bad they weren't here to help. "What have you got in here — lead bars?"

Leilani rewarded him with a withering look.

"Okay, well you're going to have to help me move it." Nick jumped up into the truck bed and got between the trunk and the cab. He shoved with his legs and the trunk moved to the tailgate. He jumped down and said, "Leilani, can you get the other side?"

Wordlessly, she grabbed the leather handhold opposite Nick.

"Okay, when I say three, we'll set it on the floor."

She nodded.

"One — two — three!"

The trunk thumped to the floor, thankfully without removing any toes or fingers. Nick rubbed his hands together while Leilani placed her small suitcase on the top of the trunk.

Nick looked through the garage door toward the kitchen. He could see Mrs. Morris but not Mr. Morris. "Come on, we'd better go speak to Mrs. Morris. I don't want to lug that thing back here if she says no."

Nick and Leilani entered the kitchen. Leilani had her purse clutched to her chest and looked over at Mrs. Morris, who looked up, teacup in her hand. "What on Earth is the matter, child?"

"Oh, Mrs. Morris." Tears streamed down her face as she dashed over. Mrs. Morris put down the cup and stood up just as Leilani reached her wide-open arms.

"There — there, child, everything will be alright. Why don't you sit down and have a nice cup of tea and tell me all about it?"

Mr. Morris came into the kitchen caring the evening paper, "Is everything alright?"

Mrs. Morris replied, "I'm about to find out. Walter. Have seat at the table."

Nick and Leilani sat opposite the Morrises. Through sobs, Leilani relayed most of the story. "So, I need a place to stay. It's only for a few days but if my parents find out I'm here, it will break their hearts."

Mrs. Morris took a sip of her now tepid tea and said, "There's no need to advertise that you are here, and they most probably won't find out. At least not from Walter or me. But I must warn you, if they ask, I will tell the truth."

Leilani leapt from her chair and wrapped her arms around Mrs. Morris. "Oh, thank you, thank you, thank you. You have no idea how relieved I am at your kindness. How will I ever repay you?"

Mrs. Morris looked into her cup and decided that the tea was too cold — even for her. "Well, you can start by keeping out of Nick's room and keeping him out of your room."

"Yes, Mrs. Morris."

Nick stood up. "Mr. Morris, can you help me with Leilani's things?"

*   *   *

Upstairs Mr. Morris and Nick heaved the steamer trunk into position in Jude's closet. Satisfied, they sat down heavily on the floor, their backs propped against the trunk. Morris eyed Nick, "What's in that thing, bricks?"

"I thought it might be lead, but whatever it is — she's not telling."

Morris took a handkerchief out of his pocket and mopped his brow. "I can't believe that Mrs. Morris approved of your girlfriend living under the same roof as you."

Back in the kitchen, Nick saw Leilani and Mrs. Morris standing at the stove stirring a pot with a wooden spoon. Nick heard Mrs. Morris say, "That's perfect — keep stirring." She turned Nick. "Sit down, Leilani will serve you some stew. Walter, please pass Nick the bread and butter." Mrs. Morris placed two bowls on the table while Mr. Morris put a sharp knife, a cutting board, and bread and butter on the table.

Mrs. Morris pointed her wooden spoon at Nick. "Now young man. You are to keep out of Jude's room while Leilani is in there. Understood?"

"But-"

"No ifs or buts, young man. If I catch either of you in the other's bedroom, I will skin you alive with this wooden spoon." She looked from Nick to Leilani.

They answered in unison, "Yes, Mrs. Morris."

Chapter Eight

2316 hours, Tuesday, December 1, 1936
Aboard the Imperial Navy Submarine, I-23
30 Meters below the surface, Off the Western Coast of American
Samoa,

The captain of the boat slapped the targeting handles up and
ordered, "Down periscope!"
"Hai!" a seaman responded, and the slick black tube retreated
with a reptilian-like hiss until the eye piece was once again below
the waves.
The lieutenant commander was the sub's captain, but
Commander Miyazaki outranked him. "Commander, the coast is
dark, and the ocean is clear. With your permission I will give the
order."
Miyazaki nodded and the captain barked, "Surface – surface
– surface!"
A klaxon blared out a warning, another seaman spun a huge
wheel, and the submarine's bow angled up. The sub started to vibrate
as the sound of air venting into the ocean filled the CIC, or combat
information center. The sub's hull started to moan as the pressure
began to ease on the compressed steel plates. Miyazaki looked over
at his traveling companion. Johnson's midnight-black dungarees
showed dark stains of sweat below his armpits. The rings extended
across the front of his shirt and almost joined at the buttons. Eyes

wide, Johnson swallowed hard and nervously looked around the CIC.

The captain noted his passenger's distress and said in English. "Patience, Mr. Johnson, we will soon have you back on dry land."

Johnson leaned forward and barfed into a small bucket that he always kept close. The sour smell added to the stink of the crew's ten-day-old sweat. The sub had run submerged during the day and surfaced at night. Once her diesels had recharged the batteries, the sub slid back beneath the waves. They had agreed that it was too dangerous to allow him on deck during recharge operations. Should the lookouts see an American vessel or patrol aircraft, they would have to crash dive. That might leave the Samoan swimming home if he didn't move fast enough.

The venting noises ceased and slowly the sub leveled off to an even keel. The captain checked the depth gauge mounted on the bulkhead and then ordered, "XO, open the conning tower hatch, set lookouts to port and starboard. Gun crews – prepare for surface action and report."

"Hai!" A seaman leapt up the center ladder and disappeared. A second later a small cascade of seawater hit the CIC deck and two more seaman, wearing binoculars around their necks, scampered up the ladder, followed by the XO.

A few moments later, the XO called back down the hatch. "Captain, all clear."

The captain turned to the senior non-commissioned officer, the Chief of the Boat. "Chief, have the landing party prepare to depart."

"Hai." The chief ducked out of the CIC and headed toward the bow hatch.

The captain turned to Miyazaki. "Commander, would you and Mr. Johnson care to join me at the forward torpedo room?"

Following the captain, and with Johnson in tow, Miyazaki made his way through the cramped sub until he reached the torpedo room ladder. He passed his small rucksack, katana, and pistol belt through the hatch to waiting hands. He turned to Johnson and said in English, "Follow me."

Top side, the fresh sea air was a relief. Miyazaki took a deep breath and had a better understanding of why submariners called their small craft *Pig Boats*. Once again, he thanked his lucky stars that he had chosen naval aviation and not the submarine service.

Dark clouds scudded across a moonless sky. The sub's dark hull so low in the water would be difficult to detect. Through his binoculars, Miyazaki scanned the dark shore about 600 meters away and noticed breakers foaming halfway. Johnson had recommended this cove because local fisherman rarely risked crossing the reef that churned the swells into crashing whitewater. As the gun crews stood watch, the deck crew transferred ammunition crates, rifles, pistols, and explosives into an inflatable launch. Miyazaki watched as all the tools needed to start a revolution were stowed.

Pleased, he glanced back and addressed Johnson in English. "This is an excellent location. Let us hope that our landing goes unnoticed."

Johnson nodded. "It will. No one spends any time here. The fishing is not worth risking the boat. There are easier waters with a better catch."

The captain approached and snapped out a salute and began in Japanese, "Commander, the launch is ready. If you and Mr. Johnson would climb aboard."

Miyazaki returned the salute. "Be here every night from 0200 – 0400 hours."

"Yes, Commander. We will watch and listen for your messages."

"Good and be ready to extract me if the Americans cause trouble."

The captain raised an eyebrow, "And the Samoan?"

Miyazaki smiled. "Regardless of what transpires, Johnson will not be returning. This life is almost over for him."

A look of shock briefly passed over the captain's face before the measured calm of the professional warrior returned. "As you wish, Commander Miyazaki. We will be here to aid you so long as our fuel holds out."

Miyazaki closed the distance between them and stared into the man's brown eyes. "You will remain here, Captain, until I release you. Rendezvous with a fleet tanker if needs must. Is that quite clear?"

The captain bowed, "Yes, Commander. I will hold until relieved or dismissed."

"Good." Turning to Johnson he switched to English. "Mr. Johnson, please board the launch."

Johnson looked at Miyazaki as if to question his sanity. Then he nodded and slowly climbed over the side, and down into the

46

gently rocking rubber raft. Miyazaki saluted the rising sun naval pendant at the masthead and followed. The crew cast off and started to paddle towards the dark coast.

The breakers loomed large as the crewmen paddled toward the shoreline. The waves tossed their launch around like a cork and they bottomed out twice. Except for a saltwater shower, they crossed the last of the reef without incident.

As they approached the shoreline, the palm trees looked dark and foreboding. The two seamen forward stowed their paddles, picked up rifles and covered the exposed beach.

When they landed the same two jumped onto the sand and disappeared into the tree line. A few tense minutes later they returned and waved the others ashore. It took the crew several trips to unload the crates of ammunition and the weapons. After stashing it behind a grove of palm trees, the ensign in charge of the away party approached Miyazaki and snapped out a salute. "Commander, your equipment is ashore. Do you want us to help you move it to a more suitable location, sir?"

"Idiot! If I wanted your help, I would have demanded it." Then with stone cold eyes he whispered. "Never presume to question me again. Get into you raft and leave – now."

Rattled, the young ensign turned and screamed at his men. "Get aboard. We are leaving."

Miyazaki seethed and wondered if the fool's yells had alerted everyone within a mile. As the men paddled toward the breakers Miyazaki strained his ears listening for a telltale sound of discovery. As the raft cleared the reef, he relaxed. There had been no alarm or curious locals coming to investigate.

He turned to Johnson, "When will your men arrive?"

Johnson looked a good deal better after a few minutes on *terra firma*. He eyed Miyazaki with a wry smile. "They are here, Miyazaki." As he spoke, a group of armed men stood at the edge of the jungle. One motioned for the others to stay in place. He shouldered his rifle and walked toward Johnson. They hugged and started talking Samoan with excited voices and a great deal of hand gestures. Miyazaki listened but could not make out what they were saying. "Johnson, what is going on? What is this man saying?"

Johnson turned on Miyazaki. "This is my cousin, Sam. He says you are as loud as a herd of pigs and smell just as bad." With that all the men at the tree line started to laugh. Miyazaki ground his teeth and gripped his katana so hard his nails bit into the cloth wrapping.

Johnson shouted something and the Samoans were quiet. "My men will carry the supplies to a safe house. We need to move now if we are to get over the Rainmaker before the sun comes up. Come."

Johnson turned his back on Miyazaki and spoke to the Samoans. Wordlessly, they hefted the heavy crates on broad shoulders and moved off at a good pace. Miyazaki shouldered his pack and followed. The trail led into the jungle and soon the dense triple canopy swallowed all trace of the stars.

Chapter Nine

12:58 PM, December 16th, 1936
Liberal Arts Building
University of California, Berkeley

Nick exhaled and closed his blue exam booklet. He looked at the wall clock and noted that in two minutes Oriental Studies would be over, and with it his first college semester. It had been a slog but not as tough has he had imagined. Studying with Nancy and Leilani had helped a lot. They were both great at Rhetoric 101 and humanities – he was not. They were also good at math and science. He told himself he was a bit better but sometimes he wondered if that were actually true.

Seated at his desk in the front of the classroom, Professor Smith opened his pocket watch and noted the time. He looked up and said, "That's time. Stop all work. Please put your pencils down and close your examination booklets."

Some students let out a low moan, but everyone did as Professor Smith directed. The students stood, shuffled up to Smith's desk, and placed the blue exam booklets on the corner of his desk. When Nick got to the desk, he placed his booklet on the pile. "I really enjoyed your class, Professor. Your China travels and insights were very interesting. Will you be returning at some point?"

Smith looked up at Nick over his glasses. "Yes, perhaps next summer. I've applied for a State Department grant."

Nick nodded. "Great, be sure to fly Pan American when you do."

"You mean on the *China Clipper*? Why would I do that?"

"Two reasons. If you fly on a government ticket, there's a huge discount. Second, I might be on the crew."

Smith looked up confused. "Grant, you've been to China?"

Nick smiled. "Indeed, Professor. Look me up if that State Department grant comes through. Hope to see you around, Prof." Nick turned, waved, and walked out of the classroom.

Outside the Liberal Arts building, Nick glanced up at the azure blue sky and sighed. His first semester of college was over, and he would be free for five weeks. He would have a few maintenance shifts at the Pan American Airways hangar, but his flight schedule was light, and he was looking forward to showing Leilani the bay area sights. He sat down on a bench and let the late autumn sun warm him while he waited for her.

Sometime later he felt a finger gently poke his chest.

"Hey, sleepy head, wake up."

Nick opened his eyes. The sun cast a halo around Leilani's face as she looked down on him. He smiled. "Hey, gorgeous. I guess I nodded off."

Leilani sat next to him on the bench a kissed his cheek. "I've got some bad news."

Nick sat up rubbing his eyes, instantly awake. "What? What is it?"

She held up a yellow slip of paper. "Dad sent me a telegram. He bought me a ticket on the next clipper. I'm going home for the holidays."

"Oh, no. We have so much planned during the break. I can't believe that you have to go home."

She took his hands. "It's worse, Father knows I'm living at your house."

Puzzled, Nick asked, "How could he know?"

"Well," she began, "Father called the residence, and the old bat Mrs. Malice told him I had been kicked out. Then he called your house. Mrs. Morris answered, and Father asked for me. Mrs. Morris said I wasn't home from school but would-be home in a few hours. That clinched it – my goose is cooked."

"Our goose you mean. Your parents aren't going to let me see you again. That's so unfair, we didn't do anything! I'm going to call your parents and set this straight."

Leilani squeezed Nick's hand. "No, you're not. I will explain what happened when I get home. If they don't believe me, they can talk to Mr. and Mrs. Morris."

Deflated, Nick brushed his hand over Leilani's cheek and ran his hands though her long dark hair. She leaned forward and their lips met. She broke the kiss far too soon for Nick and leaned back. "Please drive me to your home, I've got to pack."

*   *   *

Nick dropped Leilani off at the Grant house then drove to Alameda Airport and Pan American Lagoon. He crossed the railroad tracks and drove past Mac's old hangar. Memories flooded his mind as he remembered the good and bad times he'd had there. Things had changed forever the night Charles and Anne Lindbergh landed. Anne Lindbergh had inadvertently involved Mac and Nick in an espionage war between Japan and the United States. Nick was still fighting the war, but it had cost Mac his life.

Nick parked Mac's old pickup truck under the Pan American Airways Pacific Division sign. It showed the image of a Martin M-130 Clipper below the title. The clipper was 'on the step,' the last stage before she got airborne. It was an inspiring logo and Nick felt proud to be part of the grand enterprise. He walked in through the personnel doors and ducked into the locker room. He quickly changed into his work overalls and stepped into the hangar high bay.

The *Hawaii Clipper* sat high and dry on her beaching cradle undergoing routine maintenance. Men in similar white overalls clambered over the Martin flying boat, making last minute checks on every aspect of the airliner. One man stood on the horizontal stabilizer and polished the vertical stabilizer emblazoned with NC-14714 – the registration number. Tomorrow morning, if everything checked out, the ground crew would launch the clipper into the Pan American Lagoon. There they would complete preparation for the first Trans-Pacific passenger fight to the Philippines. With a pang, Nick realized that Leilani would be one of them.

Nick heard his name and turned to see Mr. Nieshi walking towards him. Nieshi was first generation Japanese. His cropped black hair was short and seemed to accentuate his five-foot-two stature. "You going to stand there all-day gaping or you going to get to work?"

As he was about to reply a thought crossed his mind. "Neither, Mr. Nieshi. Have you seen Colonel Young?"

"He's over in the admin offices." Nieshi cocked his head. "Why?"

"I need to speak with him about something." Nick trotted across the high bay toward the administration offices. "I'll be right back, Mr. Nieshi."

He slowed to a walk when he reached Colonel Young's outer office. Betty, Colonel Young's secretary, tucked a lock of graying hair behind her ear and looked up from her typing. "Hello, Nick. What can I do for you?"

"Hi, Betty, do you have the final crew manifest?"

"Why, yes, I've just finished typing it." She extracted the page from the typewriter and handed it to him. "Colonel Young still needs to sign it, but it is current."

Nick scanned the Flight Engineer position and saw the name he was looking for. He handed the manifest back. "Thanks, Betty." He jogged down the hall to the crew ready room and walked in. The room was large with a large weather map of the Pacific Ocean on the adjacent wall. The opposite wall held clipboards hanging on hooks. Broad cloth tape divided the wall into specific functional sections. Nick found the Fight Engineer section and the hook where the *Hawaii Clipper* clipboard should have been hanging. It was empty.

Nick scanned the tables and found John Houston flipping through a clipboard and taking notes. Nick walked over, "Hi, John."

John Houston looked up from his work, "Hey, Nick. What's up?"

Nick sat across from Houston. "I saw that you are scheduled to fly on NC-14714 tomorrow."

"Yeah, and it sucks. The wife is sick, and we've got that new baby."

"Well, maybe I can help out. You've just got the Hawaii leg, right?"

Houston looked dubious. "Yeah, then a 10 day lay-over before the return hop to Alameda. But how can you help?"

Nick leaned in. "I'm scheduled to fly in January on all the hops to Manilla and back. I won't return until after school starts. You

52

want to stay home, take care of Clara, and the new baby. I don't want to miss any classes. What if we swap?"

Houston's expression changed to hopeful. "But I thought you were in school now?"

"I had my last final today. What do you say?"

"Sure, if you can clear it with Young."

Nick stood up. "I'll be right back."

Nick returned to Young's office and asked, "Betty, can I have a word with the Colonel?"

She got up from her desk. "Let me check." She knocked and then disappeared behind Young's door. A moment later, Betty reappeared. "Yes, but be quick. I've got a long-distance phone call booked to New York in five minutes."

"Thanks, Betty. You're the best." As he swept by her, he planted a kiss on her cheek and watched as she blushed bright red. "Nick, you are incorrigible!" Then to his surprise she giggled like a schoolgirl.

Inside the office, Nick saw Young sitting behind his huge mahogany desk. Young looked up from his paperwork. "What's so urgent, Nick?"

"Thanks for seeing me, Colonel Young. I need a favor."

"Can't say I'm surprised. What is it this time?"

"I want to swap flight engineer assignments with John Houston."

Young reached for his glasses and picked up the manifest Betty had typed. "Impossible, the *Hawaii Clipper* leaves tomorrow. You know that company policy – Priester's policy – states that the manifest is frozen forty-eight hours before departure."

Nick leaned in, "Yes, but the policy also states that a division chief can make last minute changes."

Young put his glasses back on the desk. "I'm aware of that, but why should I? Is Houston sick?"

Nick shook his head. "No, but his wife is, and they have a new baby. If I switch, he can stay home and take care of her."

Young stared at Nick and started tapping his index finger on the desktop. "What else, Nick. What's your angle?"

Nick spread his hands in what he hoped would convey surprise and innocence. But he could see by Young's expression that he wasn't buying it. Young hit the intercom button next to the phone. "Betty, bring me tomorrow's passenger manifest."

Betty walked in and handed Young a sheet of paper. As she left, she shot a quizzical look at Nick. He shrugged. Young scanned the manifest. It didn't take long, as the list comprised only seven passengers. He tapped the paper. "I knew it." He looked up at Nick. "Grant, I seem to recall that one Leilani Porta has a boyfriend, a Flight Engineer, who works for Pan American. Who might that be?"

"Okay, Colonel Young, my motives aren't entirely altruistic. But you see I got a problem…" Nick explained how Leilani wound up under his roof for the past week and how Mr. Porta found out.

Young sat back in his leather-bound chair and folded his arms behind his head. "Why do you want to go see Porta? Are you nuts? He'll probably shoot you on sight."

Nick hung his head. "I swear, we didn't do anything, but I can't let Leilani face her parents alone."

Young shook his head and buzzed Betty again. "Yes, Colonel Young?"

"Betty, strike out Houston's name on the crew manifest and substitute Nick's name."

"Yes, Colonel Young. Is there anything else?"

Young leaned forward on his desk and rubbed his temples. "Yes, when you've completed the changes, please bring me a glass of water and two aspirin."

Nick smiled. "Thanks, Colonel Young, I owe you."

"Yeah, yeah, now get out of here before I change my mind."

Chapter Ten

Brian O'Malley leaned on the ship's railing, removed his hat, and wiped his kerchief through his hair. His sweat-soaked shirt stuck to his skin and he could feel the heat from the steel deck plates through his cowboy boots. Glancing at the sun, he estimated it was 11:00 am. He sighed, aware that the day's heat would not peak for another four hours. The ship had been at anchor for almost 36 hours and still they did not have permission to get off this furnace. The crew had rigged canvas shade awnings over the foredeck and amidships, but the temperature often reached 100 degrees. Brian wasn't sure which was higher — the humidity or the temperature. There wasn't a breath of air blowing either. Underway, a breeze blew across the deck and the tropical heat was bearable. But at a standstill the sun made the ship's deck as hot as a branding iron.

Down below decks, the horses had it bad. The cowboys took turns fanning the horses with palm fronds in an attempt to keep the horses cool. It helped some, but Brian was starting to get worried. The dairy cows were doing a tad better, but he knew that he had to get the livestock off the ship soon.

Shorty emerged from below and spit a stream of tobacco juice over the side. "Brian, how long they going to hold us on this frying pan of a tub?"

"I don't rightly know, Shorty. First Mate says the vet from the local US Department of Agriculture has to certify our bovine cargo as disease free."

"Well, if it gets any hotter, I'm fixing to jump overboard and swim to shore."

"Shorty, you can't swim." Brian turned his attention back to the shore and pointed to the only pier in the harbor. "Part of the holdup is the pier. It's occupied by that German freighter. Even if the vet cleared us, we'd have to wait until Herr Hitler's ship finished unloading." He looked at the swastika emblazoned on the fantail and shook his head in disgust. No good would come of Hitler and his cockeyed regime.

Shorty removed his hat and scratched his balding head. "What's a Nazi ship doing here anyway?"

Brian shook his head. "Don't rightly know, Shorty. It's something about a Great War Treaty. Irregardless, we can't unload until they're finished. Where are the other boys?"

Shorty jerked a thumb over his shoulder, "They're both below. Leslie is fanning the horses. Buck's in his bunk. He claims it's cooler down there. I think he's nuts. It's like being inside an oven below decks."

Brian stood up. "Go get 'em up here, pronto."

"What's so dang important?"

Brian pointed to the German ship. "Black smoke is pouring from the funnel."

Shorty squinted at the ship. "So what?"

Brian smiled. "They've fired up the boiler and are fixing to leave."

"But," Shorty stammered, "what about the vet?"

Brian smiled and pointed, "See that white panel van that just pulled up on the pier? The one with the USDA letters on the side?"

"Yeah. Hey, is that the first mate in the passenger seat?"

"Sure looks like it, Shorty. Go roust the boys. Looks like our ocean cruise is coming to an end. I believe we'll be off this tub this afternoon."

8:55 pm, December 19th, 1936
Village of Vatia,
American Samoa

Toshio Miyazaki sipped his tea seated in the shade of a palm-fronded hut. As he listened to Johnson make his pitch to the local elders, he watched their faces closely. Johnson and he were making the rounds on the island, going from village to village in an attempt to enlist others to the cause. Miyazaki didn't understand the Samoan dialect but picked up a few English words. He could hear the passion in Johnson's voice as he railed on about their American overlords. Miyazaki was dressed in the local garb of a lava-lava, a cotton wrap that substituted for trousers, and a bright floral print shirt. Most of the locals looked him over once then ignored him.

The mission seemed to be going well, but he had to rely on Johnson's version of events. Johnson claimed that things were great, but based upon the elder's expressions and body language, Miyazaki had his doubts. Perhaps he was unable to read the cultural subtleties accurately.

Johnson turned, pointed at him, and rattled off some heated Samoan. Miyazaki recognized his name in the tirade. Johnson switched to English and beckoned with a finger, "Commander, come over here."

Miyazaki felt his blood rise as he fought back the anger at the insult. He was not some servant to be ordered around by the likes of that native, Johnson. He stood slowly, masking his anger, took a couple of steps, and sat cross-legged on the floor next to Johnson. Through a forced smile, he whispered in English, "Never use my rank again in front of your people. My mission here is secret and the fewer who know about my country's involvement, the better. I will not warn you again."

Johnson stiffened but quickly recovered his wits and began in English, "Mr. Miyazaki, may I introduce Chief Sam, Chief Tonga, and Chief Gwa."

Miyazaki bowed at the waist and responded in English, "I am honored to meet you."

Johnson translated Miyazaki's greeting. Chief Tonga appeared to be in his sixties, with close cropped gray hair and a deeply lined face. Miyazaki could see he was still fit. He had a flat

57

stomach, and his skin was tight over taught muscles. To his surprise, Tonga spoke in American-accented English. "Mr. Miyazaki, why should the Samoan people trade the American yoke for a Japanese one?"

Miyazaki smiled, "The Emperor has no territorial claims or ambitions for Samoa. We only wish to deny to the Americans the use of your island home to attack our homeland."

Tonga eyed his guest coldly. "So, you say, Mr. Miyazaki, but what guarantee could you possibly provide?"

Miyazaki stood. "I personally pledge, on my honor as an Imperial Envoy, that Japan has no desire to colonize or otherwise occupy Samoa. We only wish to help you gain your freedom – your independence from the Americans."

Tonga smiled ruefully. "You must think us ignorant savages, Mr. Miyazaki. But perhaps I should call you Commander, a commander of Japanese Intelligence? The American newspapers are full of Japan's actions in China. Some might call them atrocities. Why would Japan treat us any differently?"

Miyazaki rubbed his chin, then responded. "You can call me what you wish, Chief Tonga. However, I ask that you refrain from using my rank outside your village. It could cause problems with the American authorities for both of us."

Tonga bowed, "Of course, Commander. You are a guest in our council and our village. As such, I will honor your request."

"Thank you, Chief. Our Emperor has decreed the creation of an Asian Co-prosperity Sphere — where European and American Colonialism have no place. Where free trade can exist between all the Asian peoples."

"I see," said Tonga, "but who will rule the sphere? Who will keep the white devils from returning?"

"Why, the Imperial Navy of course."

Tonga took a sip of tea, "And who would protect us from Imperial excesses such as we've seen in China?"

Miyazaki understood Tonga's question. He was shrewd enough to grasp Japan's true intentions. Miyazaki decided to sidestep the issue. "All nations in the Co-prosperity Sphere would have a role in the Imperial Council — including Samoa."

"An Imperial Council you say? Not an Asian Council? And who would rule this Imperial council – your Emperor?"

Miyazaki was growing tired of this banter. He was a warrior, not a diplomat. "Yes, he would preside over the council to lead and guide you."

Tonga abruptly stood causing all those in attendance to do the same. "I have heard enough. Tomorrow we will sit in our council and vote on whether to join your revolution. Tonight, I have much to consider before my vote." Tonga left the hut, followed by the other two chiefs.

Miyazaki followed them out and watched as two guards holding flaming torches led the way to an adjacent hut. The elders ducked inside, and the two guards remained outside, one on each side of the entrance. He tuned to Johnson, "You did not tell me Tonga spoke English."

"I swear, I did not know."

Miyazaki frowned. "How do you think they will vote in the morning?"

Johnson considered. "Tonga's the key. The others will vote as he does."

"And how do you think Tonga will vote?"

Johnson gazed at the hut and the two guards. "I can't say for sure. He distrusts all off-islanders but has no particular dislike for the Americans."

"Are you saying he will argue against?"

Johnson looked around furtively. "I can't say for sure, but I'm thinking he will vote against."

"Do you think he will betray me to the Americans?"

Johnson shrugged.

Miyazaki nodded and looked out across the vast expanse of the Pacific Ocean. He smiled as he flexed his muscles and thought about the exciting night ahead.

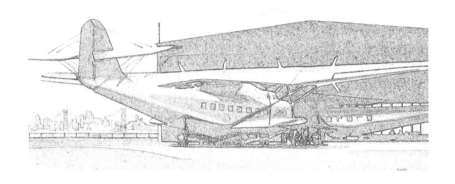

Chapter Eleven

2:03 am, December 20th, 1936
Village of Vatia,
American Samoa

Johnson's rhythmic snoring had not changed for an hour, and Miyazaki was confident that he was deeply asleep. Silently he rolled off the bed and crouched on the hut's dirt floor. He counted his heartbeats and waited a full minute before slowly crawling to the opening. He stopped just inside the shadow of the Moon and peered outside. The village was deathly still, with only the occasional muffled cough or groan.

The hut Johnson and he shared was unguarded, but across the village common, two guards remained outside the chief's hut. Both were slumped forward, their heads resting on their chests, and appeared to be asleep. Ever cautious, Miyazaki waited and watched for several minutes before he was certain.

He slipped around the rear of the hut with the stealth his years of ninja training allowed. Cutting across the village common was too dangerous – he could not risk being seen. Instead, he moved wraith-like as he drifted from one moon shadow to the next. It was slow going, but speed was unimportant. Remaining unseen was paramount as he made his way around the perimeter of the sleeping village.

As he stepped into the shadow of another hut, a dark shape suddenly jumped up and started a low growl. Miyazaki quickly reached into his pocket, pulled out a piece of his dinner, and tossed it to the dog. It stopped growling and sniffed the offering. Glancing at Miyazaki, it snatched the piece of meat and ran off into the surrounding palm forest. Miyazaki thought it a better use for the wretched pork than for his dinner.

Finally, at the chief's hut, Miyazaki cautiously checked for another entry point but found none. Disappointed, he would have to slip past the sleeping guards. He moved around to the other side and picked up a pebble, tossing it in between the two sleeping figures.

He tensed, ready to spring if need be, but nothing happened. He tossed another pebble, but neither man stirred.

Someone watching the hut might have seen a dark shadow momentarily pass between the guards and vanish, but Miyazaki doubted it. Inside he located Chief Tonga's sleeping figure and knelt beside the cot. He withdrew a small vial from his shirt pocket and uncapped it. Slowly, he leaned over the sleeping form and poured a drop of the clear liquid onto Tonga's forehead. Tonga stirred, and Miyazaki dropped prostrate to the floor and capped the vial. Tonga rubbed his forehead and then turned onto his side, still asleep.

Miyazaki crawled out and retraced his steps back to his hut. Inside, Johnson was sitting up on his cot and eyed him with suspicion. "Where have you been?"

Miyazaki smiled and sat on his cot. "Nature called."

"You were gone a long time."

"I don't know how you could stomach that foul pork they served for dinner. I swear it was rancid. Regardless, it did not agree with me and gave me the trots. Satisfied?"

Johnson did not look convinced. "Maybe." After a minute he lay back.

*   *   *

Miyazaki awoke to shouts of alarm. The locals were quarreling in their native tongue. He looked over at Johnson who was hurriedly pulling on his trousers. "What is it?"

Johnson started to button his shirt. "They're saying Tonga is dead."

61

"Is that so? How tragic."

Johnson stopped at the opening and looked back. "Is there something you want to tell me?"

He eyed Johnson coldly. "I'm not sure what you are implying?"

"You know full well. You were gone for over an hour last night — maybe longer. You could have decided to remove some objections to our plans."

Miyazaki glanced at his katana and then at Johnson. "If you accuse me of something nefarious, honor would demand that I challenge you."

Johnson patted the revolver strapped to his hip. "I'd never let you near me with that katana."

As Johnson hurried off, Miyazaki smiled to himself. The fool would never see him coming.

*   *   *

Alameda Airport,
Alameda, California,
2:50 pm, December 20th, 1936

Mac's pickup truck rattled across the railroad tracks at the airport entrance. Nick hauled on the wheel and downshifted as the ancient truck lurched and then backfired. He gave it the gas and glanced at Mac's old hanger as he drove on. The new occupants had repainted the building and removed Mac's sign. His mind flashed back to the last time he's seen Mac, the night he'd talked his way onto the S.S. *North Haven* and began his career with Pan American. He wondered if Mac would be proud of him. Mac had always said he'd go far if he ever got his head out of his behind. Mac's murder at the hands of Miyazaki still rode hard on his emotions. *Someday, Miyazaki, someday...*

Over to the left he could see the *Philippine Clipper* moored in what the locals called the Clipper Lagoon. The mechanics and service personnel had worked through the night to get her ready to go. Once they completed their final checks, the flight crew would board and start preparations for the twenty-plus-hour flight to Honolulu.

Nick parked in the employee lot, grabbed his remain overnight (R-O-N) bag and his gold PAA logo-embossed leather briefcase. It had been a gift from Colonel Young upon passing the PAA flight engineers' examination. Nick was thrilled. Young had said, "Normally, only pilots get these."

Nick asked, "Then why did you give it to me?"

"Let's just say a leather case for a Sikorski S-42 flying boat is a fair trade."

"It wasn't just me that saved the *Pan American Clipper.*"

"I know that!" snapped Young. Then in a softer tone, "But the others already have one."

The screech of metal-on-metal when he closed the truck door brought his mind back to the present. He had forgotten to grease that hinge again.

Inside the hanger, Nick stopped at the full-length mirror. Above the mirror Andre Priester's words challenged every crew member. "Are you ready to meet the passengers?" Nick checked his reflection. His navy-blue uniform fit well. He'd continued to build muscle and fill out. His daily workouts at Mr. Nieshi's Dojo not only honed his mind – it honed his body, too. His white uniform cap finally fit. It had taken a while, but the supply clerk eventually found the 7 5/8th size. Heck even his tie was straight. He was ready.

The door opened and Captain Edwin Musick walked in. He looked Nick up and down and said, "You'll do. Let get inside and start the pre-flight briefing."

"Yes, sir." Nick followed Musick into the large briefing room. One side of the room held a wall-to-wall and floor-to-ceiling map of the Pacific Ocean. On it, Nick saw the clipper's route traced out in a thick black line that left Alameda, crossed to Honolulu, then proceeded west with stops at Midway Atoll, Wake Island, Guam, and terminated at Manilla, Philippines.

The staff meteorologist stood up and walked to the wall map. "Captain Musick, if your crew is assembled, I will begin."

Musick nodded and the meteorologist began his briefing describing the predicted weather along the route. "According to the shipping reports and our out stations, you can expect moderate headwinds and no major tropical depressions along the planned route to Honolulu."

As he droned on Nick's mind began to wander. He couldn't remember a time that the meteorologist had been even close in his forecast. He often wondered why Pan American Airways paid this guy.

After the weather brief, First Officer Harold Grey stood up and handed out the duty schedule. Normally, they would work four hours on and four hours off. But most crew members stayed at their posts after their shift. There was just so much work that often it took an extra hand to complete it on time. The navigational calculations, and those for rate of fuel consumption, the distance to point of no return, and countless other aspects of flying an airliner 2,400 miles constituted an enormous workload.

Captain Grey waved Nick over. "I don't believe we've met." Grey stuck out his hand. "I'm Harold Grey, transferred in from the Caribbean Division."

Nick took the proffered hand. "Nice to meet you, sir. Do you have much time in the Martin?"

"About 100 hours – you?"

"At the controls, about 50, but a lot more on the S-42, which I prefer."

Grey smiled, "Don't we all. However, we do what Priester says."

"True enough. But don't get me wrong, I love working for Pan Am even if I have to fly the Martin."

Grey checked his clipboard. "I see that you are scheduled for second watch."

"Yes, that's right."

"Finish the pre-flight checks with Wright. He tells me your girlfriend is aboard?"

"Yes, she's returning for the holidays."

Grey smiled, "You can go back and sit with her for take-off. She might need some hand holding."

"Thanks, Mr. Grey. But my Leilani won't need any reassurance. She's a pilot in training, flown a Jenny and flown with me in a Staggerwing. She's as tough as woodpecker lips."

Grey's eyebrows arched. "A Staggerwing, you? Who did you have to kill to get one?"

Nick chuckled, "Nobody. Mr. Hughes asked me to deliver it to Oakland. I flew it from the Hearst Castle. Leilani accompanied me."

Grey pushed his cap back and scratched his head. "You know Hughes and Hearst? And I suppose you know movie stars, too?"

64

"I never met Mr. Hearst but I did have dinner with Katharine Hepburn. But I can't say I know her well, or any other movie stars. Do you?"

"What? No, of course not." Grey looked down at his clipboard, flipped through a few pages, then looked up at Nick. "Grab your things and line up for the parade."

The parade was what Priester demanded every crew do when approaching the aircraft and when deplaning. It was more of a procession, ordered by rank, with the captains first, then the first officer, navigators, flight engineers, and finally the stewards. They marched in step, by twos, with the passengers, press, movie newsreel cameramen, and hundreds of spectators looking on. Priester was known to secretly watch crews boarding and deplaning. If they did not meet his standards, he would hold them over and make the crew do it again until he was satisfied.

Captain Musick looked over his shoulder at the two lines, "You ready?"

The crew nodded in unison.

Musick ordered, "Open the doors."

Two ground crewmen held the double doors open and Musick said, "Forward, march!"

Nick stepped off on his right foot instead of his left and was immediately out of step with the rest of the crew. "Darn it." He did a quick skip and regained the cadence but tripped on the threshold. Flight Engineer Victor Wright caught his shoulder before he slammed into the back of the Grey.

"Thanks," Nick whispered.

Wright shook his head. "And they let you fly clippers? God help us."

Grey turned around and glared. "Can it, you two, or you'll be doing double watches."

Nick suppressed a smile.

Situated between engines number two and three, the Flight Engineer position sat high above the flight deck and had a narrow ladder access. Only a quarter-of-an-inch of duralumin separated the engineer from two 850 horse-power engines streaming at full throttle. It took fifteen minutes or more to take off and climb to cruising altitude. A guy could go deaf really quick at the Flight Engineer position.

Wright looked up from his clipboard. "That was the last item on the checklist. You ready to go see your girl?"

"Are you sure you don't need any help finding the engines start switch?"

"Very funny, smart ass. Get out of here or I'll go sit with Leilani."

Nick tossed out an exaggerated salute. "Aye, aye, Captain Bligh."

Wright waved him off. "Give my best to Leilani. I haven't seen her in a while."

Nick reached for the ladder. "Will do." He started down from the flight engineer perch.

At the rear of flight deck, he stepped through the hatch and closed it behind him. He marveled at the quiet afforded the passengers. Their compartment was sound proofed, unlike the flight deck and crew compartment. He descended the four steps down to the passage compartment deck and where Mr. Staves, the chief steward, stowed some dishes. When he noticed Nick, he asked, "Nick, what can I get you?"

"Nothing, Mr. Staves, I'm going to ride out the take-off in the passenger's compartment."

"Do you mean by that pretty dark-haired beauty, Miss Porta?"

Nick shook his head, "Are there no secrets in this company?"

Staves cocked his head, "Well, Nick, I can't rightly say about the entire Pan American Airways. But I can tell you there are darn few aboard this flying boat."

"Great." Nick patted Staves on the shoulder and moved aft toward Leilani's seat. A male passenger looked up, white-faced. "Is everything all right, Captain?"

"Everything is fine, sir. But I'm not the captain. I'm Flight Engineer Grant at your service."

"R.F. Bradley, Standard Oil, then why haven't we shoved off yet?"

"Mr. Bradley, the engine run up is not complete. As soon as Captain Musick is satisfied with his final checks, he will order the ground crew to cast off from the pier and we'll be on our way."

Bradley looked out the window and at the whirling props of engines three and four. "If you say so, young man."

"Situation permitting, Captain Musick will come back and brief details of our flight after take-off. If there's nothing else, sir, I need to get back to my seat."

Bradley waved a dismissive hand and Nick walked on. Leilani looked up just as he entered the compartment through the rear hatchway. "There you are. I thought I might have to live this adventure all alone."

She had pinned up her long hair into a French braid and her long ponytail was secured with a red bow. She wore a simple pink cotton dress and Nick admired her legs, crossed at the knees. "Caught you looking, flyboy."

Nick sat down and took her hand, "How could any man resist." He reached across and kissed her cheek. He pointed out the window. "See, the ground crewman just tossed a mooring line to the bow. We're off."

Leilani glanced out just as the engines began to pick up speed. You couldn't really hear the difference, but you could feel the entire ship vibrate. Leilani grinned at Nick, "This is so exciting. To be one of only seven passengers on the first Trans-Pacific flight. It will be something to tell my grandchildren."

"If we live."

Leilani playfully slapped his hand. "Nick, what a thing to say. You'd never let me aboard if you thought it unsafe. Right?"

He smiled and gently squeezed her hand. "We'll see."

Chapter Twelve

0214. Tuesday, 22 December 1936
25°32'47.6"North Latitude, 137°41'06.9"West Longitude
8,000 Feet Above Sea Level, Over the Pacific Ocean

From the depths of a deep sleep, Nick heard Victor Wright's voice. It had an ephemeral quality – like part of his dream but also part of the real world. The clipper's lurch and some incessant shaking brought him awake. He rolled over and opened his eyes.

Wright gently shook Nick's shoulder. "Rise and shine, buddy boy. It's your shift."

Nick groaned and rubbed his eyes. He glanced at his wristwatch. "Has it really been four hours?"

Wright sat down on the empty bunk across from him. "If you want to spend your off hours chatting with Leilani, and stealing the occasional kiss, that's on you. Not that I blame you, she's a lovely girl."

Nick squinted across the compartment and saw Wright lift a steaming cup of coffee. "Sit up and drink this. It will help you come back to the land of the living."

Nick took the cup and sipped it slowly. "Thanks, where are we?"

"I don't know, and neither does Noonan." The Martin flying boat hit another air pocket and lurched downward. Nick steadied himself and managed not to spill his coffee.

"What? How can that be?"

Wright replied, "We flew into the soup a few hours ago and it obscured the stars. Mr. Grey is at the controls and he descended to a couple of hundred feet above the ocean. Noonan dropped a few drift bombs, but we never broke through the clouds. So, Grey brought her back up to eight thousand to conserve fuel."

Nick took a sip. "Have we passed the point of no return?"

Wright nodded. "About an hour ago as far as Noonan can determine. We'd better get back to the flight engineer position. I'll give you the rest of the skinny there."

The crew rest compartment was in the tail of the Martin, behind the last bulkhead. They stepped gingerly past the sleeping passengers so as not to wake them. Passing Leilani's Pullman sleeper, Nick saw her fast asleep, oblivious to the bumpy ride. He ducked his head through the open curtain and checked that she had her restraining straps in place. He glanced back at Wright, "Vic, she's more than good looking. She's smart, and strapped in like a pro."

Nick mounted the flight deck steps and stopped between the pilots. "Grant reporting for duty, Mr. Grey." Even though Grey held the rank of Captain, on the clipper there was only one Captain. On this flight it was Captain Ed Musick.

Grey, perspiration dripping down his face, looked over his shoulder and nodded. "I may need you to relieve the co-pilot. He needs to get some chow and a rest. It's taken two of us to keep this beast on course."

Nick nodded, hiding his pleasure. "I'd like to get the FE shift transition brief first, if that's okay."

The Martin shook violently and yawed to port. Nick grabbed a handrail and hung on as Grey fought the aircraft back onto an even keel. "Copy that but be ready to get down here when I call."

Up on the flight engineer perch, Victor Wright began the change-over brief. "Number three engine has been running rough and a little hot. I adjusted the fuel-air mixture to rich and it smoothed out. The intermittent rain squalls helped cool it too, and I was able to lean out the mixture for a while. You'll have to keep an eye on it. Our fuel burn is above the curve."

Wright pointed to the *How-Goz-It* graph. "We are here, and we passed the point-of-no-return about here. You can see by the fuel consumption rates and my estimate we've got a three-hour reserve once we reach the islands. However, that's only if we can remain at 6,000 feet AGL or higher."

"You mean ASL – above sea level?"

"Same thing, smart-ass."

"I'll keep that in mind, Vic."

Wright continued through his brief, answering all of Nick's questions, then had one of his own. "Do you want me to hang around for a bit?"

Nick smiled. "No thanks, I got this. It'll be fun. Usually, during the mid-flight shift, the toughest thing I'll have to do is stay awake."

"Careful what you wish for. You know where to find me." Wright climbed down the ladder, said a few words to Mr. Grey, and disappeared aft.

Nick signed into the flight engineer log, noted the remaining fuel levels, and the engine readings. He had just finished his maximum range estimate when the clipper tumbled and seemed to fall out of the sky. His stomach lurched. He tasted bile as he jammed his hand up to stop his head hitting the cabin roof. The engines began to race as the Martin pointed nearly straight down. Nick watched as the four tachometers moved from the black into the red. Much more time at this rate and they would come apart. Without waiting for a command from Grey, Nick reduced the throttles to bring the engines back into the black. Then he heard a scream from the flight deck.

Mr. Grey yelled, "Nick, get down here now!"

Nick unbuckled his seatbelt and swung hand-over-hand to reach the flight deck. The angle was so severe that his feet hung perpendicular as he descended the ladder. Mr. Canaday, the radio operator, and Navigator Fred Noonan were helping the co-pilot, First Officer Jerry Weber, out of the right seat. He was cradling his left hand. Nick asked, "What happened?"

Grey, straining with the control yoke, said, "Later! Strap into the co-pilot seat and help me get this beast back under control."

The cockpit tilted in the opposite direction as Nick squeezed into the seat and tugged his harness straps tight. "I'm in."

Grey never took his eyes off the instruments. Outside, the rain beat like a drum on the duralumin skin. "We're in a downward spiral. Grab the yoke and help me get her nose up. Call out the altimeter and airspeed readings."

The clipper bucked and everything not stowed came cascading down toward the nose. Something hard hit the back of Nick's head. The clipper bucked again, and his flight engineer logbook thumped into the wind screen. Nick ignored the pain and called out. "Passing through seven thousand feet. Airspeed two-hundred-three knots. We are close to exceeding maximum velocity."

"Tell me something I don't know." Grey struggled with the wildly oscillating control yoke. "She'll hold together."

Nick patted the instrument panel. "Hold together, baby."

"Nick, when I give the word, jam all throttles forward to maximum take-off power. Then help me pull back on the yoke."

"Copy that." Nick released his grip on the yoke and reached up toward the four throttles located on the overhead between the two pilot positions.

Grey looked over. "I'm going to count down then you slam the throttles to the stops. You Ready?"

"Ready, Captain."

"Three, two, one, now!"

Nick slammed the throttles forward, dropped his hands to the yoke, and pulled back with all his might. Still the Martin dove.

A high-pitched whine permeated the roar of the engines and gradually rose in intensity to rival the engines' scream.

Noonan, strapped in at the navigator station, yelled over the din, "What's that noise?"

Nick responded, "Air rushing through the struts and guy wires."

Grey said, "I never exceeded two-hundred knots before. Ease your pull and let the yoke move forward."

Nick complied never letting go.

Then Grey added. "Pull, Nick, pull!"

Biceps trembling with the strain, Nick pulled with all of his strength. He glanced at the instrument panel and saw the artificial horizon start to roll back toward the horizontal. "Altimeter at five-hundred. Unwinding slowing." He thought about what he would feel when they hit. He wondered, would there be much pain? What would the searchers find? Would they find anything?

Grunting with effort, Grey said. "My God, she's heavy. We must have exceeded maximum wing load."

Together they continued to pull back on the yokes, but the Martin continued its mad race toward destruction in the Pacific

Ocean below. Nick's hands burned, his arm muscles ached, and sweat beaded on his forehead.

The Martin lurched to port, but they quickly corrected. The clipper leveled out and started to slowly climb. He glanced out the starboard window and saw the ocean waves in the dim moonlight. It seemed they had passed through the storm.

Grey eyed the stars and called out calmly, "Fred, perhaps now you can determine our position."

Noonan replied, "I'm on it, Mr. Grey."

Nick exhaled hard and stared at the altimeter. The needle moved slowly upward. The rate of assent was painfully slow, but they were climbing out of a watery grave. Ten minutes later, they reached two-thousand feet.

Grey said, "Take her, Nick."

Nick slid his feet onto the rudder pedals. "I've got the clipper."

Grey slumped back and loudly exhaled. "I don't *ever* want to do that again."

The controls felt heavy in Nick's hands, like they were flying through molasses rather than air. He turned to Grey. "What just happened?"

"We encountered severe turbulence that caused an upset."

"An upset?" questioned Nick. "It felt like the bottom fell out of the sky." Nick grimaced, "I think Jerry's wrist might be broken." He shook his head in disbelief. "We lost seven-thousand five-hundred feet in less than two minutes. How is that possible?"

Grey nodded solemnly. "The extreme turbulence caused us to roll off a wing and we went into a steep spiral. The yoke snapped out of my hand and hit Jerry's wrist. Jamming the throttles forward produced just enough air blast on the elevators to bring her nose up."

Fred Noonan unstrapped and moved between the two pilots. "I've seen this before. When I was a navigator on a steamer out of Yokahama. We used to call 'em White Squalls. Never thought they reached up to eight-thousand feet." Noonan paused. "I thought we were goners this time."

Grey mopped his brow. "It seems we cheated death yet again. You got our position yet, Fred?"

"Right here." He handed Grey a 3 by 5-inch card with a compass azimuth written in pencil. "Come west, north-west to course 278 degrees. We're at 25 degrees, 52 minutes north, 105 degrees, 12 minutes west."

Grey let out a low whistle and tucked the card into a clip below the windshield. "We're south of Oahu?"

Noonan continued. "The storm was pushing us south but there was no way to know it. What with the cloud cover above and below, I was dead reckoning. And our earlier position was a SWAG at best."

Nick asked, "What's a SWAG?"

In unison, Grey and Noonan answered, "A sophisticated wild-ass guess."

Feeling a little foolish, Nick looked out the windscreen, "Oh."

Chapter Thirteen

0758 hours, Wednesday, 23 December 1936
2,000 Feet above Sea Level,
Over the Pacific Ocean

Four hours later, Nick made his way back to the passenger compartment. After the terrifying nosedive, the remainder of his shift had been uneventful. Captain Musick had come back to the flight deck and taken over from First Officer Grey, who moved to the co-pilot position.

As he walked back through the passenger compartment, he saw the stewards converting the cabin from Pullman style sleepers into the daytime configuration. He stopped at the galley. "Rough night back here, Mr. Staves?"

Staves closed the overhead compartment and turned to Nick. "I'll say. The galley was six ways from Sunday. What a mess! But we put it right soon enough and got the passenger's breakfast out on time."

"Sounds rough, Mr. Staves. Anybody hurt?"

"No, thank God. But we had some grumbling from a few passengers."

Nick nodded. "Good to know. Should I ask the Captain to come back and talk to them?"

Staves shook his head. "The captain is busy. I think it best to let things lie."

"Okay, let me know if you change your mind." Nick continued through the compartments until he saw Leilani and sat down beside her. "Hello, beautiful."

She pulled a strand of hair out of her eyes and frowned. "I don't feel very beautiful right now."

"Oh, I think those red flannel pajamas are just charming."

Leilani frowned. "It's getting late and I need to get ready to meet my parents. There's only two female and five male passengers on board. The men have shaved, changed, and freshened up. But not ol' Mrs. Clara Adams, who is hogging the ladies' room. *First Flighter* or not, she's a poor traveling companion."

Nick snapped his fingers. "I know. Since all the guys are done, why not use the men's room?"

"I don't know. What if someone comes in on me while I'm changing?"

"Don't worry, I'll stand guard."

Leilani thought about it for about half a second and jumped up. "Okay." She grabbed her travel bag and walked aft towards the toilets with Nick in tow.

At the men's room, Nick knocked loudly, "Is anybody in there?" There was no reply. Nick opened the door and peeked inside. It was empty. "Okay, Leilani, the coast is clear."

Once Leilani was inside, Nick took up station outside, arms crossed, trying to look as professional as possible. Twenty minutes later Leilani emerged wearing a bright red *muu-muu* emblazoned with a white and yellow hibiscus flower print. Her long hair was unbound and cascaded down her back almost to her waist. She wore a simple leather band that crossed her forehead and held her hair away from her face.

She twirled. "Well, flyboy?"

"Wow, you look great. Is that the same dress you wore when we first met?"

Leilani shook head. "No, silly — wrong color."

"Oops, sorry." He was never quite sure why things like that eluded him.

Back at their seats, Leilani gazed out the window. Below, the western shore of Maui passed from view. She turned to Nick. "I had the strangest dream last night."

"Really, what?"

Leilani looked into Nicks eyes. "I dreamed I was in an elevator in a tall building. Suddenly the elevator dropped. The operator moved the controls this way and that but still we fell."

Nick squeezed her hand.

"When I woke up all my bed clothes were piled at the head of my sleeper. What do you think it means?"

While Nick listened, he tried to decide if he should mention their mishap. In the end he decided that, as a pilot-in-training, she needed to know these things. He told her.

She looked up at him. "Nick, I knew that I would be safe as long as you were flying this boat." She squeezed his hand then turned to look out the window. "Look, ahead! That's Diamond Head. We're so close."

Nick craned his neck to see the dormant volcano on Oahu in the distance, then directly down as the island of Molokai passed beneath Leilani's window.

A few minutes later, Leilani said, "Oh Nick, I can see Pearl Harbor and the road to Mama and Papa's house." She turned back to Nick. "It's so good to be home. I've missed the islands so much."

Straining to see over Leilani's shoulder, he saw Aliamanu Crater, a large dormant volcano, west of the white sands of Waikiki Beach. They crossed over Honolulu on route to Pearl Harbor at about 200 feet. People on the streets below shielded their eyes to stare up that the silver clipper as she passed. Many waved. The boat's four engines throttled back as Captain Musick gently eased the clipper down towards the water. His light touch on the control column was evident as they circled Ford Island.

The details around Pearl Harbor grew and Nick saw the familiar landmarks. He'd landed here a few times and he always found it fascinating. "Look, Leilani. There's the *USS Arizona*. She's putting out to sea."

Black smoke belched from the *Arizona's* stack as she made her way south towards the exit. Leilani looked out at the steel gray battleship steaming past Hospital Point. "Wasn't that the ship where you met Commander Bolts?"

"Yes, eighteen months ago."

Leilani took Nick's hand. "I'm proud of your choice. A lot of guys don't believe in serving our country."

"Don't be too proud – it was self-serving too. I could never have afforded college if not for the naval ROTC scholarship."

Leilani leaned over and kissed Nick's cheek. "You talk tough, flyboy. But your past actions have betrayed you. There's more to your actions than a scholarship."

Pearl Harbor consisted of three lagoons, or locks, as the navy referred to them. The Pan American terminal was at the tip of Pearl City which was situated on a peninsula of land between the West and Middle Lock. The clippers always landed in the Middle Lock. The engines throttled back to idle and the clipper's hull came down and kissed the water. The landing was so smooth that only the spray spreading out from the hull indicated they had touched down.

The clipper spread huge plumes of water off each side as it planned on the step much like a power boat. Decelerating, the clipper came off the step and settled deeper into the water. The engines throttled up as Captain Musick eased the Martin towards the Pearl City pier. A gentle bump announced that the *Hawaii Clipper* had slid alongside the pier. One by one the engines shut down and then Mr. Staves opened the top hatch directly in front of the tail . Two members of the ground crew pushed the boarding stairs into place. Captain Musick walked through the compartment, greeting the passengers as he passed. Near the tail, he climbed the steps, stepped over the top of the fuselage, and down the boarding stairs. He would be waiting on the pier to farewell the passengers as they left.

Leilani craned her neck and looked out the window and started to wave frantically. "Nick, my parents are there on the dock. I'm so happy to see them." Then she started to sob.

Nick put his arm around her. "It's okay, Leilani, it's okay. It was a tough few months, but now you're home safe." He pulled out his handkerchief, handed it to her and wondered if she'd ever come back to the mainland again.

The other passengers gathered up their things and filed off. Composed now, Leilani stood in the aisle. "Are you coming?"

"Can't. We have to form up on the pier and march in step to the office building."

Leilani leaned over and kissed his cheek. "Okay then, see you on the shore."

Captain Grey got the crew lined up on the pier and Musick marched them toward the admin building. They passed the maintenance crew heading towards the clipper. Dressed in white overalls, they would check the aircraft from stem to stern overnight. The crew had to ensure that the airplane was 100% ready when she made the flight out to Midway Atoll tomorrow. Pan American had yet to build a hangar at the Pearl City location, so the maintenance men would hang from harnesses, over the harbor, as they checked the wings and serviced the engines.

The aircrew reached the operations building and Musick halted the odd parade. "Men, those on the flight tomorrow, meet up at the Royal Hawaiian Hotel Coffee Shop at 3:30 a.m."

Those affected let out a low moan.

Musick continued, "Alright. You knew what you signed up for. No late night and watch your booze intake. I'll have no hangovers on tomorrow's flight. Dismissed."

As the crew broke up and each headed hism own way, Station Manager Mr. Burst stepped out in front of Nick, "Good to see you again. Please step inside. I've got a cable with your name on it."

"Hello Mr. Burst, it's good to see you, too." They shook hands. Nick had worked in the machine shop under Mr. Burst during a layover between flights almost a year ago.

Burst pushed his cap back and scratched his balding head. "I saw Leilani deplane. She's such a nice young lady."

Nick smiled. "Yep."

Burst raised an eyebrow, "Can't see what she sees in you, though."

"Very funny, Mr. Burst. Now where is that cable?"

Burst motioned Nick to follow and walked into his office. He opened a wall safe and handed Nick an envelope marked SECRET//EYES ONLY//for Cadet Nicholas P. Grant. This couldn't be good. He swallowed hard as a sense of foreboding settled over him. He ripped open the envelope and read.

SECRET//EYES ONLY

TO: Naval Aviation Cadet Nicholas P. Grant,
SUBJECT: Call to Active Duty.
1. You are hereby ordered to active duty for a period of not less than 30 days.

2. You are assigned to US Naval Intelligence Office, San Francisco with duty as set forth by Commander Steven Bolts.

3. You are directed to proceed to Naval Intelligence Office, Building 142, Pearl Harbor, ASAP for mission brief and equipment draw.

William D. Puleston,
Captain, USN
Director,
Office of Naval Intelligence
Washington, D.C.

SECRET//EYES ONLY

Chapter Fourteen

9:43 a.m., Wednesday December 23rd, 1936
Pan American Airways Facility,
Pearl City, Hawaii Territory

Nick looked up from the message. "I guess I won't be working for you this layover, Mr. Burst."

"Why's that, Nick?"

"I've been ordered to active duty." Nick picked up his overnight bag and walked into the passenger lounge. Mr. and Mrs. Porta stood speaking to Leilani. Mr. Porta's face hardened the moment he caught sight of Nick. He put his hands on his hips. "What do you have to say for yourself, young man?"

Nick was stung by Porta's stern tone. "How about, 'hello'?" It was all he could think of in reply.

In contrast, Mrs. Porta's broad smile warmed his heart. She embraced Nick and kissed him on both cheeks. "Aloha, Nick. Thank you for taking such good care of Leilani. You acted like a perfect gentleman. Didn't he, Guilherme?"

Mr. Porta scowled, leaned in, and stabbed a finger at Nick's chest. "Have you no propriety? The damage you've done to Leilani's reputation is ruinous. What self-respecting man would want to marry her now?"

Nick looked Mr. Porta in the eye. "I would."

Porta's eyes went wide then narrowed. "What? Why? Do you mean you have too?"

Leilani grabbed her father's arm and spun him around. "Papa! How could you think such a thing? Nick was a perfect gentleman. Besides, I only want to marry Nick."

Porta turned back to Nick. "Marriage? Are you two nuts? She just turned eighteen. No way!"

The other passengers were beginning to stare, and Nick heard their low murmured conversation.

Mrs. Porta cut him off. "Guilherme! Don't make a scene. We'll discuss this like adults." She turned to Nick. "You must come with us to lunch." It wasn't a request.

Puzzled, Nick eyed Leilani's father, then addressed her mother. "My friends said I'd be nuts to get within pistol shot of Mr. Porta."

Mr. Porta looked daggers at Nick. "Don't think it hadn't crossed my mind."

"Guilherme! Watch your language!"

"Yes, dear. At first, I was terribly angry about the situation. But after I heard Leilani's explanation, I was somewhat relieved." He pointed a finger at Nick's chest. "But think what you could have done to Leilani's reputation. Tongues will wag."

Leilani broke in. "I don't care what people say. I love Nick and I know he'd never do anything to harm me."

Nick tried to calm Mr. Porta. "We were chaperoned twenty-four/seven."

Porta rubbed his chin. "I don't know, Nick. I was young once, and I remember how overpowering those feelings can be. You had a lot of time alone. I have to ask you man-to-man – did anything happen?"

"Are you kidding me? Dora and Walter never left us alone for a second. We'd have had more privacy on a park bench!"

Porta hoisted a questioning eyebrow.

"No, that came out wrong. We did nothing to impinge on your daughter's honor."

Porta slowly shook his head then, surprisingly, he stuck out his hand. "Good, I'm glad to hear it. Let's keep it that way."

Nick took the offered hand, "You have my word. I love your daughter."

Flustered, Porta said. "Er, okay." He turned to Mrs. Porta. "Let's get some lunch. Nick, are you ready to leave?"

Nick shook his head. "I'm sorry, I won't be able to join you." He turned to Leilani, "I've been ordered to active duty."

"Oh, Nick. What is it this time?"

"I don't know yet. Got my orders as soon as I landed. I have to report ASAP."

"For how long?"

Nick sighed as a wave of fatigue washed over him. It felt more intense than just simply flying across the world's largest ocean. It seemed as if the world conspired to keep them apart. "Thirty days or longer. It's up to Commander Bolts."

Leilani crossed her arms. "I have a mind to ring him up and give him a piece of my mind."

"Please don't. Although I'm sure he'd love to hear from you again. It'll only make matters worse. Besides, I have no idea where he is located."

She ran into his arms. "Nick, why are we always saying good-bye?"

He kissed the top of her head. "As soon as I find out what's happening, I'll get in touch."

Mr. Porta gently pulled Leilani away. "Come, dear. Nick will call as soon as he knows something. Nick, your room in the pool house is available if the navy lets you bunk off base."

Nick nodded, "Thanks, Mr. Porta. I'll let you know one way or the other."

As the Portas left, Leilani glanced back over her shoulder. Nick couldn't tell if her expression was worry or annoyance. He dismissed the thought and went to the crew ready room. Inside, Captain Musick and Captain Grey poured over charts and the flight logs. As Nick entered, Grey looked up. "Nick, Captain Musick wanted a word." Grey looked over at Musick. "Ed?"

Musick snubbed out his cigarette. "Grant, I understand that you took over from Weber after he was injured."

"Yes, sir, that's right." Nick swallowed hard and fought the urge to defend himself and his actions. Musick had a reputation for dressing down junior crew members for the slightest infraction. He braced himself.

82

Musick looked over at Grey, then broke into a broad smile. "That was some excellent flying. Harold here tells me that without your help, it could have been a very different outcome. Well done."

Nick felt a wave of relief flood over him as he relaxed. Musick was quick to rebuke and slow to praise. "Thank you, sir."

Musick held out his hand. "Give me your logbook."

Nick rummaged around in his travel bag then handed it to Musick. Musick opened to the last page and wrote a few lines. Then he handed it back. Nick read the lines added below his flight engineer entry. "Wow, Captain Musick, thanks. It says qualified M-130 pilot. Does this mean I get a raise?"

Musick and Grey burst out laughing. Musick recovered first. "Not as long as that ol' skinflint Trippe runs the company."

Grey stifled a laugh and added, "He'll probably charge you for the privilege of flying his latest clipper."

*   *   *

The gray Navy sedan made its way east along Kamehameha Highway towards the US Pearl Harbor Naval Base. Nick looked out at Ford Island and the anchorage. Battleship Division Four was in port and three battleships, the *Nevada* (BB-36), *Mississippi* (BB-41), and the *Pennsylvania* (BB-38) were moored there. The fleet aircraft carrier, the *USS Lexington* (CV-2), was out to sea with the *USS Arizona* (BB-39), probably conducting battle drills. Nick hoped he'd see the *Lady Lex*. She was one of the Navy's first aircraft carriers and key to developing and refining carrier tactics.

As they waited in line to enter the base, Nick asked the driver, "So how long you been stationed out here?"

The sailor was about the same age as Nick. He looked at Nick in the rearview mirror. "Eighteen months, sir."

Nick smiled. "No need to call me 'sir.' I'm a college kid, not an officer."

"Orders, sir. We's to treat all Pan American flight crew as officers."

"Huh, is that right?"

The sailor pulled up to the marine standing guard at the gate. The marine saluted Nick. Feeling a bit silly, Nick returned the marine's salute, and they were waved through.

A few minutes later, the sailor wheeled the sedan to a stop in front of Building 142, Naval Intelligence Center, Asiatic Fleet, Hawaii Annex. He opened his door and ran around the car to open Nick's door. As Nick stepped out the sailor snapped to attention and saluted. "Sir, the marine sentry will direct you."

Nick returned the salute and grabbed his bag. "Thanks for the ride, sailor."

"Yes, sir."

Inside, Nick showed the marine his ID. The marine handed him a NO ESCORT REQUIRED badge. "Mr. Grant, Lieutenant Commander Layton is waiting for you in Room 214." He pointed down the hall. "At the end of the corridor, take the stairs to the second floor. Room 214 is the second door on the right. Knock and then go right in, sir."

Walking down the corridor he thought about the last time he was in the building. Then he wore an ESCORT REQUIRED AT ALL TIMES badge and had two marine guards escorting him. His life had certainly changed in the last six months.

Upstairs he knocked and went in to find Commander Layton sitting behind his desk dressed in tropical khakis. Layton's dark hair was plastered over his rapidly receding hair line, and his glasses resembled the bottom of *Coca-Cola* bottles. He looked up and asked in Japanese, "*Ohayegozaimasy, Grant-san. Anata wa dokoni ita? Clipper wa sūjikanmae ni jōriku shita.*"

It took Nick a moment to do a quick translation in his head — Ah there you are Grant-san. Where have you been? The clipper landed hours ago."

Nick bowed formally while he hastily translated *It's a long story* into Japanese. "*Ohayegozaimasy, Reiton chūjō.*"

84

Chapter Fifteen

1051 hours Wednesday, 23 December 1936
US Naval intelligence office, Building 142, Pearl Harbor,
Pearl Harbor Naval Base, Hawaii Territory

Nick snapped to attention and continued in English. "Midshipman Nicolas Grant reporting as ordered, sir."

Layton continued in Japanese. *"Nihongo o tsukau, Grant-san."*

"Kashikomarimashita." Nick wasn't sure if he had told Layton "Yes, sir" or "Close the door." Layton gestured toward one of two wooden chairs located before his ancient metal desk. Nick sat. Their conversation continued in Japanese, forcing Nick to think hard. He knew Dojo Japanese and could carry on a simple conversation. However, despite Nancy's best efforts, she said he still sounded like a *Gaikoku hito* – a foreign person.

At length, to Nick's great relief, Layton switched back to English. "Your Japanese is passable. How long have you been studying?"

"I just finished my first semester at UC Berkeley, sir. I work out at our local Dojo and my sensei insists that all discussions on the mats be in Japanese. And I have a friend –"

85

"Nancy Tanaka."

Nick nodded wondering if any part of his life was private.

Layton opened his desk drawer and retrieved a pipe, lighter, and a tobacco pouch. "Do you mind if I smoke?"

"No, sir. It's your office."

Layton slowly cleaned out the pipe bowl, packed in fresh tobacco, and snapped open his lighter. After a few puffs, the room filled with the not unpleasant scent of maple tobacco. "So, tell me about Mr. Nieshi."

"He's a great guy and Nancy's uncle. But I'm sure you already know that."

Layton's stare gave nothing away and Nick continued. "He taught me most of what I know about aircraft and engine maintenance."

"Not Mac?"

Nick shook his head. "I got the basics from Mac. Usually delivered as a tirade about how dumb I was. Mr. Nieshi's instruction was much more in depth. He's a patriot and was instrumental in alerting the *China Clipper* crew to the danger of sabotage about a year ago."

"Yes, I've read the FBI report. You were there too."

Nick nodded, wondering where this was going. Layton removed his glasses and rubbed the bridge of his nose. "Let me cut to the chase. Bolts wants you to go to Samoa and sniff around. We've had some disturbing reports from the Naval Base Security Office and a request for assistance."

Nick slumped back in his chair and closed his eyes. His eyelids felt like sandpaper and burned as waves of fatigue washed over him. He had slept less than four hours out of the last thirty-six and felt like he was about to fall out of the chair. Wearily, he opened his eyes. "Why me, sir? Surely you have trained counterintelligence agents that would do a much better job than me. Someone who's not an ROTC cadet."

Layton placed his pipe in the ashtray and leaned in. "Because you are one of the few people who has come face-to-face with Miyazaki and lived."

Nick sat bolt upright, suddenly fully awake. "How do you know he's in Samoa?"

Layton smiled. "You do not have a need-to-know!" that."

Cold fury jolted Nick as he leaned in. He wanted to reach across the table and grab Layton by the collar. Fortunately, Mr. Nieshi's centering training kicked in and he was able to calm himself. Nick leaned forward and spoke just above a whisper. "You want me to risk my life to ID Miyazaki, but you won't tell me how it is you know he's in Samoa?"

"That's right. Are you refusing the mission?"

"Can I?"

Layton replaced his glasses and handed Nick a sheaf of heavily redacted teletype papers. He held the yellow paper up to the light but was unable to see through the black redacting ink. "What's this?"

The Commander stiffened. "You are on active duty now. You will address me by my rank and respond to me with 'sir' attached to every utterance. Is that clear Midshipman Grant?"

Leaning back, Nick drew out his reply. "Yes, sir." The words seemed to hang in the air as each looked at the other until Nick broke eye contact. He was too weary for this game and just wanted to find a place to sleep.

Layton picked up his pipe and re-lighted it. "Read those intercepts and see if they motivate you. Maybe you'll have more interest in the mission."

"Do I have a choice?"

"Actually, you do. I'll only send you if you volunteer. I won't order you to go."

Nick settled back and started reading. The reports noted a Japanese sub, the I-23, leaving Yokohama Naval Base. She submerged immediately and they lost contact with her. Next there were several reports of sub sightings off Samoa a week later. Then there were sentry reports of possible observation of the Navy Base during the hours of darkness. A local reported seeing men lugging heavy boxes up over the Rainmaker pass. He also reported a man in a blue uniform directing the local men. The final report could have been unrelated, but Nick wasn't so sure. A local chief known to be friendly with the Americans died under mysterious circumstances a few days later. This was after an off islander visited the village. It had the hallmark of Miyazaki's past actions. Actions that held no regard for human life.

After he finished, Nick looked up to see Layton making his way through a pile of paperwork. Nick leaned over and placed the reports on the desk. "There's no mention of Miyazaki here, Commander."

Layton looked up. "It's him. There are sensitive methods and sources involved that strongly indicate that Miyazaki is on the island. Furthermore, those same sources confirm that the Japanese are trying to ferment a rebellion."

"What sources, Commander? I have a right to know."

"No, you don't. You do not have a need-to-know!"." They eyed each other again but this time Layton broke contact first. "Commander Bolts is on a mission elsewhere and can't make it here for weeks. However, he told me that he's convinced Miyazaki is on the island and stirring up trouble. He said that you're the perfect man for this mission."

"Sir, why didn't you lead with that? Bolts and I go back a piece."

Layton exhaled a cloud of pipe smoke. "Because we both wanted you to read the intel first – then make up your own mind. He also said that it's your choice – no harm, no foul."

Nick considered it for a few seconds. He had hoped to spend time with Leilani this holiday season, but it seemed the Gods had other ideas. "When do I leave, sir?"

Chapter Sixteen

12:10 p.m., Wednesday, 23 December 1936
Porta Home, Manoa Heights,
Honolulu Oahu, Hawaii Territory

Nick grabbed his bag from the back seat and then waved at the sailor behind the wheel. "Thanks for the ride."

"You bet, sir." He reached out and handed Nick a card. "Call that number in the morning if you need a ride back to base."

"Okay."

Nick closed the back door and the gray Navy sedan crunched across the coral gravel. It reached the pavement and started the drive back down the valley. Nick turned to look at the house surrounded by lush tropical vegetation. He inhaled deeply and smiled at the sweet fragrance of the plumeria and hibiscus flowers that framed the house. The large, two-story house was pink — the result of the crushed coral that had been mixed with concrete. On an earlier visit Mr. Porta told Nick that he wanted to be sure their house would stand up to any hurricane. Even the shutters that flanked the windows were made of steel. The effect was subtle, and the house's outward appearance belied its inherent strength.

Nick picked up his bags and walked under the portico towards two large doors of carved koa wood. The door flew open and Leilani jumped into his arms. He kissed and hugged her. "Hello, my island princess." His joy at seeing her never seemed to wane.

She pushed back in his arms and cocked her head. "Nick, in Hawaii we say aloha."

"Yeah, I know. I guess I haven't adjusted to island time yet."

She hugged him again. "Well, there's plenty of time for that now that you're here."

"Leilani, there's something I need to – "

Before he could continue, Consuela, the housekeeper, stepped into the open doorway and squealed. "Nick, so good to see you!"

"Aloha, Consuela." He glanced down at Leilani.

She nudged him in the ribs, "That's better. We'll make a *Kama'aina* out of you yet."

Consuela smiled at Nick, her white teeth in sharp contrast to her nut-brown complexion. "Mr. and Mrs. Porta are waiting for you at the dining room table. Have you had lunch?"

Nick chuckled, "Lunch? I haven't eaten breakfast."

"You go greet the Portas and I'll make you a plate. They have just finished." She hurried off to the kitchen, humming.

The dining room was as elaborate as he remembered. Two crystal chandeliers hung from an ornate ceiling. Along the west wall, floor to ceiling French doors were open to the garden. A large swimming pool covered much of the immediate view, but Nick could see trails that led off into the denser foliage of the tropical garden. He remembered fondly that was where Leilani and he had first kissed.

The Portas stood when Nick and Leilani entered. Mrs. Porta rushed over to Nick and she kissed him on both cheeks. Mr. Porta walked over and extended his hand. "That didn't take long. We got your room prepared in the guest house."

Nick took the offered hand and shook it. "Thanks, Mr. Porta."

He turned to Leilani, "I tried to tell you earlier, but I'll only be staying tonight. I'll be shipping out in the morning."

Leilani put her hands to her cheeks. "Oh no, Nick. You've only just arrived. What about our Christmas plans?"

90

Mr. Porta put a hand on Leilani's shoulder "Now, now, dear. Nick's got a job to do. What can you tell us, Nick?"

"Sadly, not much. I only know I must report to Fleet Intelligence tomorrow for my orders, and I'll be shipping out for a week or more. But I'm coming back through Honolulu." He smiled at Leilani. "I'm looking forward to spending some time with your daughter exploring the island."

He turned to look at Leilani. "Is that okay with you?"

"No, Nick it is not all right!" Leilani stood, knocking over her chair. "Hana was right about you."

Confused, Nick asked, "What did your sister say?"

"That being with you would be extremely hard. That you're impossible. You'll always show up in the middle of the night unannounced, then leave unexpectedly – like now. I just don't know, Nick. I've got to think if we even have a future." She turned on her heel and stalked from the room.

Nick reeled, unsure of what just happened. "Mr. Porta, I seem to have lost my appetite. May I be excused?"

Mrs. Porta reached over and put her hand on his. "Nick, give her some time. It's been a tumultuous first semester."

*   *   *

Nick took his R.O.N. bag and climbed the steps to the second floor of the pool house that served as guest accommodations. He tossed his bag on the bed and started to strip down. He hung the wool Pan American uniform on a hangar and placed it in the closet. He pulled on a pair of gym shorts, a T-shirt, and a pair of rubber-soled gym shoes. The sun was still high in the afternoon sky and it was humid — without a breath of air. Still, he needed to blow off some steam. He descended the stairs and took off running around the pool towards the garden path.

The path snaked through the lush tropical foliage, past lemon, lime, papaya, and banana trees. On he ran. Past the gazebo where he and Leilani had first kissed almost eighteen months ago. The memory further darkened his mood. At the end of the garden path, a gate led out into the jungle above. Nick decided to explore and ran up a narrow trail as fast as his burning lungs would allow.

Leilani's outburst had taken him by surprise, and he was troubled that he might lose her. Running or swimming always cleared his mind. Mr. Nieshe said he should try meditation, but that never worked like an all-out run or a one-thousand-yard freestyle swim.

The rutted trail was as steep as it was slippery, and Nick tumbled a time or two. After twenty minutes of running, stumbling and occasionally crashing into the mud he reached the summit, a little muddy and a little bloody. He stood on the knife edge crest balancing precariously. Looking back the way he came, he could just see the roof of the Porta house peeking through the thick green canopy below. Further down the valley the land leveled out and he saw the pink walls of the Royal Hawaiian Hotel on Waikiki Beach. Off to his right, in the middle distance, he saw ships of the Navy's Asiatic fleet moored at Pearl Harbor. Aloud he mused, "I wonder which ship I'll be on tomorrow?"

The rest of the Koolau Mountains lay further off to his right and climbed into the clouds that always seemed to cling to their peaks. He yelled, "You drive me crazy, Leilani. What do you want from me?"

He pulled off his sweat soaked T-shirt, mopped his face and tied it around his head. It would absorb some of the sweat that was stinging his eyes. He took one last look around and started back to the Portas' at a trot.

When he reached the pool, he stripped off his socks and shoes. He rinsed off the accumulated mud at the poolside shower and dove into the pool's deep end. He swam freestyle laps until he was exhausted. He hauled himself out, grabbed a couple of towels by the shower, and started up the stairs. Inside, he dried off and flopped onto the bed. The Koolau's cool breeze had followed him down from the mountain top. It wafted through the louvered door and window, bringing with it the sweet smell of tropical flowers. Nick peeled off his sopping wet trunks, crawled under the sheets, and promptly fell asleep.

Later that afternoon, Nick awoke and dressed in slacks and a shirt. He was lying on his bed reading *Coming of Age in Samoa*, but that was proving troublesome. He had borrowed the book from the Portas' extensive library, and it was fascinating. Author Margaret Mead had written a study of the Samoan people a few years earlier. According to Meade, the Samoan people were different from Americans in many ways. Men and woman only wore lava-lavas, a cloth wrap that covered them from navel to mid-calf. But his mind kept drifting back to Leilani's angry words.

There was a soft knock on the door. Nick put the book down and said, "Come in."

Leilani stepped inside. Nick slid off the bed and stood, not quite sure what to say.

She stopped a few feet from him, her hands clasped at her waist. "I wanted to apologize for snapping and walking out on you earlier."

Nick reached out and took her hands, "Come, please sit." They sat on the brightly covered bedspread facing each other. Nick took her hand and kissed it. "You've got nothing to apologize for. I was thinking that maybe you're right. I just pop into and out of your life with little warning and expect everything to be hunky-dory. I'm the one that needs to ask for your forgiveness."

"That's as may be, Nick. But I was rude and you're a guest in my father's house."

"I hope that I'm more than that to you."

She did not answer, and they sat in silence for what seemed like an eternity. Finally, she spoke, "I'm not sure how much longer I can live this crazy life. We've been run off the road by an insane cabbie and I was attacked walking to my home. Then there was that business on Santa Clara Island. We got shot out of the sky and then armed men chased us all over the island. I thought we were dead."

Nick couldn't meet her eyes. "I asked you not to come along, but you insisted."

"Nick, you don't get it! It's not me. I'm scared for you. I go crazy every time you leave. I wonder if I'll ever see you again."

He reached out to lift her chin and meet her eyes. "I don't know what to tell you except that I love you."

She glanced away. "That doesn't help with the worry."

He looked down at the bed cover. "No, I suppose it doesn't. I believe in what I'm doing. You said that you were proud of me. I guess I hadn't given much thought about how you must feel. Waiting for me to return from whatever crazy mission Naval Intelligence has cooked up must be maddening."

She put her hand on his. "It is, Nick."

Nick sighed, and a huge lump seemed to well up in his throat. "Does this mean you want to end our relationship?"

93

She stood and walked toward the door. "I'm not sure, Nick. I have much to think about."

Nick jumped up. "We can talk about it when I get back."

She stopped at the door and looked over her shoulder. "If you get back."

Chapter Seventeen

Leilani sat at the breakfast table and ate her mango in silence. She had not slept well, and felt a headache coming on. Sensing her mood, her parents had settled down and eaten their soft-boiled egg and toast in silence. They glanced at her from time to time, then at each other with worried expressions.

She looked up as Nick walked into the dining room. He looked so handsome, dressed in the navy-blue Pan American uniform, white shirt, and tie. Her parents jumped up and made a fuss over him. It was quite embarrassing. He walked over and kissed the top of her head. "Good morning, Leilani."

Her voice sounded cold in her ears as she replied, "Good morning, Nick." Yet it was all she could do not to stand up and throw her arms around him. She loved him so much, but she was also weary of the endless worry. Her emotions roiled as she sat there frozen by her indecision.

Nick sat down and reached for the egg platter. "Mr. Porta, can I use your phone to call for a ride?"

Mr. Porta dabbed his mouth with his napkin. "Nonsense, Leilani can drive you. Right, dear?"

Leilani put her fork down. "Dad, I'd like to be excused. I'm not feeling well, and I want to lie down."

Her mother stood and stepped over to her. "Come on, dear, I'll take you up." She eyed Nick and said, "You are to stay with us upon your return."

Nick started to object, "I'm not sure that's what Leilani – "

Mrs. Porta held up a hand to cut him off, "That is not a request."

Nick sighed. "Yes, Mrs. Porta. I would be delighted."

Leilani looked at Nick. "Yes, I agree. We have much to discuss upon your return."

Her mother put her arm around her shoulder. "Come on, dear, let's get you settled." Together they left the dining room.

*   *   *

Nick sat in silence in the back seat of the Navy sedan. He gazed absently out the window as the driver slowly navigated the twisting turns in the road from Manoa Heights. The sailor took the turns much slower than Leilani — to Nick's great relief. Besides, the Navy sedan couldn't hold a turn like the Portas' Cord convertible sportscar. Consumed by Leilani's words, Nick closed his eyes as the waves of despair washed over him. He needed the ROTC scholarship to pay for college and he'd signed a contract with the Navy. If he reneged, he'd have to spend four years as an enlisted sailor. That meant his dreams of becoming a naval aviator were finished. He also needed to continue his part time job with Pan American Airways. The money kept him in food and essentials. Besides, he loved flying the clippers almost as much as he loved Leilani. It seemed like his world was teetering towards chaos.

The sailor stopped at Kamehameha Boulevard, then turned right, merging with the early morning traffic. "Mr. Grant, we should be at the gate shortly. Please have your ID ready to show the MPs."

Nick grunted his assent and dug out his wallet as he continued his train of thought. The Navy and Pan American were intertwined. Could he choose one without the other? He couldn't bear the thought of losing Leilani and up until now he had not given her fears much thought. He'd have to do a better job. He would ask Leilani how he could make it better when he returned. He wondered if he could decline any further Naval Intelligence missions. He thought so. His mentor, Commander Bolts, had always given him the choice, it seemed. Or maybe he was fooling himself.

96

But refusing more missions meant giving up the chance to make Miyazaki pay. He owed that to Mac, to Roger Tanaka, and the countless others that had fallen to Miyazaki's *katana*. Nick sat back and sighed. He wished he was back on Wake Island with the other Pan American construction workers. Life was simple then. "When did it get so hard?"

The sailor looked in the rearview mirror and eyed Nick. "Did you say something, sir?"

Nick smiled. "No, just some wistful thinking."

The sailor turned left and got behind the line of cars entering the base. "Beg your pardon, sir. But sometimes a bit of wistful thinking can chase away the blues… even the troubles of the world. If you get my meaning, sir."

Nick chuckled as he handed his ID to the gate MP. "Good advice, sailor. Say, you're pretty smart – for a swabbie."

The sailor chuckled. "Thank you, sir. And you're pretty smart — I mean for an officer want-to-be."

Nick tucked his ID back into his wallet and smiled. "Fair point."

"But for heaven's sake don't tell my chief. I'd get a month's extra duty for speaking out of turn to an officer."

Nick laughed his mood lifted. "You have my word as an officer want-to-be and an occasional gentleman."

The sedan pulled up in front of a building with a sign reading, Naval Intelligence, Asiatic Fleet. Nick grabbed his gear, thanked the sailor, and entered. Two armed marine guards stood on either side of the reception desk manned by a sailor wearing Petty Officer Second Class rank. The sailor raised an eyebrow from behind his desk and had a look of mild amusement on his face. "Can I help you, …*sir*?"

Nick dug out his wallet and produced his Navy ID card. He handed it over. "Midshipman Grant reporting per my orders."

Out of the corner of his eye, he saw the marine guards turn their heads and smirk.

The petty officer took the ID and checked a ledger on his desk. "We don't get many Midshipmen here, *sir*. Especially, all dressed up as a Pan American aviator."

Nick caught the petty officer's tone and his emphasis on the word 'sir'. He was in no mood and decided to heed the words of

Chief Ellis, his senior enlisted mentor. "Never take any crap." Nick straightened up and boomed, "On your feet, Petty Officer!"

The petty officer jumped to his feet perhaps as much from reflex as shock. Nick spun on his feet and pointed at each marine. "Something funny here, marines?"

They snapped to attention, eyes to the front. In unison they answered, "No, sir!"

Nick slowly picked up his ID and tucked it into his wallet. Leisurely he returned his wallet to his pocket. Glancing around at the trio still at attention he said, "As you were."

The marines went to the position of parade rest and the petty officer sat down. "No disrespect, sir. It's been a long morning."

Nick nodded but said nothing.

The petty officer reached for the desk intercom and spoke. "Lance Corporal Cayse, report to the front desk, ASAP."

The doors on Nick's left opened and a marine one-striper entered. "Yes, Petty Officer."

He handed Cayse a sheet of paper. "Take Midshipman Grant to the supply room and then the armory. Be sure he gets issued the items on the list."

Cayse nodded. "Yes, Petty Officer."

"Mr. Grant, once Cayse issues you your equipment, he will take you to your ship. Is there anything else I can do for you, sir?"

Nick looked down at the petty officer. "I'm here dressed like this to do a job – just like you. How about you treat everybody that comes through the door with some respect?"

The petty officer lowered his eyes, "Yes, sir. Sorry, sir. The boys and I thought some of the guys were playing a joke on us. You know, like a practical joke? Are you going to report us?"

"Not this time. But there is one more thing I want to say to all of you." He scanned the two marines before turning back. "*Mele Kalikimaka.*" He extended his hand. "Let's let bygones-be-bygones."

The petty officer asked, "Excuse me, sir?"

"That means Merry Christmas… in Hawaiian."

The petty officer took Nick's hand and smiled, "Oh, well thank you, sir. Merry Christmas to you, and a Happy New Year too."

Nick rubbed his chin, "I hope so, but we'll have to see about the latter. Cayse, lead on."

*   *   *

The sedan slowed and stopped dockside next to a sleek gray destroyer. She was one of the newer models with only two funnels – or smokestacks – instead of the more common four. She had two single five-inch gun turrets forward of the bridge, two four-torpedo turrets aft of the stacks, and three more five-inch guns aft. The large white letters and numbers DD-348 were painted on her bow. Nick turned to Cayse, "What's her name, Lance Corporal?"

"She's the *Farragut*, sir, named after Admiral David Glasgow Farragut, Union hero of the Civil War. The Farragut was laid down by Bethlehem Shipbuilding Corporation's Fore River Shipyard in Quincy, Massachusetts, on 20 September 1932, launched on 15 March 1934 by Mrs. James Roosevelt, daughter-in-law of the President, and commissioned on 18 June 1934, with Commander Elliott Buckmaster in command. I'm assigned to her with some shore duty when we're in port."

"So, how is it you know so much about the *Farragut*?"

"Learned it for a promotion board, sir."

"Ah, if I want to be a brown-shoed aviator, I have to know all the details of every aviation asset in the inventory for my boards."

"Gee, sir, I didn't know officers had to endure questions from board members, too."

"Yep." Nick wondered what else he'd have to learn for future promotion boards.

Cayse parked and jumped out as Nick grabbed his gear. "Let me take that, sir."

"Thanks." Nick started up the gang plank. "Will you be sailing with us?"

Cayse, heavily laden with Nick's gear, replied, "Yes, sir. As soon as I drop off the car and hoof it back."

At the ship's railing Nick saluted the stars and stripes flying at the fantail – or stern, then turned to salute the officer of the deck – or OOD. "Request permission to come aboard, sir, to join the ship's company."

The OOD looked young. He wore an ensign's insignia on the collar of his khaki uniform and sported only one lonely ribbon over his left breast pocket. He returned Nick's salute. "Permission granted." Then he dropped his salute. "You must be the super-secret agent." The ensign put his hand to his chin in thought. "Although, I must compliment you on your disguise. Who would ever suspect you of being a spy, dressed as Pan American flight crew?"

"Look, I just do what I'm ordered. And as it happens, I am a Pan American flight crew member. The name's Grant, Nick Grant."

Cayse, caring Nick's sea bag bumped into Nick. "Oh sorry, sir, can't see much with this bag on my shoulder."

Ignoring Cayse, the ensign extended his hand. "Welcome aboard, Nick. I'm William Jones but my friends call me Bill. The captain wants to see you right away."

Taking the hand Nick asked, "But what about my stuff, Mr. Jones?"

Jones looked around Nick. "Oh, it's you Cayse. Stow Midshipman Grant's gear in my cabin. Then hustle." He checked his wristwatch. "We shove off on the hour."

"Aye-aye, Mr. Jones."

They stepped out of the way as Cayse hustled past. Nick eyed the bridge. "Where do I find the captain?"

"He's in his cabin off the bridge. You can find the bridge, can't you?"

Nick got the sense he was being teased and replied in kind. "It's that big, tall thing in front of the forward smokestack – right?"

Jones shook his head. "Oh my, a land lubber." He looked to the heavens. "Lord, you do test your faithful."

Nick smiled. "Perhaps." Climbing the ship's ladders that led to the bridge, he caught the all too familiar smell of a ship. Oil, grease, and fresh paint combined to remind him of his travels aboard the *S.S. North Haven.*

The bridge was occupied by the watch consisting of a chief petty officer and two seamen first class sailors. The chief turned as Nick entered. With a quizzical look on his face, he said, "Can I help you, …ah, …sir?"

"Chief, I'm Midshipman Grant. Ensign Jones said the captain wanted to see me."

The chief raised an eyebrow. "Midshipman? But the uniform…"

Nick sighed. "It's a long story, Chief."

"Right, sir. I'll see if the captain is available."

The chief knocked and entered through a door marked CAPTAIN. A second later he reappeared. "Mr. Grant, the captain will see you now."

"Thanks, Chief."

"Yes, sir. Welcome aboard."

Nick knocked on the door and waited. Almost immediately he heard a gruff voice say, "Come in."

Nick entered, stopped in front of a small desk, and saluted the seated officer. "Midshipman Grant reporting as ordered, sir."

The captain was a short man and thick around the middle. He wore his graying brown hair moderately long and swept back from a widow's peak. His gray-green eyes were deep set among many lines on his weather-beaten face. He returned Nick's salute. "Sit down, Grant."

Nick sat in front of the desk with his Pan American cap in his lap.

"My name is Lieutenant Commander Albert Lockett Hutson, captain of the *USS Farragut.* While aboard you will address me as Captain. Is that clear?"

"Aye-aye, Captain Hutson."

Hutson reached behind him into an open safe, withdrew an envelope, and handed it to Nick. The envelope was stamped SECRET EYES-ONLY NICK GRANT. Hutson's chair squeaked as he leaned back. "My orders are for you to open the envelope and read your orders in my presence. Then hand them back to me."

Nick tore open the letter and read:

SECRET EYES ONLY

DTG: 240945Z DEC 1936
From: DCMDR, ONI, WASHINGTON, D.C.
To: AVIATION CADET and MIDSHIPMAN Nicholas P. Grant
1. You are ordered to proceed to American Samoa, Pago Pago Naval Base at best possible speed. There you are to conduct a counterintelligence investigation with the assistance of Lieutenant Gregory Walker. He has orders to provide whatever support needed to accomplish your mission.
2. You are not to engage any hostile foreign intelligence agents. Your mission is to observe, provide security suggestions to the local commander, and gather evidence of foreign influence to foment acts of aggression,

sabotage, and other nefarious acts against the United States of America, its citizens, or members of the U.S. Armed Forces. Report all actions that are contrary to the U.S. national interests and those of the President.

3. You are to provide daily SITREPS on your progress to Office of Naval Intelligence, Asiatic Fleet, Pearl Harbor via encrypted means.

Signed
Ellis M. Zacharias,
Commander, USN
Deputy Chief, Office of Naval Intelligence,
Washington D.C.
Copy Provided: Commander Steven Bolts,
Office of Naval Intelligence, Western District,
San Francisco, California

SECRET EYES ONLY

Nick handed the orders back to Hutson. "I understand, sir." Hutson held the letter over a large desk ashtray and flicked open his lighter. The orders caught and they curled before Hutson dropped them onto the ashtray. The smell of burning paper filled the tiny compartment and competed with the smell of old tobacco.

Chapter Eighteen

Captain Hutson continued. "You will join the officers in the Wardroom at 1800 hours and take all your meals there. You are not restricted unless we go to General Quarters. Then go to the Wardroom and assist the surgeon. I don't suppose you have any medical experience, do you?"

"Yes, sir, I was the surgeon's mate on the *S.S. North Haven* for six weeks?"

Captain Hutson only grunted. "Go there and stay out of the way until the surgeon releases you. You can exercise with the Marines on the starboard deck between the number-one torpedo station and the whaleboat station. But stay out of the crew's way. You got that?"

"Yes, sir."

Hutson eyed Nick's uniform. "Do you have anything else you can wear other than that ridiculous outfit?"

Nick looked down at his Navy-blue wool uniform. "I was issued two sets of tropical khakis and one set of duty dungarees."

Hutson lit a cigarette. "Wear your khakis. You naval aviators – Airedales the lot of you – always carry khakis and brown shoes. Don't know what's wrong with regulation black shoes like the Blue Water Navy wears."

"Captain, I wear black Oxfords, just like you. I finished basic flight school last summer and the Navy awarded me the gold aviator's wings. However, I'm not a brown shoe naval aviator until I complete specialty training next summer and earn my V-5 device."

Hutson blew smoke rings at the ceiling. "And I suppose you want to fly fighters off carriers?"

Nick shook his head. "No, sir. I serve as crew on Pan American Airways flying boats. I'd like to stay in flying boats, like the Navy's new Consolidated Patrol Bomber the PBY-1. I saw a couple on Ford Island during our approach yesterday. They may not be as sleek or as fast as Pan American's flying boats, but man, do they have duration."

"Humph, thought all you Airedales wanted to fly off carriers."

"I'll ask for flying boat training, but I'll serve in any capacity the Navy requires."

Hutson inhaled deeply then snubbed out the cigarette into the still smoldering ashes of Nick's orders. "And what about this foray with Naval Intelligence? If that's what it is – a foray."

"Sir, I hope this is the last time they require my services. I've got to finish college and my flight training. All this messing about with Naval Intelligence has put a real damper on my life."

Hutson nodded but did not look convinced. "You'll be bunking with Ensign Jones. I'll see you at dinner. Dismissed!"

Nick saluted, "Aye-aye, sir, and *Mele Kalikimaka*."

Hutson looked up, "What, Grant?"

"Merry Christmas in Hawaiian."

Ensign Jones' cabin was on the main deck just aft of the bridge superstructure. The passageway led from amidships, through the superstructure, towards the bow. Nick imagined the wind howling through the passageway when both hatchways were dogged open and the *Farragut* was steaming at thirty knots. The passageway was lined with officer cabins and most had two names on the doors. This was 'Officer Country' as the crew referred to areas off-limits to the enlisted men.

Nick knocked on Jones's door and, hearing no reply, entered. He found his gear piled on the top bunk of a two-bunk compartment a bit larger than a closet in his parents' house. The bunks were opposite a narrow desk with a chair and lamp. The far wall held two lockers, one marked Jones and the other with no nameplate. Nick opened the empty locker and started to unpack. He placed his newly issued M-1911A1 .45 caliber automatic pistol, three empty magazines and pistol belt with holster and ammunition pouch on the top shelf. Next to it he placed a box of .45 caliber ammunition. Then he carefully placed his picture of Leilani next to the ammunition box and continued to unpack. As he did, he felt the deck vibrate under his shoes. The engines rumbled to life, and the ship's ventilation systems picked up a beat. She was coming to life for their high-speed dash to Samoa. The ship creaked then shifted slightly to starboard. Why couldn't they just drop him off with one of those new PBY flying boats? Oh, well, he thought, it is what it is — the Navy way!

The cabin door opened and the young ensign who greeted him earlier at the gangplank walked in. Nick jumped to his feet and stood at attention. "Hello, sir."

The ensign tossed his cap on his bunk and extended his hand. "Most people call me Bill."

Nick took the offered hand, shook it once, then resumed the position of attention. "Nice to meet you, sir."

Jones smiled. "Stand easy, Midshipman. May I call you Nick?"

Nick relaxed and said, "Yes, sir."

"Look, Nick, we're going to be bunking together for the foreseeable future. I can't have you hoppin' and poppin' every time I walk in. Call me Bill inside the cabin and when we're alone, with Doc Wilson, or the other ensigns. But better call me Ensign Jones or Mr. Jones when the captain or the XO are about. The old man's a stickler for doing things by the book."

"Thanks, Bill. Where'd you get your commission, the Academy?"

"Heck, no. I'm no ring knocker. I graduated from the University of Nebraska, a proud product of Naval ROTC."

Nick relaxed. "Me too. I'm a freshman at UC Berkeley. So, I got a few years until I graduate. I'm studying aerospace engineering and I'm also in the Naval Aviation Cadet program."

Bill sat on his bunk and gazed into Nick's open locker. "An aviator too. I see you're wearing wings on your uniform. I thought that cadets got their wings after they graduate and receive a commission."

Nick glanced down at his suit coat. "This is actually a Pan American Airways uniform."

Chuckling, Bill replied. "I get that." He pointed to Nick's open locker. "I see you've got wings on the navy uniform too."

Feeling a bit foolish, Nick responded, "Oh, well yes. Since I'm already a qualified Pan American Clipper pilot –"

"Wait – what? You're a Clipper pilot?"

Nick started to unbutton his uniform jacket. "No, I'm a flight engineer. That's a third officer. The navigator, Fred Noonan, is a second officer, and the co-pilots are first officers. And then there are the captains. A Captain is sort of like a God while airborne. And everywhere else, come to think of it. We live in awe – no more like terror – of them really. Except for the navigators, we're all cross-trained."

Bill rubbed his chin. "Makes sense, but why isn't the navigator cross-trained?"

"He's got a full-time job just figuring out where the heck we are. And along with the flight engineer, determining if we have enough fuel to get where we're going."

"Oh, who'd have thought. So, you work for a Sky God and fly the clipper when needed."

"Sky God… I like that. Though I'd never have the guts to say that to a captain's face."

Bill lay back on his bunk and crossed his arms behind his head. "Anyway, did the captain discuss your actions during battle drills?"

"He said to report to the Wardroom and assist the ship's surgeon during General Quarters."

"It's the same thing." Bill reached under his bunk and pulled out a battleship gray steel helmet and a huge kapok-filled navy-blue life jacket. You'll need to wear these when you go there. I'll introduce you to Doc Wilson at dinner. He's a Lieutenant

Commander, one rank below Captain Hutson but not in the chain of command. Plus, he's old."

Nick pulled on his khaki trousers and tucked in his shirt. "Old? How old?"

"He's got to be at least forty."

Nick nodded. "Yeah, that's pretty old."

Bill stood. "Finish dressing and I'll take you on a tour of the *Farragut*."

Nick tied his last shoelace and stood. "Great, let's go."

Chapter Nineteen

1156 hours, Thursday 24 December 1936
Aboard the *USS Farragut,* DD-348,
Pearl Harbor, Oahu, Hawaii Territory

     Ensign Jones led Nick back through the passageway and onto the foredeck. Nick's view forward was blocked by a five-inch gun turret. Its huge bulk extended almost to the railings on either side of the destroyer. Bill motioned Nick to follow as he walked around the turret and toward the bow. The *Farragut* was steaming towards the harbor entrance at a leisurely five knots as launches and gigs dashed across the calm waters all around. They reminded Nick of water bugs scooting across the pond at Alameda Airport.
     The bow provided a clear view of the harbor where the Asiatic Fleet was conducting refueling operations. Off to port, the hull of the Navy's first aircraft carrier, the *USS Langley,* rose three

stories above the *Farragut's* deck. Nick craned his head back. "Wow, the Navy's first aircraft carrier."

Bill shielded his eyes and looked up at the towering hull. "Yep, the Navy converted an old coaler after the fleet switched to fuel oil. They tacked on a wooden flight deck and wall-la, instant carrier."

Nick reflected on the newsreels he'd seen at the local movie house. "Lot of Naval Aviators died on the *Langley*, learning how to operate off a moving ship."

Bill nodded. "For a while, the Navy was seriously reconsidering the idea of launching and receiving fighters and bombers while at sea. Then the aviators figured it out and now we have honest-to-God aircraft carriers."

"Bill, our carriers are all converted cruisers. We need to do what the Brits and the Japanese did. Purpose build an aircraft carrier from the keel up."

Bill laughed. "Next you'll be telling me the aircraft carrier will replace the battleship."

They passed Hospital Point to port and Nick replied. "Maybe not today, Bill. But some day I'm sure they will."

"Ha! Not in your lifetime buddy. I'm going to be a battleship captain – just you wait and see."

Nick turned back to his new bunkmate. "I'm sure you will, Bill." The ship's bow lifted slightly as the *Farragut* put on speed at the harbor mouth.

The headwind off the bow ruffled Bill's brown hair and lifted his officer's cap. He grabbed it just in time. "What about you, Nick, you want to command an aircraft carrier?"

Nick snatched his khaki garrison cap off his head before it went sailing away with the increasing headwind. "No, I plan to do the active time required by my ROTC contract then serve the rest of my time in the reserves. I want to become a Master of Ocean Flying Boats with Pan American."

Bill raised an eyebrow. "What's that?"

Nick smiled. "A Skygod, as you so aptly put it. A flying boat captain."

Bill led Nick aft. Amidships, at the number one torpedo launcher, the ship passed the Pearl Harbor channel entrance. The *Farragut* rounded the outer channel marker and piled on speed. Her foaming wake spread as far as the eye could see. It also whipped up ocean spray. She reminded Nick of a thoroughbred racehorse exploding out of the starting gate. Nick felt her engines rumbling through his oxfords and the salt smell of the open ocean flooded his senses. It brought back fond memories of his time on the *North Haven*. The wind whipped at his uniform and howled in his ears. He leaned over and shouted into Bill's ear. "How fast do you suppose we are moving?"

"I'd say twenty-six, maybe twenty-eight knots."

"Can we maintain this speed all the way to Pago Pago?"

Bill pointed to the area between the forward and aft torpedo launchers and yelled. "Let's get out of this headwind."

Behind the shelter of the torpedo mounts, Bill tried to plaster his hair back into some semblance of order. "I've been with the *Farragut* almost a year and never seen the old gal move so fast. What's the hurry anyway?"

"Got to get to Samoa."

"Why?"

"Sorry, Bill, that's classified and under strict need-to-know criteria."

"You intel weenies. And here I thought we were off to such a great start."

Nick pursed his lips. "Navy regs, Bill. I don't make the rules and you know that. But we both have to follow them." He stuck out his hand. "We good?"

Bill gripped Nick's offered hand and shook it. "Yeah, we're good. It's just frustrating not knowing what we're doing and why."

"Look on the bright side. At least you know where we're going."

"That's as may be Midshipman Grant," said Bill, "but it's going to take about three-and-a-half days to get there – even at twenty-eight knots."

*   *   *

Lance Corporal Joseph Cayse stood to attention and called out. "Marines, a-ten-shun!" as Nick appeared at the starboard side of torpedo launcher station one. Nick tugged at the brown belt that held his workout Keikogi together. He looked up and called out, "At ease men. Good to see you again, Lance Corporal Cayse."

110

The marines wore sweat suits without identifying ranks or names. Cayse said, "Yes, sir. May I introduce you to our NCOIC, Sergeant Gurley." He turned to Gurley. "Sarge, this is Midshipman Grant. He was the one I was telling you about. The Clipper pilot."

Gurley was in his mid-thirties, stood about five-foot-eight, and was built like a fire plug. His face was deeply tanned from years on deck or standing guard duty. Gurley stepped forward. "Have we met, sir?"

Nick cocked his head. "You look familiar, Sergeant, but I can't place you. Regardless, the captain directed me to use this area to work out, but I can come back another time."

"Not a problem, sir. I was just giving the boys a little hand-to-hand combat instruction. You're welcome to watch, or," Gurley rubbed his chin and gazed at Nick's brown belt. "Or, err, you could join the class, if you like, sir."

"You go ahead, Sergeant. I've got to stretch and warm up first."

"Aye-aye, sir." He turned to the other three marines. "All right you meat-heads. Give me a good horse stance."

The marines placed their feet shoulder-width apart, pointed their toes out slightly, then squatted down with their knees bent out about 45 degrees.

As Nick stretched, he watched in astonishment as Gurley moved the marines through kicks, punches, and blocks that looked very similar to the Japanese Jujitsu that Master Nieshe practiced. When the sweaty marines took a break, he motioned Gurley over. "Sergeant, what martial arts form is that?"

"Sir, that's my poor attempt to pass along the Shaolin Kung Fu I learned while stationed with the China Marines in Shanghai."

"Shanghai? When were you stationed there, Sergeant?"

"I left in June. I'd been there since I was a private. But once I earned my sergeant stripes, the C.O. said time to move on. And I got assigned to fleet duty with the *Farragut*. Why do you ask, sir?"

"Were you involved in a certain Naval Intelligence operation in Shanghai last spring? Against the Japanese?"

Gurley shifted nervously. "We ain't supposed to talk about that, sir." He took a closer look at Nick's face. "Say, ain't you that civilian pilot that made the snatch?"

Nick smiled. "I ain't supposed to talk about that, Sergeant. But if I was, I'd commend the China Marines for their dedication and great support."

Gurley looked dumfounded. Then he smiled and nodded. "Yes, sir. I fully understand. As I recall you was pretty good, with your Kung Fu."

"Thank you, Sergeant. But it's Jujitsu. The Japanese martial arts form."

"So, what do you think, sir?"

"About what, Sergeant Gurley?"

"You know – which is better, the Japanese style or the Chinese?"

"One way to find out, Sergeant. Care for a little light touch sparring session?"

"That's a great idea but I'd like to choose one of the men. They need the practice, and I wouldn't want to embarrass you." Then with a sly smile he added. "I mean in front of the men, sir."

"Certainly, Sergeant. Perhaps we could spar another time then. Without the audience."

Gurley's sly smile returned. "Of course, sir. Another time then." He called out. "Cayse, get up here."

"Aye-aye, Sergeant!" Cayse jumped in front of Nick.

Gurley said, "Cayse, you need the practice against a different opponent. You know the Midshipman. This is a light contact spar. No landing full force kicks or punches."

"Yes, Sergeant."

"And watch those flailing elbows."

"Yes, Sergeant."

Gurley continued. "Sir, and Lance Corporal Cayse, the first one to land three strikes wins. Any questions?"

The contestants shook their heads. Gurley raised his arms to move them about six feet apart. "All right then, bow and begin."

Nick put his feet together, bowed, and looked up in time to see Cayse's right foot rocketing towards his head. He ducked. Then he back-pedaled as Cayse threw kick and punch combinations. Nick blocked left, right, and then center, but was unable to counter Cayse's unrelenting attack.

Nick ducked and rolled under Cayse and sprang to his feet. He aimed a snap kick at Cayse's torso. Nick pulled it just in time but still hit hard enough to wind his opponent.

112

Cayse stumbled backward and Nick pressed his advantage. He stepped forward, landed his left foot, and then raised his right to deliver a roundhouse kick to Cayse's chest. He didn't connect. Too late, Nick realized the stumble was a feint. Designed to draw him in, get him over-extended, and off balance. Cayse ducked under Nick's extended leg and slid his foot toward Nick's left leg.

Wham!

Cayse's foot pushed Nick's foot aside like so much straw. Nick toppled onto the deck. Before he could recover, Cayse dropped low on one knee and delivered three pulled double punches to Nick's stomach and chest.

Gurley called out, "Match goes to Cayse."

Cayse stood and offered a hand down. Nick took it as Cayse hauled him to his feet. Still reeling from the marine's attack, Nick extended his hand. "Cayse, that was a hell of a match."

Cayse grinned, "Thank you, sir. Are you all right?"

Nick rubbed his stomach. "Yes, I think so. You know what, Cayse?"

"What, sir?"

"I'm glad we're on the same side."

No longer focused on the bout, Nick noticed that about twenty or so sailors had gathered around. Some were exchanging money. Some were moaning, some smiling, but the mood was festive. He wondered how they found out about the bout and how they had time to place bets.

Then he heard a roar that could only be coming from a seasoned chief petty officer. "All right you lay-abouts. Back to work, the lot of you! Uncle Sam ain't paying you to goof off. You need something to do? I'll find it for you."

The men scattered like leaves before a strong wind until only Nick and the marine contingent were left next to torpedo station number one. Nick looked around at the four marines then addressed Gurley. "Sergeant, I've got another mission not unlike Shanghai. Think I could borrow Cayse once we reach Samoa?"

"Yes, sir. That is… providing you don't break him."

Chapter Twenty

Aboard the USS Farragut, DD-348,
2°49'23.1"North, 161°11'37.4"West
128 Nautical Miles East of Howland Island, North Pacific

At *Oh-dark-thirty* Nick awoke to a grinding metal-on-metal sound and a violent shudder that reverberated through the three-hundred-forty-foot ship. It was as if a huge hand had reached up from the depths and stopped the *Farragut's* headway cold. The fantail lifted as her following wake overtook the stopped ship. She settled as the wake passed under the bow and out into the dead calm ocean.

The ship's crew address system blared. "General Quarters. General Quarters. Damage assessment team to engineering. This is not a drill."

The General Quarters klaxon sounded, and Nick leapt from his bunk. He snapped on a light and looked around for Bill. Then remembered Bill was standing the third watch on the bridge. Nick threw on his khakis, grabbed his steel pot and life jacket, and raced for his General Quarters station – the Wardroom. When he entered through the hatchway, he found Doc Wilson looking as disheveled as Nick felt. "Morning, Dr. Wilson. Do you have any idea what's going on?"

Wilson stood at the coffee urn pouring himself a cup. He shook his head. "No clue." His salt-and-pepper hair stuck up in vertical spikes at odd angles and his black rimmed glasses were askew. He ran his hand through his scalp trying unsuccessfully to tame his unruly hair. "I had just dropped off when all hell broke loose. Then I high-tailed it here."

Nick glanced around the empty Wardroom. "Should I lay out the surgeon's kit, Doctor?"

Wilson shook his head. "Let's hold off until we find out what is going on. Grab yourself some coffee. It's bound to be a long night."

The coffee's aroma greeted Nick as he poured a cup, and he smiled remembering how much he used to hate the smell. Now it seemed an essential part of shipboard life. He added cream and sugar, then sat down at the long central table that doubled as an operating theater in less peaceful times. Removing his helmet, he asked, "Commander Wilson, how long have you served in the Navy?"

Wilson took a seat across from Nick. The harsh neon lighting made the wrinkles around his brown eyes apparent. "Too long. It feels like forever. I volunteered for the Navy after I graduated from medical school. It was the spring of 1917 – right after America entered the Great War. It seemed like every able-bodied man rushed to sign up. I remember standing in line for hours at the recruiting station."

Nick had heard similar stories. "My dad said the same thing. Did you serve overseas?"

"I served *at sea*. Navy assigned me to a destroyer squadron. We chased U-Boats, or maybe I should say U-Boat ghosts. We sure dropped an amazing amount of depth charges. Killed a lot of fish but, as far as I could tell, not one U-Boat."

"But you stayed on? I mean after the war?"

Wilson took a sip of coffee then continued. "Nope. Like a lot of guys, I got mustered out after the armistice. Went into private practice with a friend from medical school. Got married then divorced – no kids. It was okay. Then the Navy recalled me to active-duty last year."

"But I thought you'd resigned your commission?"

"Nope. I still held a commission in the Naval Reserve. Unbeknownst to me, I was promoted from Lieutenant Junior Grade to Lieutenant Commander. When President Roosevelt decided to expand the Navy two-fold, they had a severe shortage of sailors. The short answer is I was recalled for a period of not less than three years."

"Yikes. What happened to your practice?"

"The other physician agreed to cover my patient load. Things were slowing down anyway, so I thought, what the heck. Not that I had much choice in the matter. And here I am."

They sat in silence for a few minutes until the Captain's voice came over the intercom. "Now hear this. Now hear this. Secure from General Quarters. Officers not on watch to the Wardroom. That is all."

One-by-one the ships officers arrived and took seats at the Wardroom table. The din of their conversations rose with each new arrival. Rumors abounded as to why they had ceased headway and about the sound that rung the ship like some enormous bell.

The XO walked in and called out, "At ease. Gentlemen, the Captain."

The assembled officers stopped their conversations mid-sentence.

Captain Hutson took the open chair at the head and began. "Engineer tells me we've blown the main bearing on the port propulsion shaft. There's no way to fix it out here. Ordinarily, I'd return to Pearl. However, we've still got to deliver our special passenger," he nodded at Nick, "to Samoa."

Collectively, the officers moaned and turned to stare at Nick.

The XO banged his hand on the table. "At ease! The Captain is speaking."

Hutson rubbed his eyes. "We'll continue at best possible speed to reach Samoa. There we'll effect whatever repairs we can and await further orders." Hutson looked around the room. "Any questions?"

Nick glanced around the table. No one moved so he spoke up, "Captain?"

Hutson's tired eyes met Nick's. "Yes, Mr. Grant?"

"Sir, what's our estimated time to American Samoa?"

Hutson rubbed his eyes again. "Hard to say, Mr. Grant. We'll have to reduce the revolutions on the starboard shaft or risk losing that screw too. I'll have a better idea in a few hours." Hutson stood and as one the Wardroom stood at attention. Hutson looked around. "XO with me. The rest, dismissed."

Chapter Twenty-One

Five days later, the mountains of American Samoa peaked up from the hazy horizon. The starboard engine had held despite the strain of losing the left screw. It took several more hours before they reached the outer buoy marking the reef at the harbor entrance. A quiet bay lay beyond. Tall palm trees ringed the bay and shimmered in the low angle sun. Small huts lay behind the palms, and only one two-story building was visible. From Nick's vantage point on the foredeck, he realized that the two-story building was the governor's mansion, and the low buildings clustered around it comprised the naval base.

Nick studied the steep cliffs rising hundreds of feet above the harbor and pondered how a Pan American Airways pilot might shoot the final approach. The prevailing wind blew directly into the harbor mouth. That meant that the approaching clipper would have to come in over the mountains and dive for the water. Too steep a dive and the pilot might not be able to pull out before smacking into the bay. A hard hit could damage or even destroy the clipper. Pull out too shallow and the pilot risked running out of harbor before he could

118

put it down. If the clipper landed long, the crew would wind up on the reef, where the crashing waves would make short work of the flying boat. Take-off would be just as tough. Heading into the prevailing wind, with the fuel load needed to reach New Zealand, it would be a close thing. If the pilot didn't judge the take-off just right, the clipper might not clear the reef. Even a pilot with Captain Musick's skill would have a tough time using Pago Pago as a refueling stop.

The *Farragut* coasted to a stop alongside the only jetty at the Navy base. The familiar rumble of the engine died away and with it the sweltering heat of the tropical day closed in. Standing next to the bridge on the starboard deck, Nick felt the full intensity of the afternoon sun beating down on the steel deck. Sweat began to drip from every pore in his body. By the time the crew had secured the destroyer and rigged a canvas shade above the decks, his back was soaked and rivulets of sweat dripped from under his cap.

On shore, a naval officer in sweat-soaked tropical khakis stood next to a battleship gray navy sedan. When he caught Nick's eye, he casually waved. The sun reflected the two silver bars on his collar denoting the rank of a Lieutenant. Nick wasn't sure if he should salute or wave back. He decided to wave just as the officer started for the gangplank. Nick rushed to meet him there.

At the top of the gangplank, the lieutenant went through the time-honored ritual of first saluting the Stars and Stripes, hanging limply at the stern, then the officer of the deck. "Lieutenant Walker, permission to come aboard, Ensign?"

Ensign Bill Jones, who once again stood Officer of the Deck, snapped out a return salute. "Permission granted, Sir."

Lieutenant Walker's tanned skin was a deep caramel that contrasted with his indigo blue eyes. He was a rail thin man a few inches shy of Nick's six-feet-four. Walker stepped over and extended his hand to Nick. Confused by the senior officer's casual attitude, Nick snapped to attention and saluted. "Aviation Cadet and Midshipman Grant, Sir."

A smile crossed Walker's face as he tossed off an extremely casual salute back. "At ease, Grant. Welcome to the smallest and most forgotten backwater in the United States Navy, American Samoa. Or, if you prefer, Tutuila, as the natives call it."

Nick bridled and struggled to keep his voice even. "Sir, the Hawaiians taught me that they consider the use of the word 'native' an insult. They prefer 'local'. Is that also the case with the Samoans?"

Walker nodded slowly and seemed to size Nick up. "Yes, that's true, and I would never use that term in their presence. Does it bother you, Mr. Grant?"

"It's not a term I would use, sir."

The lieutenant eyed Nick for a few seconds then slowly nodded as if some understanding dawned. "Okay, Nick. Is it alright if I call you Nick?"

"Yes, sir."

"You speak your mind but in a respectful tone. I like that in a sailor. That works with me, but I'd be careful around the base commander and island governor, Captain Milne."

"Noted, sir."

Walker extended his hand again. "As you no doubt heard, I'm Lieutenant Walker. We'll be working together while you're on island."

Nick shook the offered hand. "Sir, if it's alright with you, I'd like Lance Corporal Cayse to tag along."

"Fine by me. Have you squared it with the *Farragut's* Captain?"

"Yes, sir. Cayse's NCOIC has cleared it with Lieutenant Commander Hutson. The port screw shaft failed, and they are likely to be here a while."

Walker used his handkerchief to mop the sweat from his face. "Yes, I'd heard. We don't have the facilities here for that type of a repair. There's a repair ship *enroute* from Pearl but it won't be here for a week – or more, depending on the winter storms. Then who knows how long for repairs. Anyway, get your sidekick, grab your sea bag, and follow me. This tin-can is only going to get hotter as the day wears on."

The drive to the headquarters building inside the sweltering staff car was mercifully short. The driver slowly weaved his way through sailor and civilian pedestrians until they came to a two-story building with a tall, steeply pitched roof. Nick decided it was a cross — somewhere between an official-looking government building and the local Samoan architecture.

Inside the building it must have been fifteen degrees cooler. The louver windows were thrown open to the breezes descending from the surrounding slopes. While not exactly cool, it was a relief from the destroyer's deck or the staff car. Glassless and propped open from the bottom, the windows reminded Nick of the Porta home. Briefly, he thought of Leilani and their contentious goodbye. He wondered whether they had a future. But that would have to wait for another time.

Walker led Nick and Lance Corporal Cayse into a large corner office. A stern looking officer with silver hair that matched the silver eagle insignia on his collar looked up from his desk. "I'm Captain MacGillivary Milne, Commander of United States Naval Station Tutuila, and Governor of American Samoa."

Captain Milne sat in front of a large painting of BB-39, the *USS Arizona,* moored next to Ford Island in Pearl Harbor. Ceiling fans moved the warm moist air around in competition with a large oscillating fan that sat on top of a bookcase. Milne's steel gray eyes met Nick's. "You're just a kid!"

Cayse and Nick snapped to attention. "Aviation Cadet and Midshipman Grant reporting as ordered, sir."

Milne took off his black-rimmed reading glasses and rubbed his eyes with fore-finger and thumb. "I know that Grant. But who is this with you? My orders said one Midshipman."

Cayse, still at a rigid attention, belted out. "Lance Corporal Joseph Cayse, sir! U.S.M.C., sir!"

"At ease both of you." Milne eyed Nick, "Grant, how old are you?"

Nick thought the captain looked like someone's grandfather. "Eighteen, Sir."

"You don't look a day over fourteen. But Commander Bolts says you're capable." Milne sat back in his chair and muttered, "Naval Intelligence never did have a lick of sense and now they send me a kid." Then he looked at Nick and asked, "So tell me, why you?"

Lieutenant Walker stepped forward. "Captain, I've read Grant's personnel jacket. He's served the Navy both as a civilian and ROTC cadet. He's young but he's done yeoman's service for the Navy and the nation."

Captain Milne looked from Walker to Nick. "That right, Grant?"

"I've done my best, Sir. I officially started working for Naval Intelligence aboard the *USS Arizona* in the summer of '35." Looking up at the painting Nick asked. "Were you her captain then?"

Walker tensed as Captain Milne's eyes flared and his jaw tightened.

"What do you mean by that remark, Grant?" demanded Captain Milne.

Walker blurted out, "Sir, Commander Bolts granted Nick access to special intelligence aboard the *Arizona* as the Asiatic Fleet Intelligence officer. But that was after your watch, sir. I'm sure Nick didn't mean any disrespect."

Horrified and confused Nick shook his head. "No, sir. The *Arizona*'s the pride of the fleet. I meant no disrespect."

Shaking his head, Milne looked at the ceiling. "They send a boy to catch the most dangerous Japanese spy in the Pacific. Why me, Lord, why me?"

Walker raked a hand through his sweat-soaked hair. "If you have no further questions, sir, I'll have my staff brief Mr. Grant."

Captain Milne shook his head, then turned and gazed up at the painting. "No Lieutenant. Keep me appraised of the situation as it develops. I want that spy off my island. That will be all, dismissed."

Chapter Twenty-Two

1856 hours, Tuesday 29 December 1936
Headquarters Building, United States Naval Station Tutuila,
Pago Pago, American Samoa

Outside Captain Milne's office, Walker said, "Follow me."

As Nick walked along the hallway he asked, "What was that about the *Arizona*?"

Walker stopped outside a door marked, INTELLIGENCE OFFICER. "Come in and we'll talk." Walker closed the door behind them and addressed a chief petty officer sitting at a desk. "Chief, this is Mr. Grant. Mr. Grant, this is Chief Jim Ward, he's my first shirt."

Nick reached out a hand. "Good to meet you, Chief Ward."

"Likewise, Sir." Ward gestured to Cayse, "And who's this bright-eyed jarhead?"

"This," said Walker, "is Lance Corporal Cayse. He needs a rack and directions to the chow hall."

The Chief stood. "On it, Mr. Walker. When and where do you need him next?"

Walker turned to Nick and raised an eyebrow.

"Oh, yeah." Nick looked to Ward. "I don't think I'll need him tonight. We can get started tomorrow. Chief Ward, he'll need a side-arm, holster, and extra magazines. Can you make that happen?"

Ward looked to Walker, who nodded. "No problem, sir. I'll have him back at 0730, armed and ready to go."

Nick nodded. "Thanks, Chief. Where will you billet Cayse?"

"With the marine detachment, sir."

"Great. Cayse, see you in the morning." Nick grinned. "Try not to get into trouble with the local jarheads."

"Me, sir? No way!"

Walker gestured. "Come into my office and I'll brief you."

The first thing Nick noticed was a large-scale map of Tutuila that occupied one wall of the office. The other was an oscillating fan that rustled the papers on a large gray desk. The air felt thick and Nick noticed that someone had battened down the windows, removing any chance of a cooling breeze. The coffee pot in the corner added to the stifling heat.

"Sit down, Nick. Coffee?"

"Yes, thanks. Cream and sugar?"

Walker poured a cup for himself and Nick. "Sorry, Nick. You'll have to take it black. No dairy products on this island, but that's about to change."

Nick took a sip. It could have been the world's worst coffee, but maybe not. He'd tasted a lot of bad coffee in his travels. He took another sip, suppressed a grimace, and asked, "How's that?"

"A few days ago, some California cowboys off-loaded half a hundred head of dairy cows, a couple of bulls and a handful of horses. They're setting up a dairy ranch on the other side of the bay."

"Wow, I had no idea. Hope I'm here long enough to enjoy some cream in this coffee."

Walker took a sip then placed the cup on his desk. "Now about the Old Man and the *Arizona*. When Captain Milne commanded the *Arizona,* the ship ran over a fishing boat off of Astoria, Washington."

"What happened?"

Walker grimaced. "There was a heavy fog. Visibility was down to a few yards. Apparently, the boat cut across the *Arizona's* bow and the big battleship cut it in two. Killed two fishermen. Their bodies were never recovered. Milne was relieved of command and sent here as punishment. He just avoided a court martial."

"Ouch. I really poked the hornet's nest."

"Don't worry, the old man is a good sort and doesn't hold a grudge. But I wouldn't ask him any more *Arizona* questions."

"Point taken, Mr. Walker." Nick took a sip of his coffee and was confident. It *was* the worst he'd ever tasted. "How did the island wind up with a dairy?"

"Captain Milne petitioned FDR, arguing that the Samoan children needed the nourishment. Mrs. Milne even send a note to Mrs. Roosevelt. I think the First Lady clinched the deal. FDR's private secretary, Missy LeHand, called up Howard Hughes and he made it happen."

At the mention of Hughes' name, Nick's mind started to spin. "How did Mr. Hughes make that happen?" Nick's earlier involvement with Hughes and his H-1 racing monoplane was strictly need-to-know. Nick continued, "I thought he was into fast airplanes, making movies, and – of course – the ladies."

Walker laughed. "Hughes does have that reputation with the ladies. Apparently, he owns an island off of Santa Barbara, California. Runs a cattle ranch out there."

Nick nodded and decided that Walker had a right to know some of his involvement with Hughes – but not all. "Yes, I know. I was on the island in August."

Walker sat up. "How so, Nick?"

"I was sort of working a mission for Commander Bolts."

"Sort of working, Nick? There was nothing about this in your personnel jacket."

"Commander Bolts pulled me out of flight school early and assigned me to guard Hughes' H-1 racer. It was at his private airport. That's where I first met Mr. Hughes. Things got messy at the airport and I sort of borrowed some documents to trap Miyazaki and then an airplane."

"Not sure how and aviation cadet '*borrows*' Navy documents and an airplane without landing in the brig."

Nick frowned at the memory. "Mr. Walker, it's complicated. I'm not sure how much more I can tell you. Maybe you could ask Commander Bolts for the details or have him give me permission to relay the full story. No offense, sir, but *need-to-know* and all that…"

"Need to know?" Walker sat back in his chair and shook his head. "Don't I know about *need-to-know*!"

Thinking what were the odds of running into Brian, Shorty, Slim and Lesly on American Samoa, Nick smiled. "I'll bet I know those cowpokes. If they're the ones from the island. Good guys, you'd like them."

Walker stood up. "Come over to the wall map and let's get you situated. And, just for the record, try to remember to use *sir* – or *mister* when addressing senior officers. I don't really care, but others will. That way you can avoid a needless dressing down."

Nick scratched his head. "Yeah, I'm having real trouble with that concept of '*sir*', Mr. Walker."

"Better get used to it, Nick. You've got a Navy ROTC scholarship. That means the Navy owns you for a few more years."

Nick nodded, "Aye-aye, Mr. Walker."

Walker moved to the large island wall map.

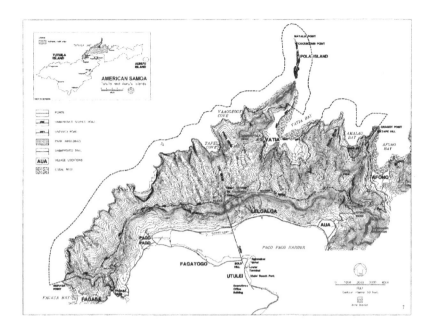

Chapter Twenty-Three

1920 hours, Tuesday 29 December 1936
Intelligence Section, United States Naval Station Tutuila,
Pago-Pago, American Samoa

At the map of Tutuila, Lieutenant Walker pointed out key terrain features, the population centers, and the villages. Then his executive officer, Lieutenant JG Harris, provided a lengthy rundown of the local chiefs and their allegiances.

Still sleepy from his travels, Nick drank another cup of truly dreadful coffee. It desperately needed cream.

The last to brief was a wizened old chief petty officer named Isaiah Bergen. Bergen explained that most Samoans were peaceful and approved of the US Territorial rule and the Naval presence. "There have been no open protests or appeals to Captain Milner as governor. However, our sentries have spotted shadowy figures observing the oil and aviation fuel storage facility. They seemed especially interested in the new aviation fuel storage and refueling area."

Nick asked Lieutenant Harris, "Description?"

Walker shook his head. "Nothing solid. Black on black and whoever they were kept to the shadows. At first, we thought the reports were a result of overactive imaginations. But Chief Bergen went out last week and he caught a glimpse of — well something. Chief, tell Mr. Grant what you saw."

"There's not much to tell. I noticed a glint — like moonlight on steel. As I stared into the darkness, I saw what looked like a disembodied face. It seemed to be floating in the trees. I moved forward, training my flashlight, and caught a fleeting glimpse of a figure. He was dressed head-to-toe in black and retreating into the wood line."

Nick leaned in, "Did you notice anything else?"

"Yes, the figure had two objects, like sticks, rising from his back that crossed to form an X just below his head." Bergen paused and eyed Nick. "Does that mean anything to you?"

Nick nodded, "Yes, it does. You ever heard of the Black Dragons? *Ninjas* — Japanese assassins?"

*　　*　　*

Lieutenant Harris showed Nick to his room in the Bachelor Officer Quarters or BOQ. It was small — just a bed, an even smaller closet, and a chest of drawers. The louvered window was closed but allowed a little air into the room. A large wall-mounted fan stood silent.

Harris reached over and turned it on. "It does help somewhat."

Nick guessed that the room temperature was somewhere close to a hundred degrees Fahrenheit. "It can't be any worse than the three months I spent on Wake Island."

Harris turned and looked at him. "What were you doing on Wake?"

"I work for Pan American Airways — when I'm not playing Navy spy catcher. In 1935, I was on the crew building the *China Clipper* flying boat bases."

Wide-eyed, Harris asked, "Have you flown on the *China Clipper*?"

"A few times. Mostly I crew another M-130 — the *Philippine Clipper*. But I actually have more time in the S-42s."

Harris scratched the back of his sweat-sodden hair. "As a pilot?"

"Yes, when I get the chance. I'm rated as a Flight Engineer. I'm qualified to fly both the M-130 and the S-42 but only when the captain or first officer gives me permission."

"Do you want to be a flying boat captain?"

Nick sighed, "Yes, but that's years away. I have to finish college first."

Harris removed his hat, mopped his brow, and frowned. "So why are you in Naval Flight School if you already fly the most advanced flying boat in the world?"

Nick smiled at Harris, remembering what his old mentor, Chief Ellis, said in answer to one of Nick's questions. "Orders."

"Oh, orders huh." Harris nodded. "I get it. Well let's head over for supper. Then Lieutenant Walker wants to take you out for a walk along the perimeter."

Nick's stomach growled at the mention of food. Navy chow was usually good and sometimes excellent. He hadn't eaten since breakfast and any chow would be welcome. They walked across the street and joined Walker in the mess hall. Famished, Nick ate quietly.

After dinner, they moved out onto the veranda, and they waited for the sun to disappear behind Rainbow Mountain. Nick grimaced as Harris handed him a cup of black coffee. He sipped the bitter brew as the last rays illuminated the palm trees that ranged along the ridge line. The cumulus clouds that towered thousands of feet above them cycled through a series of orange and reds. The sky turned a deep indigo blue, and the stars began to appear in the heavens. Soon the sky was a curtain of thousands of twinkling lights. Nick sipped his coffee and tried not to gag. He looked up at the glorious night sky and said, "I've always enjoyed the tropical sunsets."

Walker cupped his hands around a cigarette as Harris held a lighter to the end. Walker took a long drag then offered the pack to Nick.

"No, thanks. I don't smoke."

"You don't look old enough anyway." Walker chuckled. "So, tell me, what's your favorite part of the Pacific?"

"Hawaii – especially Oahu."

"You got a girl there – name's Leilani, right?"

129

Nick frowned. "Just how detailed is my personnel jacket anyway?"

"Oh, it's thorough. We can't have just anybody hanging around with you — especially any undesirables. And for the record, there's nothing undesirable about the Porta family."

Nick drained his coffee cup and wondered if any part of his life would ever be private again.

Walker looked up at the now inky sky and stabbed out his cigarette. "Let's get going." He handed Nick a large metal flashlight. It must have contained five D cell batteries.

Two sailors wearing Navy Shore Patrol blazers appeared and handed Walker and Harris pistol belts with .45 caliber automatic pistols. Nick noticed that the sailors cradled M1928A1 Thompson Submachine Guns. He wished he had brought his own .45 rather than leaving it locked in his BOQ room.

The glow of the Naval Station streetlamps cast pools of light on the pavement resembling steppingstones in the darkness. The group turned onto a narrow unlighted path that led up the cliff face. Twice Nick stumbled on some unseen rock or root during the steep assent. The path leveled out on a large plateau that contained several huge oil storage tanks. On the far side Nick saw an eight-foot-high chain-link fence topped with rolls of barbed wire.

Walker stopped and pointed toward the fence. "That's where the sentries noticed the first person observing the area."

Thick jungle crowded the fence line. Nick scanned the green wall but saw nothing beyond. "You could hide a company of marines in that underbrush."

Harris turned to Nick. "We've started clearing the vegetation on the far side, but it grows back fast. It's an endless job."

They moved on and took a path at the other side of the plateau. It led down toward a clearing where two large aviation fuel storage tanks stood. Reading the data plate, Nick saw that they each contained 300 gallons of high-octane AVGAS. They stood 6 feet off the ground on metal legs that kept them above the rocky soil. They connected to a series of pipes that led downhill toward the docks.

Nick asked, "Can I see the aircraft refueling station?"

"Sure," Walker said. "Harris, lead the way."

The group followed two pipes down a gentle slope until they came out on a pier. On the pier, the pipes connected to a hand pump and hoses that were coiled onto big storage wheels. Nick recognizedd the type. They were the same as the refueling fittings he'd seen at Pan American bases. Looking out over the dark harbor, he noticed a fishing boat festooned with lights chugging toward the harbor mouth. It appeared to be the only activity on the bay tonight. Just off the end of the pier they heard a large splash.

Harris offered, "Could have been a shark. There's lots of them in the harbor. They feed on the fish offal that fisherman toss overboard."

Nick shuddered. He dismissed thoughts of the night he'd spent in Pearl Harbor batting away sharks. The hammerheads were distracting him from pulling an explosive device off the Clipper's hull. He asked, "What security measures do you plan to use when the Clipper is refueling?"

Walker replied, "We'll have two armed sentries on the pier at all times."

Nick nodded. "Do you post a launch off the pier?"

"No, we haven't. You think that's necessary?"

"Lieutenant Walker, I'm not sure how much you know about the attack on the *Pan American Clipper* during its R.O.N. at Pearl Harbor. Frogmen, most likely Japanese, placed a limpet mine on the Clipper. Fortunately, we were able to remove the explosive before it exploded."

Walker looked at Nick. "I was unaware. Harris, take a note to add a patrol gig during the clipper's stay." He clapped a hand on Nick's shoulder. " Now, let's get back to the Officer's Club, such that it is. We'll be meeting the New Year's Eve party and New Year's Day services committee. You might as well come along. You're bound to be a while."

"Aye-Aye, Captain Bligh."

"Grant, you are such a smart ass."

Chapter Twenty-Four

0710 hours, Wednesday 30 December 1936
On the Bay Road
Pago Pago, American Samoa

The truck's horn blared, causing Nick to jump off the asphalt and onto the shoulder. Deep in thought, he had failed to hear the truck approach from behind. He slowed to a walk while catching his breath and turned to see a beat-up flatbed truck hauling produce roll slowly by.

The passenger, a local Samoan man not much older than Nick, leaned out the window. "Watch it, swabbie. You don't own the road. It belongs to the Samoan people, not the Navy."

"Sorry," Nick yelled at the truck as it accelerated away.

The only reply was a rude hand gesture as the men drove on.

Puzzled, Nick picked up his pace and continued his run along the bay road. It seemed that Naval Intelligence might have underestimated the extent of the Samoan people's anti-American sentiment. He'd have to relay this brief encounter to Lieutenant Walker after his workout.

Dressed in gym shorts, a UC Berkeley T-shirt, and gym shoes, he estimated that the run would cover about three and half miles. The round trip was a decent start to burning off the heavy Navy chow he'd scarfed down aboard the *Farragut*.

Few clouds greeted the sun as it rose above the calm Pacific Ocean. Nick continued his run to the headland at the tip of the adjacent shore. Sweat dripped off his nose and drenched his T-shirt. The day promised to be a hot one and he was glad that he had decided to run early. Later he planned to hit the Base gym to continue his workout. Perhaps Cayse would be there, and they could spar once again.

Rounding the bend that followed the bay, Nick noticed a corral under construction up ahead on the left. As he closed the distance, he made out two men bent over a fence post attaching a wire strand. Both wore wide-brim Stetson hats, long sleeve shirts, and cowboy boots.

Nick slowed and then stopped a few feet from the men. "Howdy, boys. You seen any cattle around here?"

Without straightening up, one said, "Now that is a pretty stupid question, pilgrim. You must be a sailor."

The man straightened up and turned with his gloved hands on his hips. Then a broad smile lit up Brian's face, "Well, I'll be hornswoggled. Shorty, it's Nick Grant!"

Shorty straightened up and turned. "Nick Grant? Well, don't that beat all?" Shorty rushed forward, ripping off his gloves, his right hand extended. "What on God's green earth are you doing in this godforsaken place two days before the New Year?"

"Shorty, Brian. Good to see you too. Heard you were over here starting a dairy farm. Seems an odd place for a couple of dedicated range cowboys."

Shorty leaned in. "It ain't no dairy farm, Nick. We are building a dairy herd."

"And what's the difference between a dairy farm and a dairy herd?" Nick asked.

Brian removed his Stetson and wiped his bandana across his face. "I suppose there's not too much difference really. It's more a matter of a man's pride. We're cowboys — not farmers. Either way we get paid and paid well."

Shorty wiped the sweat from his face with his sleeve. "Hughes is paying us triple. Three years' pay for six months work."

133

Brian wacked Shorty on the shoulder with his glove. "Shorty, it's not three times our pay – it's six times. No wonder you're so bad at cards."

Nick smiled, thinking back. "It's great to see you boys again. You saved our bacon back on Santa Clara. I wouldn't be alive if it weren't for you guys."

Brian looked down and scraped his boots in the dust. "Aw, shucks, Nick. It weren't nothing."

Shorty snorted, "I don't ever want to do that again. I tell you what though, life has gotten far worse on Santa Clara Island."

"How's that?" Nick asked.

"Mr. Hughes insisted on putting a telephone in the bunk house. Dang thing rings all the time. I'm telling ya, it's disturbing the natural order of things."

Perplexed, Nick looked at Brian.

Brian shrugged, "Rings maybe two to three times a month."

Nick shook his head, chuckling." I can see your point, Shorty. No phones around here I'd wager?"

Brian shook his head. "Nick, if you got no plans for tonight, the locals are throwing us sort of a special dinner. You're welcome to join us. It's sort of like the Samoan version of a Hawaiian luau."

"Sounds great — can I bring a friend?"

Brian's eyes widened. "Is it Nancy? Is Nancy on the island with you?"

"No. 'fraid not. She's back in Berkeley still working for the FBI – full time during our school break. I'll tell her you said hi if you like?"

"Yeah, do that. So, who's your friend?"

"His name is Lance Corporal Joe Cayse. He's a good guy... I mean for a Marine?"

The three laughed at the implied slight about marines. "Well boys, I got to be getting back. What time tonight?"

"Seven p.m., but that's island time. Certainly, no earlier."

"Great, we'll see you then."

Nick tossed a half-hearted salute, "See you later, boys."

The run back to the Naval Base was faster than the run out, or at least it seemed that way. Still, he was sweat sodden when he reached the base gym. The attendant handed him two towels and asked him to shower before he used the pool.

Nick took a seat next to the basketball court. A pickup game was in full swing and that made it much more enjoyable during his cool-down. After he'd cooled down, he stood and crossed over into the weight room.

Inside, several sailors were working the free weights but paid no attention to him. In the corner sat Joe Cayse stretching on a floor mat.

Cayse looked up. "Mr. Grant, good morning, sir." He started to rise but Nick waved him back.

"As you were, Lance Corporal."

Cayse sat back down and Nick sat on the mat next to him.

"Care for a sparring match after you stretch, sir?"

"Sure, all I've got to lose is my pride."

Cayse stiffened, "Sir, I didn't mean to – "

"No harm, no foul – no insult. You bested me fair and square. But I do want you to show me that leg sweep."

"Will do, Mr. Grant."

*   *   *

To his surprise, Joe Cayse found that he liked the young middy. Maybe it was because they were so close in age. But probably it was more to do with Grant's easy manner. He'd never met an officer or midshipmen that was so down to earth.

Cayse jumped to his feet. "Do you need to stretch out, sir."

"No, I'm good. Let's work through a few katas to warm up. Then you can put on your best instructor hat."

Cayse smiled, "Yes, sir."

After a ten-minute warm-up, working through several scripted exercise routines, or kata's, Cayse said, "As far as that fake and double-tap strike, it's all about a good demonstration and excellent execution. Your fake must convince your opponent that you are hurt. That means you have to let your opponent strike you hard."

"No, wait," Nick said, "I pulled that kick."

"Yes, sir, you did. But I moved into the blow."

"You're right. I recall being surprised at the force of the impact."

"And you saw the pain on my face."

"Lance Corporal Cayse, I thought I might have inadvertently hurt you."

"Even so, you pushed your advantage. And that was part of the demonstration. Yes, it did hurt — but that was the point. I had to convince you that you had scored a solid hit. "

Nick sighed, "I guess I was caught up in the moment. You were clearly dominating the match. I saw an opportunity and I took it."

"You saw what you thought was an opportunity, but it was in fact a trap and you waltzed right in."

Nick shrugged. "I'm just glad that my sensei didn't see you trounce me. I'd be doing knuckle push-ups until he got tired!"

Cayse smiled. He really did like this middy. "Now, let's go through a couple of drills step by step."

"Aye-aye, Lance Corporal *Sensei*."

Chapter Twenty-Five

7:30 p.m., Wednesday 30 December 1936
Dairy Ranch, Bay Road,
Pago Pago American Samoa

The drive out to the Dairy Ranch in the borrowed governor's car was short and wonderfully cool. The Navy had splurged and had installed an air conditioning unit. The unit looked like a small torpedo attached to the passenger side rear window. It blew cool dry air in the open window vent. The driver, a Seaman 3rd Class, was old enough to be Nick's father and even more cranky.

On orders from Lieutenant Walker, Nick and Lance Corporal Joe Cayse wore tropical khakis. Nick's midshipman rank was attached to his collars and the coveted gold naval aviator wings were pinned over his left pocket. Next to him in the back seat, Joe Cayse was dressed in his khakis and wore two rows of awards and overseas ribbons over his left shirt pocket. He also carried a small khaki duffle bag. Cayse looked over at Nick. "Mr. Grant, are you sure we'll need all this heavy artillery?"

"Two pistols, web belts, andholsters do not qualify as artillery — let alone heavy artillery, ."

"All the same, sir. I'm the one carrying the darn things."

"Quit your belly-aching and think of all the young Samoan ladies you'll meet tonight."

Cayse sat back and grinned. "Yes, sir!"

Nick glanced over at Cayse and smiled. "Just stay close to me and don't get distracted by some fair maiden you just met."

Cayse groaned, "Yes, sir. Duty first always. Still, it's a crying shame…"

The driver pulled into the crowded parking lot in front of the corral where Nick had met Brian O'Malley and Shorty earlier. The driver looked back. "We're here, sir. Do you want me to wait?"

"Yes. You can go and get some chow at the feast. But I want you to bring your food back here and stay with the vehicle. If we need to move, I want to be sure you're ready."

The sailor turned back around. "Yes sir, I'll be here and ready."

"Thanks." Nick glanced out the window towards a large open-air pavilion that was festooned with flaming torches interspersed with hanging electric lights. Nick could hear music and see people sitting around a center stage. Looking closer he saw a troop of Samoan teenage girls performing. Dressed in local garb, they danced to the beat of a carved-out log that served as a drum, and a ukulele.

The music stopped and the girls froze, bent at the waist, with their right hands palm-up just above the floor and their left arms straight up into the air. Everyone clapped and the girls left the center stage. "Okay, Lance Corporal, it's showtime."

They stepped out of the car and walked to meet Brian. Nick offered his hand. "Brian, this is Lance Corporal Joe Cayse. He was the friend I was telling you about. Lance Corporal Cayse, this is Brian O'Malley."

Brian turned to Cayse and extended his hand. "Glad to meet you Lance Corporal. Any friend of Nick's is welcome here."

Cayse took Brian's hand, "Nice to meet you Mr. O'Malley. But please call me Joe."

"Fair enough, Joe. And you can call me Brian. I've saved a spot for you close to the stage where all the action is. Let's grab some chow and then take our seats."

The food table was laid out in buffet style. Some of the food Nick recognized, some he did not. A young Samoan girl standing behind the table said with an impish grin, "You must be a new arrival."

Nick gazed at the girl. She was perhaps 13 or 14 wearing the same dress the earlier performers had. The flowers were still pinned in her hair. He smiled back. "And you must be one of the dancers I saw earlier?" Although he had not seen much of the performance, he offered, "Great performance."

She curtsied. "Thank you. Now let me tell you a little bit about our local food. We have roast pig, and chicken and rice." She pointed to a bowl of purple colored paste. "This is poi."

"Yes, I recognize it from my time on Oahu. A friend introduced it to me last year."

That impish grin returned. "A girlfriend?"

Chuckling, Nick nodded. "Yes. What's your name?"

"Tavalia. Did you like the poi?"

Nick decided not to mention his dislike. "That is a very pretty name. I'm Nick, Nick Grant, at your service." He bowed. "And this is Joe Cayse." He pointed to Cayse behind them in the line.

Tavalia pointed to the dishes on the table and started naming them.

Cayse did not hesitate. He piled his plate high with a wide variety of the food. As Nick did the same, a familiar feeling crept up his spine. It was like someone was staring at his back. Slowly, he turned around and gazed across the crowd. There, at the far side of the pavilion, Toshio Miyazaki was speaking to a Samoan man with strangely light-colored hair. Miyazaki said something to his companion, who turned sharply and looked directly at Nick. Nick grabbed Cayse by the arm. "Put the food down and follow me. He's here."

Cayse put his plate down. "Who? Who's here?"

"It's Miyazaki. He's with a local I don't recognize. They spotted me and may bolt. Come on!"

Nick and Cayse jumped down from the pavilion and ran along the outside to intercept Miyazaki. Cayse trotted alongside Nick. "Mr. Grant, we're supposed to observe and report. I'm not sure Mr. Walker said anything about confronting anybody."

"He tried to kill my family and he murdered two very good friends. I'm going to deal with him personally." Nick charged on as the crowd parted before them. When they closed the distance, they stopped dead in their tracks. Miyazaki was gone.

"Cayse, pass me a pistol."

Cayse dug into the duffle bag and handed Nick a .45 automatic, holster, and pistol belt.

Nick strapped the pistol belt around his waist as Cayse did the same. Then he scanned the crowd. "Do you see him anywhere?"

Cayse looked over the area. "What exactly am I looking for, sir?"

"A Japanese man in the company of a local man with dark skin and light hair — possibly blond."

Brian O'Malley trotted up. "What's happening, Nick?"

"It's Miyazaki. He's here."

"Well don't that beat all. Let me get the rest of the boys. Will be back here armed and mounted in ten minutes."

Nick shook his head. "Not a good idea, Brian. We were lucky last time. Miyazaki likely had no idea you had come to our aid. I can't authorize civilian involvement. It's too risky."

Brian eyed Nick. "That's as may be, Nick, but you can't stop me."

Nick smiled, "No, I don't suppose I could. Thanks, but be careful." He continued, "Miyazaki knows that I made him and –"

Brian raised his hands. "Wait, made him? What does that mean?"

Nick closed his eyes in frustration. "Miyazaki knows that I spotted him. He's bolted and I can't let him get away. Cayse and I will head up the trail that goes toward Rainmaker. You guys could mount up and comb the flats. But remember he's a killer."

"Sure. What do you want us to do if we locate him?"

"Nothing. Send word to the naval base and keep tracking him. But don't get close enough to feel his katana."

Brian nodded. "Not to worry. My Colt .45 can out-distance a sword any day."

Nick looked away towards the Rainmaker, the highest peak on the dark mountain spine that split the island in two. "Just remember he's very smart and has surprised everybody who tracked him."

"Got it. We'll go out in pairs."

"Great. Cayse, you ready to go?"

"Yes, sir."

Nick turned and trotted across the corrals and paddocks until he reached the edge of the jungle. Looking around he saw an opening. "There. Come on!" The opening led to a trail that disappeared into the dark foliage. At the entrance, the moonlight provided sufficient illumination to make out footprints — many sets of footprints.

Cayse looked down at the well-trodden path. "How will we know if they came this way?"

Nick squatted by the footprints. "Here, see this set of tracks?"

"Yes?"

"These boot prints are Japanese military. Pretty rare on Samoa I'd say." Nick's mind raced with the implications. "I need you to run back and alert Brian. Ask him if he can find another way across to the other side of the Rainmaker. Maybe cut off Miyazaki. Then come find me."

"What are you going to do, sir?"

"I'm going to go up the trail and put some pressure on Miyazaki."

"But sir, our orders…"

"The situation has changed. And I'm taking the initiative. Now go!"

"Yes, sir." Cayse turned to go, but then turned back. "I sure hope you know what you're doing, Mr. Grant."

"So do I, Joe. So do I."

Chapter Twenty-Six

7:45 p.m., Wednesday 30 December 1936
Dairy Ranch, Bay Road,
Pago Pago American Samoa

Cayse ran towards the pavilion lights searching for Brian. He spotted Brian talking to three other cowboys and trotted over. He shouted, "Brian."

Brian turned around. "Here."

Cayse stopped beside the cowboys, panting. "Nick says Miyazaki has gone up a trail that leads to the Rainmaker. Maybe to get to the other side for pickup." He gasped for breath. "Nick asked that you find another way to cross and cut off Miyazaki." Cayse bent at the waist, hands on his knees, gasping for air.

Brian looked up at the darkened mass of the mountain chain that split the island in two. "Shorty, you was on the other side a few days ago. Can you lead us over?"

"Can do, Brian. But it's rough going. It's a dangerous ride — especially at night."

"We'll just have to be careful. Okay boys — saddle up. Bring rifles and pistols. It's the same crew we chased off Santa Clara Island a while back."

Leslie, chewing on a straw, shrugged. "Seems we got us a new gig."

Buck frowned. "I knew this job was too good to be true."

Brian spoke up. "Sometimes a man's got to do the hard right — rather than the easy wrong. Defending America from her enemies is hard. Yeah, I know it's a new gig, but one worth doing. If you don't want to come, I understand. There's no shame in not wanting a part of this. But if you're coming, let's ride."

Cayse listened in admiration to Brian's words and thought that he had the makings of a fine Marine. As all the cowboys moved toward the stables, he decided to make one more stop before he rejoined Nick. Running hard, he headed back to where they had left the staff car. Pulling up short he noticed the car was still running and knocked on the driver's side window. The driver jerked awake and rolled down the window. "What's up, Lance Corporal?"

"Grant said to drive back to base. Find Lieutenant Walker. Tell Walker that Nick has identified Miyazaki and is following him up the Rainmaker Mountain trail. Ask Lieutenant Walker for his orders."

The sleepy driver scratched his bald head. "Who's Miyazaki?"

"Never mind, just go. Mr. Grant might need backup."

"All right. Hold your horses. I'm going."

The driver rolled up the window and pulled the car back onto the Bay Road. Cayse watched as the taillights disappeared around a curve.

"Okay," Cayse said aloud. "Now to stop Mr. Grant from getting himself court-martialed or maybe killed." Wearily, Cayse turned and jogged back to the trailhead. He put his he down abd leaned into the run. He had to catch-up with Mr. Grant ASAP. *Officers, they cold never be trusted on their own.*

*   *   *

Brian tugged on the saddle's rear cinch which caused Sarge to flinch and turn his head toward his rider. The horse eyeballed Brian as if to say, "Do you mind?"

Brian tapped the horse's flank. "Don't you bloat on me you old nag. I know your tricks."

Sarge exhaled, which sounded a lot like a sigh, enabling Brian to tighten the cinch one more notch. Sarge never seemed to mind the bit and halter but was squeamish about the strap across his belly.

Brian looked around the stable and saw that the others were mounted. He climbed up into the saddle and leaned forward to check that his granddaddy's Winchester was secure in its case. He checked the holster strapped around his waist. The leather strap that secured his Colt revolver was in place. Satisfied, he called out, "All right, Shorty, lead the way."

The four horsemen left the stable single-file with Shorty leading, followed by Buck and Leslie. Brian road trail. He could see the puzzled look on the faces of the revelers as the four mounted cowboys headed into the night.

Shorty called back, "It's easy going for a mile or so before we start hitting the switchbacks. Then the trail gets mighty narrow. Best to keep a tight rein."

The trail was steep and narrow as it wound its way up the side of the Rainmaker. About 15 minutes later, they reached the first switchback. This one turned a hard right. Looking to his left, Brian saw the lights of the dinner party below, then, across the bay, the naval base lights. Sarge stumbled. Loose rock fell away under his hoof as the horse scrambled to regain his footing. Then the animal found his feet and continued up the steep trail.

The moon was past its zenith and he estimated they had two maybe two and a half hours of moonlight remaining. It would be very dark before the dawn's first light. An hour later they crested the trail and Brian called a halt. "Let's give our mounts a short rest."

Brian dismounted and threw the reins over Sarge's head. The horse immediately ambled over to a small stream cascading off the hillside and started drinking. The other horses followed suit.

Leslie took out a pack of cigarettes and was about to light up when Brian put a hand on his arm. "Better not, Leslie. Think about it, fellas. How far do you suppose a match or even a cigarette would show at night?"

Leslie put the pack back into his shirt pocket. "I catch your drift, Brian. We are pretty exposed here. Daddy always said to leave your tobacco at home if you was a hunting. Guess that's even more true if you're hunting two-legged game."

A few minutes later, Brian called for them to mount up, and Shorty led the way down the steep trail. The moonlight reflecting off the ocean contrasted sharply with the darkness that must be the western shore of the island. From their vantage point they could see many miles out to sea. The Pacific was calm and empty, but just as Brian looked back to the rocky trail, something flittered in his peripheral vision. "Hold up, boys. Look out there just beyond the peninsula."

The three dutifully looked in the direction Brian pointed.

Buck said, "What? I don't see — wait a minute. What is that?"

Brian dug out his binoculars and searched for a few moments then stopped. "It's a submarine on the surface."

Shorty reach for Brian's binoculars. "Let me see."

Scanning the ocean from left to right, Shorty stopped abruptly. "Yep, it's a sub alright. I wonder whose it is?"

Brian retrieved his binoculars. "I'll give you one guess. Wish there was a way to alert Nick."

*　　*　　*

Nick's foot slipped backward in the inch-deep mud. Warm muck flowed over the top of his Oxfords and filled his shoe. It was the third time in as many minutes. His khakis were covered in mud from the time he tumbled forward and landed on the slippery trail.

Breathing hard, Cayse trotted up and stopped next to Nick. "Message delivered, Mr. Grant."

He bent forward at the waist with his hands on his hips. He was covered much the same as Nick and hadn't fared any better. Standing at the crest of the trail, they both tried to catch their breath.

Nick leaned on a tree trunk and looked over at Cayse. The jungle, close at times, was sopping wet, and every time they brushed up against the vegetation their clothes absorbed more water. Nick couldn't tell if his soggy state was from the vegetation, his own sweat, or a combination of both. Whatever it was, he was soaked clear through.

Cayse, still leaning forward, straddled the trail. "Looks like they came this way. No idea how long ago, though." He took two deep breaths then went on. "Gee, that climb kicked my butt."

Nick nodded, breathing hard. "Me, too. You ready to continue?"

"Yes, sir."

Silently, Nick took the lead and started moving as fast as he dared down the treacherous path. Out of the west, dark clouds, occasionally illuminated by lightning, rolled toward the moon.

Cayse said, "Looks like we might be in for a storm."

Nick looked at the angry clouds that formed a squall line as they advanced rapidly. "Yeah, just what we need. A downpour."

Chapter Twenty-Seven

9:42 p.m., Wednesday 30 December 1936
Rainmaker Trail
American Samoa

Toshio Miyazaki trotted down the steep slope trying hard to maintain his balance. Risking a glanced behind, he did not see Johnson. Miyazaki stopped at the next bend and waited. When his companion rounded the turn, Miyazaki reached out and grabbed Johnson by the throat. Johnson flailed uselessly as Miyazaki squeezed. "Do you want to get caught? You know what the Americans do to spies, don't you?"

Johnson gasped for air and shook his head. Miyazaki released Johnson, who fell to his knees and grabbed at his throat. "What'd you do that for? I was moving as fast as I could."

"That is not good enough. If the Americans catch you, they will throw you in the brig, torture you, and execute you. Is that what you want — you worthless sack of fish offal?"

Gasping, Johnson got to his feet. "I haven't done anything. I could just disappear into the jungle and be done with all your intrigue."

147

Miyazaki took a step toward Johnson. "What about Chief Tonga? You are an accomplice to his murder. You'll hang for that. What about guiding a foreign agent to a landing?"

Johnson took a step back. "I had nothing to do with Tonga. You did it, not me!"

Miyazaki stabbed a finger into Johnson's chest. "Tell that to the authorities if you must. I should draw my Katana and cut you down where you stand. You are a weak coward."

"I wanted help ridding my homeland of the Americans. I didn't request your help to murder my countrymen. There was no need to kill Tonga."

"You are wrong! He was trouble. He would have reported you and me to the authorities the moment we left the village."

"Maybe, but you can't know that for sure."

Miyazaki shook his head. "What a fool you are. This is not a game for children. Loose ends end up compromising the mission. You said that you were willing to do anything to rid the island of the Americans. Is that no longer true?"

A stab of light as bright as a flashing neon sign followed immediately by a crash of thunder interrupted Miyazaki's tirade. Then the skies opened with sheets of thick rain. Momentarily night blind, Miyazaki blinked. When he opened his eyes, Johnson was gone. "Ah yeee!" Miyazaki drew his katana and whirled around. "Come back here, you coward. Come back now and I'll let you live. If I have to hunt you down your death will be slow and painful."

The thunder and sheets of rain concealed all trace of Johnson. Miyazaki stabbed into the underbrush again and again with no results. The pounding rain had also washed away any trace of Johnson's footprints. As he looked around in frustration, he started to calm himself – to force himself to think rationally.

He knew that Johnson must die, but he'd hoped to get some more use out of him before he tied up that loose end. Now he'd have to spend precious time hunting him down and dispatching him. Time that he needed tonight — to make the sub rendezvous. If he missed the pickup time, he'd have to hide through another day. Since Grant had spotted him, the whole island would be crawling with marines and sailors hunting him. And those cowboys, Miyazaki wondered, what were they doing? No doubt they were mounted. He'd never be able to outrun them. He looked up into the raging storm and bellowed, "I curse you, Grant! By all the Gods, I curse you!"

148

Nick had never experienced rain like this. The sheets poured down so hard he could barely see two feet in any direction. It also made it difficult to breath. Every breath contained as much water as air. Worse, it had slowed their progress to a crawl. "Joe!" He yelled into the gale force winds.

"I'm here, Mr. Grant." Like an apparition from a horror movie, Cayse stepped out of the underbrush.

Nick leaned in to Cayse's ear. "What were you doing in there?"

"Looking for someplace to ride out the storm," He yelled back.

"No, we've got to keep moving."

"It's a mud puddle in there anyway."

Something hard smashed into Nick, toppling him backward into the muddy trail. Nick looked up into the face of a local who had bowled him over and landed on top of him. Cayse reached down and hauled the man up and was about to punch him in the face when Nick yelled, "Wait!"

Cayse stood there, one hand wrapped tightly into the offender's shirt, the other cocked back to deliver a right cross. "Who the Hell are you?" he demanded.

Nick recovered and drew his .45 automatic. "It's the local who I saw with Miyazaki." He pointed the pistol at the man. "Where's Miyazaki?" Then he had a terrifying thought. "Joe, it might be a trap."

The man cowered, "No, it's not a trap. I had to get away from him. He's a stone-cold killer – a madman."

Nick pointed the .45 at the man, "Name – quick!"

"Ta'isi Olaf Johnson. Don't shoot!"

"Cayse, I've got him. Draw your pistol and cover the trail downhill."

"Aye-aye, skipper."

Nick took one step backward keeping the pistol trained on Johnson. "You were working with him. Why?"

"He offered to help us rid the island of the likes of you."

Nick nodded as a knowing smile crossed his face. "How's that working out for you, Johnson?"

Johnson looked away momentarily then back to meet Nick's eye. "Like crap. He murdered a revered Chief." Johnson gasped for breath. "He spread lies and falsehoods to our tribal councils. He and his Japanese masters are as bad as you, Mainlander!"

Nick ignored the insult. "So why are you here? If there's no difference between Imperial Japan and the United States, why change sides?"

Hatred flashed across Johnson's face. "Who said anything about changing sides. I ran to save my skin, swabbie."

"Johnson, you're in so deep you'll never come up for air. Miyazaki has got to kill you. You know too much, and he's killed for way less. Your only chance is to throw in with us. Where is he? What was his plan?"

A glint of metal in the flash of lightning probably saved Nick's life. He ducked. Johnson wasn't so quick. The whirling disk struck Johnson's chest and sunk in. Cayse turned and fired until the pistol's slide locked to the rear. Then he dove into the mud as another steel disk whizzed past his head. Nick rolled over and sighted down his barrel but saw no target.

Cayse yelled. "Reloading!"

"Covering," Nick replied. "You hit, Cayse?"

"No, sir. You?"

"Nope. I was lucky."

Cayse said, "Locked and loaded, Mr. Grant."

"Cover me, I'm going to check on Johnson." Nick low crawled through the mud until he reached Johnson's side. A flash of lightning revealed his worst fears. Johnson lay on his back very still. Both of his hands gripped his chest. Nick pulled one hand free and felt for a pulse. It was there, but weak – Johnson was still alive. A *shuriken*, or a hidden hand blade as Mr. Nieshe had called it, was deeply embedded in Johnson's chest just above the heart. Blood soaked his shirt, but the heavy rain was rapidly washing it away, forming pink puddles around the body.

"Mr. Grant? You alright, Sir?"

"Yes, I'm coming over to you. Keep a sharp lookout, Miyazaki might still be close."

When Nick slithered over, Cayse asked, "What about Johnson?"

"Alive, a *shuriken* took him in the chest. He's going to need medical attention ASAP."

"What's a *shuriken?*"

Nick closed his eyes to the horror. So many deaths – so many wounded. He shook it off – he had to keep moving. "It's a Japanese concealed weapon. It's like a hidden dagger, or *metsubushi.* It's a favorite Ninja weapon used to distract, misdirect, or inflict a grievous wound. It has either four or six razor-sharp double-edged blades."

Cayse just stared at Nick for a long minute then said, "You know, sir, I'm beginning to think you're more than a run of the mill aviation cadet."

Nick stripped off his shirt and ripped off the sleeves. "Cayse, get over here and hold my shirt against Johnson's chest." Nick gingerly placed his knife blade into the center hole of the edged disk. "When I remove the *shuriken,* you put direct pressure on the wound. It's going to bleed like crazy. I'll use the sleeves to hold it in place."

"Got it, Mr. Grant."

Nick flicked the razor-sharp weapon into the jungle and Cayse covered the wound.

Johnson sat bolt upright. "Ouch! You trying to kill me?"

"No!" Cayse and Nick shouted in unison. Nick said, "Lie back. We're trying to stop you from bleeding out."

Johnson complied and Nick tied the makeshift binding around his torso and cinched it as tight as he could.

Johnson gasped. "I can't breathe! You've got to loosen it."

Nick loosened the binding but noticed that Johnson's blood was starting to soak through Nick's wadded-up shirt. "Cayse, you're going to have to escort Mr. Johnson back to Pago Pago."

"But, Mr. Grant! It's better if we both tackle Miyazaki."

"Got it, but you've got to get Johnson to a doctor."

"I don't like it, sir. Miyazaki – "

"Can it, Marine. That's an order."

Cayse cocked his head and opened his mouth to object, then seemed to think better of it. "I'll get him help but then I'm coming back. I don't care what you say — SIR!"

Nick smiled and put a hand on Cayse's shoulder, "Thanks, Joe. In truth I can't think of anyone I'd rather have covering my six. Hurry back."

Cayse's eyes blazed in the lightning flash. "I will, Mr. Grant. Please don't try to be a hero."

"Me? No way!"

"Yeah, right!"

Nick recalled how Commander Bolts had scolded him on too many occasions. "That's 'yeah, right,' SIR! Now go before Johnson passes out from loss of blood."

"Aye-aye, Mr. Grant."

They helped Johnson to his feet and threw his arm over Cayse's shoulder, then went their separate ways.

Chapter Twenty-Eight

10:52 p.m., Wednesday 30 December 1936
Rainmaker Trail,
American Samoa

Miyazaki slowed to an easy trot after the flat-out run he had maintained since his encounter with his pursuers. He felt confident that the wound he had inflicted on Johnson would be the end of the man. The fugu tetrodotoxin-tipped *shuriken* would do the work if Johnson didn't bleed out first. Still, he hated not personally ensuring that he had tied up that loose end.

He slowed to a stop where the trail ended before the open beach and tried to get his bearings. Checking his wristwatch, he noted he had just over an hour before the sub would send a shore party to collect him. Off to the left, a small village was snuggled up against a tall sugar-loaf-shaped mountain. The earlier rain had chased everyone inside, and he could see a couple of smoldering fire rings. He would hole up behind one of the huts, close to the shore but still away from prying eyes.

*   *   *

Brian gave Sarge his lead and slackened his grip on the reins. He'd been leaning back in the saddle for almost an hour and he felt it in his tail bone. The rain had stopped about fifteen minutes ago, leaving the air thick with steamy humidity. Up ahead, he saw Shorty break onto the beach and longed for a cool ocean breeze.

Brian called the riders to a halt and motioned them to form a circle. "Shorty, where is the Rainbow Mountain trailhead?"

Shorty cut off a wedge of tobacco and stuffed into his mouth. He answered between bites, "Up the beach about half-a-mile."

Leslie asked, "What else is up that way?"

Shorty spit a stream of tobacco juice into the sand. "There's a small village. Maybe six, seven huts and some fishing boats."

Brian reached down, pulled his grand-daddy's Winchester from its case, and chambered a round. "Time to draw your guns, boys."

The cowboys complied. They were locked and loaded. "We'll approach abreast and spread out. Shorty, you're with me on the left. Leslie, you and Buck take the right. Let's do this like we search for a lost calf, but no hollering. Let's do this real quiet-like."

The cowboys spread out and nudged their mounts down the beach toward the village and whatever lay beyond.

*   *   *

Nick trotted down the trail as fast as he dared. His white t-shirt was splattered with Johnson's blood and trail mud. Which he thought was a good thing. Nothing like a bright white shirt bounding down the trail to draw unwanted attention. At least the rain had stopped, and the partly cloudy sky let the full moon peek through from time to time. When he emerged on the beach, he stopped and looked around. The storm clouds were breaking up and patches of moonlight dappled the beach. He knelt and looked for a sign. The volcanic basalt sand did not hold water and he made out a set of tracks leading toward a small village in the distance. He strained his eyes searching for movement but saw nothing. Drawing his .45 he followed the tracks.

The deep sand clung to his feet and made the going slow. It was almost as exhausting as climbing the Rainmaker Trail. The broad beach was checkered with light and dark patches from the shafts of moonbeams. At the village outskirts, Nick stopped and

154

listened. It was all quiet, but Miyazaki's trail had ended in the myriad of tracks left by the village inhabitants. Then he thought he heard a woman's soft crying on the stiffening breeze. He moved closer and was now certain that a woman was weeping. In a low voice, almost a whisper, she seemed to be pleading. He couldn't be sure, as he did not recognize the language. At the hut's doorway, Nick heard Miyazaki say in English, "Shut up, woman. If you do as I say you will not be harmed."

The woman wailed in the universal language of fear, and then Nick heard a slap. The woman went silent. It was all Nick could do not to barge in and confront Miyazaki. Looking down, he realized his hands were shaking. He eased the grip on his pistol and tried to calm himself. Soon Brian and the boys would be here. He could wait. Quietly, he moved back away from the opening. He dropped onto the sand with his .45 trained on the opening. He listened intently, hoping to hear a horse whinny or some other indication that Brian's party wasn't too far off.

*   *   *

Inside the hut, Miyazaki grabbed the young girl by her hair, pulled her close, and put his tanto blade to her throat. "One more peep out of you and I'll slit her throat."

The woman, who Miyazaki assumed was the girl's mother, shrank back into a corner and sobbed quietly. When he entered the hut, it had looked empty. Then, what he thought were bundles of cloth erupted into this woman and the young girl. He had only just stopped the woman from screaming and alerting the rest of the village. His mind raced as he considered using them as hostages. But he realized they could both start screaming at any moment. And he could not dispatch them. Their deaths would doubtless ruin what little success he had achieved winning over the population against the Americans. For the moment he was stuck with them.

Luckily, the hut doorway faced the ocean. Looking at his watch he saw it was time to contact the sub. He tossed the girl next to her mother and pulled out a small electric signal lamp from his shoulder bag. Aiming out to sea, he flashed the recognition signal and waited. The minutes dragged by and he was about to resend the signal when he saw the response. He took a deep breath and, for the first time in days, relaxed. Soon he would be back aboard the I-23

155

and headed home. While his mission wasn't a complete success, he would return in a few weeks or months. When things had settled back into the usual American complacency. Yes, he would be back and perhaps more Naval Intelligence agents would accompany him to speed the revolt.

Looking out the doorway he could just barely make out the outline of the flat black rubber raft making its way through the surf. As before, two sailors were in the bow, rifles at the ready, as six others paddled hard. When the raft was 50 meters from the shore, Miyazaki motioned for the hostages to stand. Once again, he grabbed the girl and put his blade to her neck. He mimed for the woman to be silent, or he would slit the girl's throat. Then he gestured for them to walk toward the surf.

*   *   *

A rhythmic movement out to sea caught Nick's eye. At first all he saw were shapes reflecting moonlight as they moved back and forth. As it got closer, he realized he had seen the paddles of a black rubber raft filled with armed men. Before he could assess this new development, he saw movement at the doorway of the hut. Then, three shapes moved toward the surf. A cloud passed and a shaft of moonlight revealed Miyazaki pushing a woman and a girl toward the ocean.

The woman fell to her knees and pleaded something that Nick couldn't quite hear. Miyazaki whirled around and kicked her. "Shut up, woman!"

She fell to the ground and rolled onto her stomach. Nick locked eyes with her and saw the desperation in her face. Impulsively, he jumped up and charged Miyazaki. Pointing the .45 at Miyazaki's head, Nick yelled out in Japanese. "Stop right there, Miyazaki!"

Miyazaki stopped and slowly turned around using the girl as a shield. His tanto held to the frightened girl's neck. Miyazaki smiled. "Ah, Grant-son, we meet again. You need to drop the pistol."

"No way, Miyazaki. Let her go or I swear, I'll drill you right now."

Miyazaki laughed as he darted his head from one side of the girl's head to the other. "You think that you are that good of a shot,

156

Grant? You will most likely shoot the girl. Although that would save me the trouble of slitting her throat."

Nick hesitated. Miyazaki was right. He might be able to hit Miyazaki's head but at 50 feet it would be a close thing. And Miyazaki kept moving his head from side-to-side, further complicating an already tough shot.

"Do it now, Grant, or she's dead." He lifted the girl's head and pushed the blade a little harder into her throat.

Nick raged, "You do it and I'll empty the magazine into you."

"Yes," Miyazaki agreed. "Then she will be dead, and I will die a glorious death for my Emperor. You see, Grant, the gulf between you and me is vast. I do not fear death and you do."

Defeated, Nick threw his pistol into the sand and slumped.

"Now put your hands up, turn around, and walk backwards towards me. Any tricks and she dies."

Nick seethed but he had no choice.

He shuffled backward slowly until Miyazaki ordered, "Stop! Tuck your hands into your pants at the small of your back." That done, Miyazaki pressed his tanto to Nick's throat. Then he slipped something around Nick's wrist and tightened what must have been a thin rope or wire. It hurt like Hell, but he would not give Miyazaki the satisfaction of hearing him cry out.

Nick pleaded, "Miyazaki, let the girl go." Then something hard thumped into his temple and he fell forward onto the sands and darkness.

Chapter Twenty-Nine

12:01 a.m., Thursday, December 31st, 1936
Outskirts of Vatia Village
North Shore, American Samoa

Shorty reined in and motioned for Brian to come over. Then he dismounted and kneeled to examine something on the beach.

Brian drew up next to Shorty, "What is it?"

"Tracks. These here are strange ones – like the ones that was all over Santa Clara after we run off those Japanese sailors."

"Miyazaki's?"

"Pretty sure, and there's another set. I reckon they belong to young Nick."

Brian frowned, "Just one other track? Thought that marine was with Nick?"

"Tracks don't lie. There's Miyazaki's and one other."

"Okay, mount up. You follow the tracks. I need to speak with the others then I'll catch you up."

Brian nudged Sarge into a slow canter and then pulled up next to Buck. He waved Leslie over. "Shorty's located Miyazaki's trail and one other. We don't know if it's Nick or the marine. Something must have happened on the trail. I need you two to ride up the Rainmaker and see if they need help. Buck, you got your first-aid pouch?"

"Brian, bit late to ask, don't you think?"

"Fair point. Well, do you?"

"Yes, of course."

Brian nodded, "Great, render aid if needed, then ride back to the other side of the island. Get in touch with the Navy. Tell them about the submarine we saw in Vatia Bay. Now ride and don't spare the horses."

Catching up to Shorty, Brian asked, "Anything new?"

"Nope." Shorty spit a stream of tobacco juice just missing Brian. He hated tobacco in all forms. Brian was convinced that it had led to the early death of his granddaddy, although he couldn't prove it.

Winchester on his hip, Brian scanned the shore, still thinking about the submarine they'd seen earlier. He remembered seeing *A Woman of Experience* a few years back. In the movie a spy got picked up by an enemy sub. Well, if that were the case, even his granddaddy's Winchester wouldn't be much use.

As they approached the village, Shorty pointed. "Brian, rubber raft in the surf. There's armed men, too."

They kicked their horses into a gallop and made a beeline for the raft. One of the men, a sailor, Brian guessed, unslung his rifle from his shoulder and took aim.

Brian shouted, "Look out, Shorty! Zig-zag!" The two riders moved in opposite directions then swung back toward each other.

BAM! The sailor's shot echoed across the beach and bounced off the cliff behind the village. The first sailor worked the bolt on his rifle as two others unslung their rifles. Brian raised his rifle and waited for Sarge to rise to the top of his stride and fired. The .44-40 bullet ripped past the sailor and punctured the raft.

Two more shots rang out from the sailors. Brian looked over to see that Shorty was still in the saddle and returning fire. "Shoot the raft!"

Brian levered another round into the chamber, aimed and fired. He missed the raft but hit a sailor who crumpled backward onto the sand. Shorty fired and scored. Then Brian heard the submarine's deck gun boom and heard a whining sound that was increasing in intensity. A second later a huge geyser of sand erupted a few yards ahead. A wall of sand slammed into his face and Sarge stumbled. Brian felt himself lifted from the saddle.

He hit the sand hard, rolled, and then turned to find Sarge. A few feet away, the horse staggered to his feet and shook off what looked like a ton of sand. Brian ran over and pulled on the horse's bridle. "Get down, you silly old horse." Sarge neighed in protest, dropped to his knees, and rolled onto his side. Brian realized he no longer had the Winchester. "Oh Lordy, granddaddy's gonna rise up from the grave and cut me up one side and down another if I lost his precious rifle." Brian drew his pistol and laid down next to Sarge. "I sure hope Shorty's gonna be okay."

When the sand had settled, he glimpsed Shorty dismounted behind one of the village huts. Pecos, his horse, stood behind Shorty, winded but apparently okay. The village men started pouring out of their homes. Some were armed with ancient rifles and some with clubs. This was about to get very ugly.

*   *   *

Slowly the world came back to Nick. He heard shooting and hoped that Brian and his men had arrived. His head pounded and felt like it was about to explode. Something wet flowed down his right cheek and over the corner of his mouth. Sticking out his tongue, he tasted the coppery warmth of his blood. He felt himself being dragged along the beach and opened his eyes. Two uniformed sailors dragged him toward the rubber raft at the surf's edge. He tried to struggle but immediately felt the cold steel of a blade on his throat.

Miyazaki leaned over him and spoke in a cold and calm voice. "That will be enough struggling, Grant-san. You are about to embark on a sea voyage in one of His Imperial Majesty's best submarines. You should feel honored."

Nick spat blood mixed with sand from his mouth. "You'll never get away with this, Miyazaki. I've alerted the Navy. The *Farragut* is steaming your way."

The two sailors dumped Nick onto the floor of the raft. Other sailors urgently applied self-sticking patches to the bullet holes while several others fired their rifles into the darkness.

Miyazaki stood and gazed around, theatrically oblivious to the occasional bullet zipping by. "You think so, Nick? Let me quote that English pirate and one-time buccaneer for Queen Elizabeth, Sir Francis Drake. 'Ships? I see no ships – only hardships!' Hardships for you- you young fool." Miyazaki brought his face down close to

Nick, his dark eyes bright with delight. "You will wish you were never born when I get done with you. I have many ways to make you talk. You will tell me everything about US Naval Intelligence operations. Especially counterintelligence operations run by your mentor, Commander Steve Bolts."

Nick stared up at Miyazaki and started to laugh. "Boy did you capture the wrong guy. Bolts never tells me anything – the creep. Last time we met, he threatened to keel-haul me. Says I don't have a need-to-know!". Ha! I'm a midshipman in aviation training. I can tell you a great deal about the Yellow Peril trainer and some about the USS *Farragut*. And not much else."

A sailor working the bolt on his rifle cried out and dropped to the sand. Miyazaki pointed to the Japanese bosun and barked out an order in Japanese. The sailors on the beach shouldered their rifles and heaved wounded men into the raft. Others pushed the raft into the surf then clambered aboard. Strangely, the incoming bullets had ceased, which puzzled Nick. The Japanese were all clustered and would make easy pickings.

Miyazaki, sitting at the stern, looked down at Nick. "Your friends must have seen us toss you aboard and wisely decided not to chance hitting you."

Nick struggled into an uncomfortable sitting position. He was losing circulation and his hands were going numb. "This is so reckless, even for you. At least four American cowboys saw you abduct me – not to mention God knows how many Samoans. This is an act of war, Miyazaki."

The raft pitched up as they crossed the reef and its pounding surf. Miyazaki sheathed his *tanto* and shook his head in mock pity. "No body — no crime, Grant. As you Americans say, 'Your goose is cooked,' my unworthy opponent."

* * *

"Hold your fire!" Brian shouted to Shorty. "And tell those villagers to stop shooting, too. Nick's on the raft!" Brian heard a few scattered shots then silence. He stood and got Sarge to his feet. Mounting, he trotted over to Shorty, who was in a heated conversation with a middle-aged Samoan man.

The Samoan shouted in English, "They're getting away! Nobody holds a knife to my daughter's throat and lives to talk about it." The Samoan was almost as wide at the shoulders as he was tall. He looked strong enough to pick up Shorty, and Pecos, and toss them as easily as a sack of rice.

Brian reined in Sarge. "What's the trouble, chief?"

The Samoan turned and eyed Brian. "I'm not the chief." Pointing at Shorty, he continued. "This man ordered our men to stop shooting when we could have easily got them all. Why?"

Brian opened his palms in what he hoped was a beseeching gesture. "One of our guys was kidnapped and is on that raft. We might have hit him."

The Samoan nodded. "We've got boats. Let's go get him."

Brian shook his head. "Can't. You saw what that shell did to the beach. Can you imagine if they turned it loose on your village?"

The Samoan pounded a giant fist into the palm of his other hand. "So, what do we do?"

"We wait. I've sent two riders over the Rainbow to alert the Navy. They've got planes and a destroyer they can send."

The Samoan groaned. "That will take hours, and the Japanese will be long gone."

"Perhaps, but what other option do we have?"

The big Samoan rubbed his chin, deep in thought. "I'm not sure, but I've got an idea. Let me get with the villagers and see if we can pull this off."

"Pull what off?"

The Samoan grinned. "I'll tell you when I figure it out." He grunted, turned, and ran into the village shouting in Samoan.

Chapter Thirty

12:47 a.m., Thursday, December 31st, 1936
Rainmaker Trail
American Samoa

Joe Cayse was tiring rapidly. Ten minutes ago, Johnson had slowed down, stopped, and then toppled over. Cayse heaved the large man over his shoulder and continued up the steep and muddy path. At the top of the rise, he gently lowered Johnson to the ground and sprawled out beside him. "You are a lot heavier than you look," he murmured. Johnson did not reply. He had remained unresponsive since his collapse.

Cayse reached over and checked the wound. Nick's ripped up shirt was still in place and the blood stain wasn't any bigger. He wondered if maybe the fighting star had hit something vital, but he had no way of telling.

Groaning, Cayse got to his feet and started to lift Johnson when he heard the hoof beats. Clopping up the trail at a fast pace, the horsemen were on him before he could decide what to do.

The lead horseman reined in. "You that marine that was with Nick Grant?"

Resting his hand on the butt of his .45 automatic he replied, "Maybe, who wants to know?"

"I'm with Brian, the ones at the Celebration. You're Cayse, that right?"

"Yes, did you catch up with Mr. Grant?"

"Not exactly." The rider dismounted. "I'm Leslie Pearl, this here is Buck Thomas." Looking over Cayse's shoulder, Leslie asked. "Who's that with you? He looks hurt."

Cayse pointed to the prostrate figure. "A guy named Johnson who was in cahoots with Miyazaki. But I guess they had a falling out. He got hit by some sort of Japanese whirling knife. Mr. Grant told me to take him to the hospital and alert the Navy about a submarine we saw on the surface."

Leslie pushed his Stetson back. "We saw it too, from the top of the trail." Looking down at Johnson, he continued. "He don't look so good. Buck, get over here and take a look-see."

Buck dismounted, grabbed his first aid kit, and knelt next to Johnson. "This chest wound shouldn't have caused Johnson to be unconscious."

Cayse looked at Buck, "I didn't think the wound was that bad either, but a few minutes ago he just collapsed. Carrying him is out of the question. Say, could one of you fellas toss him over the saddle?"

Leslie nodded. "Sure. Buck, mount up, and Cayse and I will hand him up."

"Why do I get to ride double?"

"Because Cayse is going to ride double with me."

*   *   *

The big Samoan stopped in the middle of a group of villagers. "Has anyone seen Manuia?"

"I'm here, Loto." A young man wearing a lava-lava trotted over to the big Samoan.

Loto put his arm on his brother's shoulder. "Where is your *Va'a*?"

Manuia scratched his scalp absentmindedly. "It's beached on the other side of the village. Why?"

"Are your fishing nets stowed aboard?"

Manuia nodded, a puzzled look on his face.

"Great, grab Rangi and get over there fast. I'll get Tausa'afia and meet you there."

Loto ran over to Tausa'afia's hut and yelled inside, "Tausa'afia, are you in there?"

"Yes!" came an exasperated reply. "I can't find my darn rifle."

"Never mind that. Bring your abalone goggles and come with me."

Tausa'afia emerged from the hut, goggles in hand. "What's up, Loto?"

"Come on. I'll tell you on the way."

"What? Where are we going?"

Loto, who had already started trotting away, said over his shoulder, "Will you come along? We've got to hurry to catch that submarine before it submerges!"

When Loto and Tausa'afia got to the *Va'a*, Manuia and Rangi were ready to push off the beach. Tausa'afia and Loto helped push the outrigger into the surf, then hopped aboard. Manuia handed out paddles and the men put their backs into it. They crested a wave and paddled quickly toward the reef and the submarine's silhouette beyond.

Manuia asked, "Loto, what are we doing?"

Loto dug his paddle into the dark water and smiled. "We are going to pay a visit to our Japanese visitors. Give them a *pati fa'afeiloa'i.*"

Rangi reached for another stroke. "How do you know they are Japanese?"

"I heard them speaking on the beach just before the gunfire erupted."

Tausa'afia looked over from his side of the outrigger. "A warm welcome? How? With what?"

Loto smiled. "With an entanglement." He joined in the other men's laughter. They understood what he was about to undertake. He hoped and prayed the cost would not be too high.

*   *   *

Miyazaki's impatience was growing with each stroke. He turned to the bosun. "Make them paddle harder. Do you want the American planes down on us?"

"No, Shirei-kan. The two wounded cannot paddle."

Miyazaki shoved a paddle into the bosun's hands. "Then you join them in their efforts."

Wide-eyed, the bosun took the paddle and dug in. Miyazaki scanned the sky. He estimated that they had less than an hour before an American plane would arrive. If the horsemen left immediately, it would be thirty minutes before they reached a phone. Say thirty minutes to rouse a pilot and to warm up the aircraft. Once airborne, it would only take a few minutes to fly to their location. Plenty of time to catch them on the surface. He could not relax until he had Nick safely below decks and the I-23 got under way.

Grant eyed him with a wry smile. "What's the matter, Miyazaki? Afraid that an American fighter might be on the horizon?"

Miyazaki laughed, trying not to display the anxiety he felt deep down. "You are the one who should be afraid. I wonder if you will squeal like Joe MacMillan when you feel my blade?"

Hands still bound behind his back, Grant launched himself at Miyazaki. It was a clumsy move, and one Miyazaki easily dodged. "Ha! That was weak, Grant." He laughed until he heard a pop, then a rush of air blew in his face. The raft immediately started to sag in the middle with the combined weight of the crew. "Bosun, get over here and fix this leak properly."

"But Shirei-kan, we have no more patches."

"Then put your back against it, fool!"

The bosun pushed his back against the puncture just as Miyazaki heard another leak develop. It was on the opposite side of the tube that constituted the portside of the raft. The bosun reached over the side and placed his palm over the new leak. Miyazaki looked over at Grant, who looked smug. "Grant, if this raft sinks, we can all swim. Can you swim with your hands tied behind your back?"

Chapter Thirty- One

12:55 a.m., Thursday December 31, 1936
United States Naval Station Tutuila,
American Samoa

Lieutenant Gregory Walker stared at the driver in disbelief. "You're saying that Mr. Grant has taken off after Miyazaki and he's taken the marine with him?"

The driver stood at attention. "Sir, that's what Lance Corporal Cayse said to tell you."

Walker shook his head. "Okay, sailor, dismissed." He turned to the other officer. "Lieutenant Harris, get me a chart of Vatia Bay. We're going to see the old man."

"Why Vatia Bay?"

"Call it a hunch."

"Aye-Aye, Mr. Walker." Harris hurried out of the office.

Walker turned his attention to the pilot standing by the wall map. "How soon can you have your plane ready?"

Lieutenant JG Jesse Johnson checked his watch. "The men are fueling the Curtiss Seagull now. The chief will warm up the engine after he tops off the tanks. I'd say 10 minutes, give-or-take."

"Make it five. Does that thing have any armament?"

"Yes, sir. It's got a forward firing .30 caliber machine gun and another on a swivel mount at the observer's station."

Walker nodded. "Report what you see but do not fire unless given permission."

"Am I really looking for a submarine?"

"I don't know for sure. We've got the port locked down and I can't see another way off the island. Unless Miyazaki steals an outrigger canoe and paddles back to Japan. Just get over the other side of the island and report what you see."

"Aye-aye, Mr. Walker." Lieutenant Johnson tucked his leather flight helmet under his arm and exited.

Harris arrived carrying a rolled-up map under his arm. "Got it sir, but it's old. Printed in 1909."

"It will do, not much has changed on the island in the last 27 years. Come on, Harris. Let's go brief the old man. Better hang onto your hat though, this might be quite a blow."

*   *   *

Lieutenant Johnson ran from the headquarters all the way to the bay. The Curtis Seagull was tied to the dock, its engine turning over at idle, and the maintenance crew stood by to cast off. The observer, Seaman First Class Smith, strapped himself into the rear cockpit. "Smitty, do we have any ammo for the guns?"

Smith looked puzzled. "No, Mr. Johnson. Didn't know we needed any."

Ignoring Smith, Johnson turned to the maintenance chief. "Chief, how long would it take to get .30 cal ammo?"

Kowalski lifted his chief's cap and scratched his balding head. "Let me think, Mr. Johnson. I'd have to get the officer of the day. He'd have to release the keys to the ammunition bunker. Then we'd have to find the armorer because he's got the locker keys. Then count out the rounds and sign for them. Then – "

"Oh, for heaven's sake. I don't have time for all that, I've got to get airborne." Exasperated, Johnson continued. "Go get 1,000 rounds and bring it back here. I'll go make a sweep and return. Be quick as you can, Chief."

"Aye-aye, Mr. Johnson." He shouted to one of the men at the forward mooring line. "Kinney!"

"Yes, Chief?"

168

"Take over here and stay put until I get back."

"Will do, Chief!"

Kowalski turned and hurried off toward the headquarters building.

Johnson pulled on his flight helmet and swung up into the biplane's forward cockpit. As he strapped in, he ran his gaze over the instruments. Satisfied, he yelled out of the cockpit, "Cast off stern!"

Seaman Kinney repeated the order, "Cast off stern lines." The sailor at the tail loosened the mooring line and hauled it onto the dock.

Johnson yelled, "Cast off forward!"

Kinney repeated the order and the forward mooring line fell slack. Johnson eased the throttle forward and taxied the Seagull out into the bay. The storm had passed, and the moonlight provided ample illumination for a safe take-off. At the end of the bay, he turned the Seagull toward the ocean outlet. "Smitty, we good to go?"

"Ready in all respects, sir."

Johnson did a quick magneto check then pushed the throttle forward to the stop. The Seagull surged forward, plowing through the water, propelled by the Pratt & Whitney R-1340 engine. At full power, the 600 horse-power single engine pulled the float plane onto the step in a few seconds. Once on the step, hydroplaning on the surface, the Seagull skimmed across the bay rapidly gaining speed. Johnson felt life come into the controls as the air rushed past them.

When the airspeed indicator reached 65 knots, Johnson eased the yoke back and the Seagull rotated. Water streaming off the floats, they climbed eastward. Ahead he could see dark clouds and the occasional lightning flash from the recent storm. Banking the biplane, he headed west and climbed to clear the dark shape of Rainmaker. Beyond he could just make out the dark Pacific Ocean and Vatia Bay.

Johnson keyed his microphone. "Smitty, we're going to patrol the windward side of the island. Keep a look out for boats or ships close to the shore."

Smitty keyed his mic twice in acknowledgement.

Johnson eased the throttle back as he crossed the Rainmaker, and the Seagull began to gently lose altitude. He slid his canopy back and felt cool air flow into the cockpit. He checked his rearview mirror and saw Smitty also slide his canopy open. "Smitty, you concentrate on the port side and I'll take the starboard."

This time Johnson heard Smitty's voice in his headset. "Mr. Johnson, what are we looking for exactly?"

Johnson keyed his mic. "Possibly a sub on the surface or small motor craft. Mr. Walker seems to think that a spy might have been on the island and is trying to leave. We'd like to stop him if at all possible."

"Right, sir. Maybe ask him a few questions like?"

"You got it. Now the coast is coming up. Keep a sharp look out." Johnson eased the stick forward increasing the gentle dive towards Vatia Bay.

*　　*　　*

Despite the Japanese bosun's best efforts, Nick now sat in several inches of water that had collected on the raft's floor. The sailors continued to paddle the increasingly heavy raft. The sub was close, and Nick was unsure if they would make it before the raft sank.

Nick craned his neck at a familiar sound – an airplane engine coming off power. It was what a pilot might do if he'd just come over the Rainmaker. He looked back toward Miyazaki who scanned the night sky. He smiled. "Told you they'd come, Miyazaki. Untie me and surrender. I'll make sure you're treated well. Not that you deserve it."

Miyazaki reached out and backhanded Nick's face. Nick's head snapped to the side with the impact. "Shut up, Grant, or I'll gag you!"

Jerking his head back, Nick replied. "Last chance."

Miyazaki raised his hand to strike again when Nick heard the sweet sound of a radial engine roaring up the bay. Both turned their heads to see a biplane with floats about 25 feet off the water. It was headed straight for the sub.

Miyazaki drew his pistol, chambered a round, and started firing at the approaching plane. The pilot was either very brave or couldn't hear the pistol over the engine's roar. The American Curtis floatplane flew by so close that Nick could make out the face of the pilot and the observer in the back. As the floatplane roared over the sub, one of the sub's machine guns started firing. The green tracer bullets arced up toward the retreating floatplane. The pilot pulled the

Seagull up into a steep banking turn. He disappeared around the headland and was out of immediate danger.

The raft bumped into the side of the sub and strong hands lifted Nick aboard. Miyazaki said something in Japanese to a sailor who pointed his rifle at the sagging raft and fired. He repeated the action several more times. The raft lost its remaining air and sank into the bay.

A Japanese officer wearing a white officer's cap came running across the deck and started yelling at Miyazaki. Miyazaki replied in a similar heated tone. The Japanese language was coming fast and furious and Nick was having trouble keeping up. He was pretty sure the argument was about him. The captain did not seem happy that Miyazaki had brought Nick aboard.

A sailor on the conning tower pointed aft and shouted. Two sailors standing near Nick raised their rifles and started shooting at a dark shape off the stern. Gunfire erupted from elsewhere on the deck as other sailors joined in. They were firing their rifles at a Samoan outrigger and the occupants padded away for all their worth. Nick dropped to the deck and rolled. He hit two of the sailors from behind, disrupting their aim. One of the sailors tumbled into the bay, losing his rifle. The other managed to grab something but his rifle splashed into the bay.

"That will be enough!" Miyazaki yelled and kicked Nick.

Nick felt a sharp pain in his kidneys. Two sailors hauled him to his feet while another drove his rifle butt into Nick's abdomen.

"Enough!" Miyazaki shouted in Japanese. "He will feel my blade later, but first I need to interrogate him. Get him below."

The captain countermanded the order. The three sailors looked from one officer to another as if deciding whose orders to follow.

Speaking slowly, so even Nick could understand, Miyazaki growled, "Captain, you will either step aside and follow my orders or I will shoot you where you stand."

The two men eyed each other. Nick waited for one of them to blink but neither did. He saw his chance and took it. Drowning seemed a better option than dancing on the tip of Miyazaki's katana.

The captain and Miyazaki were still arguing, and the sailor's grip seemed to be loosening. Nick started to increase his breathing. Inhaling deeply, filling his lungs completely – then exhaling as fully as possible, flushing excess CO_2 from his lungs. If his biology professor were to be believed, hyperventilation could extend the time he could hold his breath. He would need those extra seconds if escape were possible.

Sooner or later the sailors would notice his breathing and return their attention to their captive. He sucked in a deep breath, alerting one of the sailors. Nick spun, breaking both sailor's grip. Catching everyone by surprise he dove off the sub's deck into the bay. Using a dolphin kick, he pushed himself deeper and deeper. Bullets zipped by harmlessly as the darkness and cold embraced him. He kicked off his shoes and his speed increased markedly. If only his hands weren't tied behind his back, he might stand a chance.

Chapter Thirty-Two

1:42 a.m., Thursday December 31, 1936
Vatia Bay
North Shore, American Samoa

Paddling hard, Loto looked over his shoulder at the submarine. The rifle fire had slackened and then stopped. "Hold up, boys. I think we're safe now."

Breathing hard, Tausa'afia rested his paddle across the outrigger's thwart. "I thought they had us. When that sentry started yelling, I thought we were all dead."

Wide eyed, Manuia and Rangi, also resting on their paddles, nodded their agreement.

Loto looked back and smiled. "I'd love to be there when they start their engines."

Rangi frowned. "Do you really think those fishing nets will foul their propellers?"

Loto shrugged, "Who can say. But at least the Japanese will think twice before they attack our village again."

Manuia laughed nervously. "That was fun! I can't believe we sabotaged a Japanese sub and lived."

Loto turned to look at his village across the bay. "Let us hope that the Japanese do not exact retribution on Vatia."

Tausa'afia straightened up. "Let's go back."

"What?" the others said in unison.

Tausa'afia continued, "We sneak back and wait close as we dare. If the Japanese start bombarding our village, we board the sub and kill the gun crews."

"With what, Tausa'afia?" asked Manuia. "We left our rifles behind."

Tausa'afia lifted his eight-inch double edged fishing knife, which briefly reflected in the moonlight. "With this. It will gut a Japanese sailor as well as it will gut a fish."

*   *   *

Nick's lungs burned as he kicked with all his might for the surface. It seemed so far away, and he was starting to experience tunnel vision. Exhaling hard, he wondered how long he could remain conscious. With a final mighty kick, he broached the surface and gasped in a breath before his weight dragged him back under. He used a scissor kick to bring him back toward the surface. This time, just before he surfaced, he rolled onto his back. He was floating and could breathe again. But every time he exhaled, his head would sink below the surface. He'd have to time his breathing with a hard kick to keep his nose and mouth above the water. With a little luck he could float like this all night.

A few minutes later he heard waves crashing over the reef. He took a deep breath and rolled onto his stomach. Kicking hard he could just keep his eyes above the water. He realized he was being pulled onto the reef's crashing waves. Rolling onto his back, Nick kicked as hard as he could. He knew he'd never be able to keep his head above water in the churning waves over the reef.

Despite his efforts, he was only slowing his progress. Frantically, he looked around for something, anything, that would keep him from certain death. Then he saw a glint of metal. It wasn't a rifle or helmet. It was much smaller. A knife, maybe?

He tried to call out and was rewarded with a mouth full of sea water. Spluttering, he cleared his lungs and yelled. "Help! Over here! Help!"

*   *   *

Manuia held up his paddle. "Did you hear that? Someone yelling for help in English."

They all stopped paddling and listened. Loto nodded, "Yes, let's take a look."

He dug his paddle in and turned the outrigger toward the cries. As they paddled the cries became louder, but still Loto

174

couldn't see where they were coming from. "We should be able to see the man as close as we are."

Rangi called out. "I see him. Only his face is above water."

Loto steered the outrigger over close to the man. Manuia and Rangi reached over the side and hauled the floater out of the water.

Rangi looked down at the victim. "Loto, someone's tied this poor fella's hands behind his back."

"Well, cut him loose!"

Rangi cut the man's bonds and rolled him over. "He's conscious, Loto. Who is this fella?"

Loto put his head in his hands. "Rangi. How should I know? Why don't you ask him?"

Rangi looked at the rescued man. "Boss wants to know who you are?"

Rubbing his wrists where the bindings had cut deep, the fella answered. "Midshipman Nick Grant. There's a Japanese agent on the sub. He captured me."

Loto looked at the sodden young man and nodded. "You with those horse fellas on the beach?"

"Yes," said the exhausted Nick.

"Good. We threw fishing nets onto the sub's propellers."

Nick shivered and rubbed his hands together. "That was brilliant. It should slow them sufficiently to let the Navy get here."

"We're going back," Loto said. "We'll approach quietly and wait. If the sub decides to shell our village, we will board to stop them. Do you want to come with us?"

"Going back may well be suicide for all of you. The Japanese agent is Commander Miyazaki and he's a vicious killer." Looking down and speaking softly, Nick continued. "He's killed the guilty and innocent alike. Including several of my close friends. He'll cut you down without hesitation if you get in his way."

Loto looked from Tausa'afia, to Rangi, and then to Manuia. "You heard what this boy said. It's going to be dangerous. Maybe we get killed. Maybe get hurt so bad can't fish no more. What I need-to-know!" is this. Are you still willing to stop them from shooting the big gun on our village?"

Each man nodded in return and Loto turned to Nick. "And you, boy sailor? What about you?"

*　　*　　*

Nick could not believe his ears, going back to the sub was not what he had in mind. "If I say no, then what?"

The boss man replied, "Then we give you a life ring and you swim back to shore."

"Oh, in that case, I'm in. Do you have any weapons?"

One of the other Samoan men handed Nick a vicious looking double-edged knife with a bone handle. Then he said in passable English, "My name is Rangi." He pointed out the others. "That's Manuia, Tausa'afia, and the boss man's Loto."

"Nice to meet you, and thanks for pulling me out of the drink. I thought I was a goner."

Loto, at the rear steering paddle, replied, "Yeah, many people say that tonight."

Rangi handed Nick a paddle. "Try not to splash. I don't want to get shot."

Nick dug the paddle in and managed only a little splash. "I'll try."

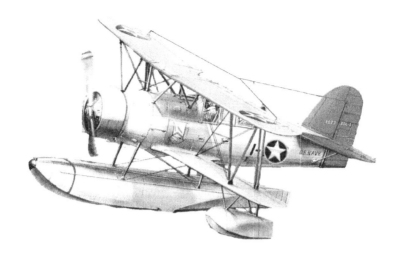

Chapter Thirty-Three

2:03 a.m., December 31ˢᵗ, 1936
Above Rainmaker Mountain Range
American Samoa

Lieutenant Johnson keyed his mic. "Tutuila Base, this is Navy Xray-one eight, over."

Johnson waited but got no response. Thinking Rainmaker Mountain might be blocking his radio signal, he tried again once they had cleared the mountain. "Tutuila Base this is Navy Xray-three-zero, over."

Still no answer.

"Smitty, I'm going to bring her in hot. Better hang on back there. Did you see that guy on the rubber raft shooting a pistol at us?"

Seaman First Class Smith keyed his mic. "Did you see the submarine's machine gun shooting at us?"

Johnson felt bile rise in his throat. "Are you alright? Did you get hit?"

"No, sir. I'm okay. But that Japanese sub ventilated the tail pretty good."

Moving his control stick back and forth and then the rudder pedals, Johnson keyed his mic. "The controls check out okay, but I'll take a look-see when we get back to the dock."

Smith keyed the mic twice in acknowledgement.

Easing the throttle back, Johnson set flaps at 30 percent and lined up with the dark bay. He hated night landings – so much could go wrong. Suddenly, to his delight, two twin rows of lights came on. Someone had placed floating landing lights in the bay, illuminating a safe landing zone. Now his touch-down would be a piece of cake.

They bounced once when they hit, a bit harder than Johnson would have liked. He remembered what one of his fight instructors had said and smiled. "Any landing you can walk away from, Johnson, is a good landing. He taxied the floatplane toward the pier and considered that, in this case, it would be *any landing you swim away from ...*

Chief Kowalski directed the crew to secure the Seagull then shouted over the engine, "Mr. Johnson, I've got your ammo!" Then pointing at the tail, "What the Hell happened?"

Johnson shook his head, "Long story, Chief." He keyed his mic. "Smitty, help the chief lock and load both guns. I'm going to check out the empennage for damage."

Smith came back. "The what, sir?"

"The tail assembly. Don't they teach you sailors anything in aircraft maintenance school?"

"I wouldn't know, sir. I'm a machinist mate. I just got drafted to be your observer."

"Wonderful, just wonderful. Go help the chief."

The empennage was riddled with 28 holes. He was amazed that the Seagull's flight characteristics didn't seem affected. Then he noticed his transmission antenna was missing.

Kowalski ran up to Johnson. "Ammo's loaded, Mr. Johnson. Do you want to top off fuel?"

"No, chief. No time. Have your heard anything from the head shed?"

"Not a peep, sir."

"My radio is out. Send a runner to the Officer of the Day. Tell them that I've been fired on by what appears to be a Japanese submarine of the *Kaidai* type. The boat was on the surface retrieving a landing party when we passed. They fired on us but did little

178

damage. I'm headed back but I'll return here in 45 minutes for orders. Right now, I'm just going to buzz them. Got all that?"

Kowalski scratched behind his ear. "Well, I think I'd better go myself, sir. No swabbie will remember all that."

Johnson tightened his helmet strap. "Whatever you think best, Chief. Just get word to the head shed."

"Aye-aye, Mr. Johnson."

Johnson swung up into the cockpit, strapped in, and yelled, "Cast off fore and aft!"

*　　*　　*

0215 hours, 31 December 1936
Aboard the USS *Farragut,* DD-348,
Pago Pago Harbor, American Samoa

Ensign Jones awoke to the General Quarters alarm that sounded throughout the ship. "GENERAL QUARTERS – GENERAL QUARTERS! Man battle stations. This is not a drill."

Jones hurriedly dressed, grabbed his helmet and life vest, and headed toward the bridge. Outside his stateroom the passageway was a scene of confusion. Half-awake officers, chief petty officers, and sailors stumbled about, bumping into each other.

When Jones topped the last ladder to the bridge, he saw Captain Hutson in deep conversation with Lieutenant Walker and a Lieutenant Junior Grade he did not recognize. Hutson seemed agitated. "I'm not about to sail my ship into a bay with that chart. It's ancient."

Walker looked exasperated, "Sir, you don't need to enter the bay. All Captain Milne asks is that you blockade the entrance. Just stop the sub from leaving."

"And what?" Hutson retorted, "get a torpedo amidships?" He looked at the Lieutenant, Junior Grade. "Harris, what type armament does a Japanese submarine carry?"

Harris didn't hesitate. "Eight torpedoes, type 89 s – six in bow tubes and two in stern tubes. She mounts a 100mm deck gun, two 12.7-mm anti-aircraft machine guns on a twin mount, and a single 7.7-mm machine gun, sir."

The XO entered the bridge. "Captain Hutson, we're building steam and should be able to cast off in about 20 minutes. Hope that jury-rigged propeller shaft holds."

"So do I, XO, so do I." Hutson turned back to Walker. "You two joining us on this fool's errand?"

Walker nodded. "Yes, sir. If you'll have us."

Hutson eyed them for a few seconds then turned back to the XO. "Get them helmets and life vests. Then park them in the C-I-C."

"Aye-Aye, sir."

Hutson turned back to the two land sailors. "Do try to keep out of the way, gentlemen. This is a working ship."

*   *   *

Loto held up his hand and the Samoans stopped paddling. They had been creeping along without speaking, gently dipping their paddles into the water, and being careful not to splash. Nick estimated they were 50 yards away on the ocean side of the sub. He could see several sailors, rifles slung over their shoulders, patrolling the length of the sub. However, their focus was on the shoreline. Only occasionally did someone on the conning tower look in their direction. And then only briefly.

The Samoan outrigger was painted a dark red and they had un-stepped the mast. The entire boat was low in the water, which, Nick supposed, made it difficult to see in the dark.

Voices drifted across the still water. Nick could make out only the odd Japanese word or two, but he was getting the gist. Loto moved quietly up beside Nick and whispered. "Do you know what they are saying? They seem to be arguing."

"They are. The captain wants to leave but that man," Nick pointed, "is Commander Toshio Miyazaki, Japanese Intelligence. He wants to shell your village as revenge for interfering with his carefully laid plans."

Loto stiffened. "Then we must attack now. My family lives there."

Nick put a hand on the Samoan's arm. "No, not yet, Loto. The captain has forbidden any attack on civilians. His rule is law."

A shot echoed across the water. Nick turned in time to see the captain slump, then slide into the bay. Sailors rushed to the sound but Miyazaki, pistol in hand, ordered them back to their stations. Nick heard Miyazaki call out a name and a young officer ran up and saluted.

It was difficult to hear but Nick heard some chilling Japanese words.

180

He turned back to Loto. "Miyazaki shot the captain and just ordered the crew to prepare to fire. Now might be a good time to strike."

Chapter Thirty-Four

2:13 a.m., December 31st, 1936
Rainmaker Mountain Trail
American Samoa

Buck leaned forward in the saddle as he reached the trail head. His left arm was cramping as he held the unconscious Samoan seated behind him. Buck had cinched his belt around the big man, but he still had to hold tight otherwise the Samoan surely would have fallen off the back of his horse. The party guests were gone. Except for a few parked cars, the pavilion was dark and deserted. "Leslie, where'd everybody go?"

Leslie, riding double with Cayse, shook his head. "What time is it, Buck?"

Buck hung his reins over the saddle horn and dug out his pocket watch. "Two fifteen, why?"

"Do you think maybe it's a bit late for the party to still be going?"

"Could be that's the case, Leslie."

Two sets of car lights snapped on. Doors opened and dim figures stood behind the bright headlights. A man's voice boomed. "Hold it right there. Show me your hands."

Buck and Leslie looked at each other and raise their hands. Cayse slipped off the back of Leslie's horse. "It's Lance Corporal Cayse from the *Farragut*. We've got an injured man here. We need your help."

The voice called out. "Joe, that you?"

"Yes, that you, McKinny?"

The headlights cut out and two marines carrying Thompson submachine guns ran up, slung their weapons over their shoulders, and helped lower the Samoan to the ground. Cayse knelt next to the prostrate local. "He's been like that since right after he got hit by some kind of flying knife. The wound's not deep and he hasn't lost much blood. He should be conscious."

Sergeant McKinny examined the Samoan. "Peterson, help me get him into the staff car."

Cayse stood aside as the two marines hoisted the Samoan into the back seat. "Mr. Grant said to guard this man. I'll get in the back with him. He may have important information — if we can keep him alive. Can you take us to the infirmary?"

"Right, hop in."

Cayse leaned out the window. "Leslie, Buck, what're you guys going to do?"

Leslie replied. "Change mounts then head back over the mountain to give Brian and Shorty a hand."

*   *   *

Loto, Nick, and the others slipped over the side of the dugout and swam silently toward the sub. Each carried a gutting knife tucked into their waist bands. The plan was simple. One would swim to the bow. Two would approach the conning tower, sometimes called the sail. The last two would head towards the stern. Once in position, Loto would count to 50, then bang on the sub's hull with the butt of his knife. The metal-on-metal sound would be the signal to attack.

Simple, thought Nick, and ridiculously dangerous. The element of surprise would work to their advantage only for the first few seconds. Then they would be facing armed sailors on full alert.

Nick's breaststroke was quiet and moderately swift, and he reached the conning tower easily. As he grabbed a handhold, he heard the rumble of the sub's diesel engines start up. Smoke erupted from the exhaust vents that would conceal the aft attack for precious seconds. Loto grabbed a handhold close to Nick, his lips moving with the count. Nick grabbed his knife and got ready to scale the slippery port side of the sub.

Men on the deck started shouting. Nick thought they must have been discovered. Then he heard the sweet sound of a radial engine in a steep dive. The heavy machine guns just forward of the conning tower fired, spitting a line of green tracers into the air. Between each glowing line arcing up to meet the American plane, there were four dark rounds. He wondered how the Japanese machine guns could miss. Then Nick heard the deck impact with repeated metallic pings. It had to be from the American plane. Its machine gun swept the deck of the submarine. Two sailors cried out and went down. Others aimed their rifles at the retreating floatplane, which returned fire from a rear-mounted machine gun.

Nick looked at Loto. "Let's go!"

Loto banged on the sub's hull and hauled himself up on the deck. Nick followed, fisherman's knife in hand. They emerged on the port side of the conning tower and looked around.

A sailor forward saw Loto, yelled, "Banzai!" and charged. Loto swatted the rifle's bayonet aside. He lifted the sailor off the deck and tossed him overboard.

Nick turned to see another sailor charging him from the stern. The space between the conning tower and the port rail was only large enough for one man to pass. There was no room to dodge the oncoming sailor. Nick whipped off his t-shirt and threw it into the man's face.

The sailor stumbled and fell on his face at Nick's feet. Nick grabbed the end of the rifle and jerked it aside just as it fired. He brought his foot down hard on the sailor's hand. The sailor yelped and he lost his grip on the rifle. Nick kicked it aside, dropped onto his backside, and pushed the sailor over the side with both feet.

Standing, Nick slung the rifle over his shoulder and climbed the conning tower ladder. He had to get to the aft machine gun mount. When he topped the ladder, the two-man crew was training the gun on the fight that had erupted on the stern. Rangi and Tausa'afia had dispatched the two stern sentries and were advancing toward the conning tower amidships. Rangi had a rifle, but Tausa'afia only brandished his knife. They would be cut to pieces by the machine gun.

Atop the ladder, Nick unslung the rifle. He raised the butt and smacked one of the sailors in the side of the head. The sailor went down. The other sailor started to draw a side-arm when Loto reached up out of nowhere and grabbed the surprised sailor from behind. He lifted the poor man like a sack of flour and tossed him over the side. From atop the gun mount, the flailing sailor made quite the splash when he hit the water.

Nick and Loto crawled forward on top of the conning tower, past the periscope mounts. They dropped into the sub's bridge, located on the forward edge of the conning tower. Two officers on duty were facing forward, one speaking into a talking tube, the other scanning the shore. Neither noticed Nick or Loto until they too were flailing toward the bay. Nick had never met someone so immensely strong. Loto was not even breathing hard.

Looking down on what would be the cigarette deck on a US sub, Nick saw a three-man crew manning a much larger twin mount machine gun. One man, probably the gun captain, pointed up at the sky and yelled. As they watched, the crew traversed and elevated the gun. Looking at where they pointed, Nick saw the American floatplane lining up for another gun-run. He looked at Loto. "We've got to take out those guns or it will make mince-meat out of the plane."

Nick unslung his rifle and Loto drew his knife. "We'll go on three. One. Two. Three!" They jumped the five feet down to the heavy machine gun mount.

This time, one of the sailors saw them leap and shouted an alarm. Loto hit the deck and charged. Once again, he lifted the first sailor and tossed him overboard.

Nick butt-stroked the gun captain and advanced on the last terrified man. The man shrieked, dropped his pistol, and leapt overboard.

Loto bent down and retrieved the discarded pistol. Then he looked at the twin machine guns, "You know how to work this thing?"

Eyeing the unfamiliar machine guns, Nick shrugged, "How hard could it be? Come on, let's swing this thing around and use it on the deck gun."

*   *   *

185

Miyazaki screamed at the deck gun crew. "Why are you so slow? I want that village destroyed!" Brandishing his katana in one hand and a pistol in the other he hit the gun captain with the flat of the sword. "Hurry up, man, or I'll flay you alive."

The gun captain shouted, "Hai!"

Looking up to the conning tower, Miyazaki yelled, "What are you waiting for? Engage the engines and get us moving before that plane returns."

The officer in the conning tower bent down to use the speaking tube and was jumped from behind. The sub's XO was next. Then both officers seemed to fly off the bridge and splash into the bay.

"What is going on?" Miyazaki yelled and watched in disbelief as two men leapt from the bridge and took out the heavy machine gun crew. It seemed like half the deck crew was swimming in the bay. One man had jumped unassisted. He would pay with his life later for his cowardice.

Enraged, Miyazaki raised his pistol and fired twice before the slide locked to the rear. He was out of ammunition. He raised his katana just as he noticed the men around him diving to the deck. Machinegun rounds plunked into the steel deck and ricocheted everywhere. He dove and looked up to see the American floatplane waggling its tail as it dove on the sub. The effect was remarkable for a single small-bore machine gun. Bullets hit the sub from stem to stern. The plane roared over not ten meters above his head. As it passed, that pesky rear gunner added insult to injury, further spraying the sub with additional bullets.

Rising to his feet, Miyazaki looked up at the heavy machine gun mount and saw Nick Grant swinging the barrel in his direction.

Chapter Thirty-Five

0300 hours, 31 December 1936
Aboard the *USS Farragut*
Steaming toward the headland, American Samoa

Commander Hutson scanned the coastline. Satisfied, he hung his binoculars around his neck and turned to the other officer standing on the bridge. "XO, how's the shaft bearing repair holding up?"

Lieutenant Commander Jordon eyed the telephone talker. "Seaman, get current bearing status from the engine room."

"Aye-aye, Mr. Jordon."

As the telephone talker rang the engine room, Jordon checked the heading. "Captain, heading is zero-three-five true, making twenty-eight knots."

Hutson acknowledged. "Zero-three-five at twenty-eight knots. Where's that status report?"

The telephone talker reported, "Mr. Jordon, the engineer reports that the bearing is holding, and shaft temperature is nominal."

Lieutenant Commander Hutson nodded. "XO, what's our projected time to reach Vatia Bay?"

"We should be there at Begin Morning Nautical Twilight, sir."

"BMNT. Good. I want our gunners to see what they're shooting at."

Jordon frowned. "Sir? We're just supposed to bottle up the sub. Not sink it."

"I'm well aware of our orders, Mr. Jordon. Regardless, I plan to be ready for anything. A warship, especially a submarine, in US territorial waters is an act of war. I plan to be on a wartime footing when we reach the headland. Then we'll go to general quarters, battle stations surface action."

*　　*　　*

0312 Hours., 31 December 1936
Aboard the I-23
Vatia Bay, American Samoa

Up on the gun platform, Loto had figured out the traversing mechanism on the twin mount Hotchkiss heavy machine guns. He slowly cranked the gun around until the twin barrels were aligned with the main deck gun. Nick was attempting to decode the Japanese characters and figure out how to depress the gun barrels. The earlier strafing run by the floatplane had bought them precious time but now the crew was starting to get up and return to their stations.

Miyazaki was first on his feet and fired two pistol rounds at them. The bullets pinged harmlessly off the armored crew shield. Loto ducked. "Hurry up, Nick."

"Got it!" Nick jumped into the gunner's seat and depressed a foot pedal. The muzzles dropped and he squeezed the trigger. A burst of 12.7mm bullets ripped into the deck a few feet beyond the gun crew. They scattered. Two ran forward but seeing the big Samoans at the bow, they decided to take their chances in the bay. The other two followed Miyazaki down the forward hatch, disappearing into the sub.

Nick jumped down to the deck, "Come on, Loto. They're going to escape!"

Loto stood unmoving. "Good, if they are fleeing, so be it. Thank you for the help. We will not forget your deeds this night." He called out in Samoan, tucked his knife and the pistol into his waist band, and dove from the gun mount into the bay some fifteen feet below. Quickly the remaining Samoans followed.

Alone, Nick raced toward the forward hatch. Reaching for a dropped helmet he jammed it into the hatch just as men inside were pulling it shut. He unslung the rifle and jabbed the bayonet at the hands attempting to free the helmet and close the hatch. He heard a muffled yelp as the hands disappeared into the sub. Nick wrenched the hatch open.

BANG-BANG!

Two bullets shot out of the hatch and missed his head by inches. Nick jumped back and searched for something – anything – he could toss down the hatch. His eyes came to rest on a stack of 100mm shells next to the deck gun. He put the rifle down and heaved up the heavy shell. Straining, he moved to the hatch and dropped it in point first and listened. The shell's delayed fuse did not detonate. But he was quite sure everyone in the compartment would be hightailing it out of there as fast as their feet would carry them. But somewhere they would stop and try to oppose him. Snatching up the rifle, Nick followed the shell into the submarine's depths.

Landing hard, he brought the rifle to the guard position and looked around. Red light reflected off the bulkheads and equipment of what seemed an empty compartment. At the sound of a metal-on-metal click, he whirled about. A sailor leapt at him from behind a huge piece of equipment and charged. Red light reflected off the sailor's tanto fighting knife.

Nick swung the rifle up and the butt caught the man under the chin. There was a sickening crack, and the man went down spitting teeth. Nick tensed for the next attack, but none came. Gathering his bearings, he moved cautiously amidships where, he supposed, the control room would be located.

The sub began to vibrate as the diesel engines fired up. They would soon be underway. Nick looked toward the stern through the open watertight hatches. He suspected that Miyazaki was somewhere close to the periscopes and the other controls for conning the sub. He eased himself through the narrow oval-shaped opening. Someone grabbed his rifle and jerked it hard. Nick lost his balance and

189

tumbled forward. Dropping the rifle, he continued through the roll and sprang to his feet facing back toward the hatch.

Two sailors advanced, one carrying a large wrench. The other carried a wicked looking screwdriver the length of Nick's forearm. Screwdriver man stabbed at Nick's abdomen in a lightning-fast strike.

Nick stepped aside, parried the man's outstretched arm, and delivered a backhand fist strike to the man's temple. He staggered but remained on his feet. Nick kicked him hard and he slammed into a large piece of machinery. The distraction allowed wrench man to move within striking distance. His arm came down aiming for Nick's head.

Nick moved into the man's swing. The wrench grazed the back of Nick's head and he felt a wallop. Seeing stars, Nick head butted the sailor, rotated around the outstretched arm, and jerked up violently. The elbow gave way with s sickening crunch. The sailor screamed and fell back clutching his ruined arm. Nick retrieved the rifle and continued aft.

In the next compartment, two sailors hid behind what looked like an electrical panel. They glared but made no move to stop him. As he approached the far watertight hatch, he heard two men arguing in Japanese. One was clearly Miyazaki, but the other Nick did not recognize. Nick's Japanese wasn't good enough to catch every word, but it seemed to center around recovering the sailors overboard in the bay.

"No, Lieutenant," Miyazaki said. "We must leave now. The men in the water must sacrifice themselves for the glory of the Emperor."

"Commander," the other man pleaded. "It will only take twenty minutes. We will be gone long before daylight. The men have served you and the Emperor with honor and deserve our help."

"Ha!" screamed Miyazaki. "Half of those men dove overboard instead of fighting the gaijin who boarded this submarine. Go aft and determine why the propellers are jammed. I want to get underway immediately. There will be no more talk of pulling those cowards out of the water."

The other man replied, "Hai!"

Nick heard the man retreat aft and decided to make his move. He gazed through the last hatch leading to the control room. He expected it to be crowded with crew members, but Miyazaki stood

190

alone. His back was toward Nick as he studied the chart table in the center of the small compartment. Nick raised the rifle to his shoulder and aimed at the center of Miyazaki's back. He had waited almost two years for a chance to exact revenge for Mac, for Roger Tanaka, for all the people this man had killed. He exhaled and started to squeeze the trigger. Then he stopped, frozen and unable to continue.

Nick hated Miyazaki with every fiber in his body. No one deserved to be cut down more than this man. But he couldn't do it.

He thought about the first time his dad had taken him hunting in the mountains east of Alameda. They had tracked a beautiful buck for hours, finally lining up a shot. His father had whispered, "You take it son. Remember what I said, aim just behind the foreleg. That will lessen the chance he will suffer."

Nick had raised the rifle to his shoulder, lined up the shot, and then he froze. He couldn't squeeze the trigger. He started shaking so hard he thought he would drop the rifle. His father lowered the barrel and gently said, "Don't worry, Nick. It's called buck fever." His father added, "It's a common occurrence for first time hunters. Next time you'll be able to shoot. Put the rifle on safe and let's head home. It's been a long day."

Years later his buck fever had returned. As much as he loathed the man, Nick was unable to shoot Miyazaki in the back.

Still aiming the rifle, he saw a lieutenant enter the control room. The lieutenant swung around the two periscope wells, saw Nick, and stopped dead in his tracks.

The lieutenant met Nick's eyes. They stared at each other for what seemed like an eternity – neither moving.

Then the lieutenant reached for his pistol and yelled a warning.

Miyazaki dropped to the floor as the lieutenant raised his pistol and fired. Nick dropped back behind the hatch as the two rounds cracked through the opening. He heaved on the hatch, pushing it into the opening, and spun the wheel that activated the dogging mechanism. Someone had reached the other side of the hatch and started turning the hatch wheel in reverse.

Nick detached the bayonet and thrust it into the space between the spokes of the wheel. The dogging latches started to move to the open position until the spoke hit the bayonet and stopped. Nick had jammed the hatch shut. He retrieved the rifle and retraced his steps forward. At the forward hatch that led to the deck, he took the ladder rungs two at a time until he was once again on the deck.

Sailors on deck were helping those in the bay clamber up the sides. Looking aft he saw others with axes chopping away at the fishing nets fouling the stern propellers. With a deep rumble and black diesel smoke belching from the exhausts, the sub started to move. It swung around to point toward the mouth of Vatia Bay and picked up headway. Sailors too far out into the bay shouted and waved but none of the sailors on the deck paid any attention to them.

Finally, one of the sailors, perhaps a chief petty officer, saw him, pointed, and started yelling. Nick dropped the rifle and dove into the bay. Bullets zipped past him as he kicked away under water. Lungs burning, he broke the surface and swam away from the sub as fast as his tired arms and legs would propel him. Thankfully, the rifle volleys ceased.

He turned to see the I-23 plowing towards the open ocean just as the first rays of light were beginning to show in the eastern sky. The high cumulus clouds reflected the reds and golds Nick had seen so often in tropical sunrises. Off to the north, Nick saw a huge bow wave as the *Farragut* steamed towards the bay. She fired her forward guns causing two huge geysers of water to spout on either side of the sub. He heard an airplane close at hand. Looking overhead Nick saw the floatplane line up for another run at the sub. But by the time the plane got within range, the bullets struck empty water. The sub had slipped beneath the waves leaving almost no trace.

Chapter Thirty-Six

0653 hours, 31 December 1936
Vatia Bay, American Samoa

"Over here!" Nick yelled and waved at the *Farragut's* launch. The small boat had been tooling back and forth across the bay picking up men from the water. The coxswain saw Nick and turned the boat towards him.

The launch stopped next to Nick and one of two armed sailors asked, "Who are you?"

"I'm Midshipman Grant. Give me a hand up, will you?"

Once aboard, Nick saw two sailors, armed with Tommy guns, warily watching a group of eight dripping wet Japanese sailors.

Nick asked one of the armed sailors. "What's going to happen to these Japanese sailors, Petty Officer?"

"I haven't the faintest, Mr. Grant. The XO said to round them up and bring 'em back to the *Farragut*."

The eight Japanese sailors sat looking very dejected. Nick thought a moment and then said in his halting Japanese, "Honored sailors of the Japanese Empire, you will not be harmed."

At that point two men jumped overboard and dove deep. The coxswain at the tiller said, "What'd they do that for? Ain't no one gonna hurt them. Captain said to rescue 'em — not shoot 'em."

Nick looked at the helmsman. "Petty Officer, perhaps the Tommy guns gave them other ideas."

"Mister Grant, Captain also said to keep a sharp eye, as they was interlopers. Whatever the heck that means."

The helmsman slowed and coasted in circles as they searched in vain for the two missing Japanese sailors. Sadly, they found no trace. Nick wondered if their *Bushido* – or warrior code – forbade them to surrender. He must remember to ask Mr. Nieshe when he returned to Alameda.

When the launch pulled up alongside the *Farragut,* Nick called up to the deck. "We've got rescued Japanese sailors aboard."

A voice Nick recognized as Ensign Bill Jones called down, "Anyone speak Japanese?"

Nick called back, "A little, Bill."

"Nick Grant? The whole island is looking for you. What are you doing here?"

Nick considered where to start. "It's a long story. I'll tell you later. What about these Japanese sailors?"

"I've got the marine detachment here to escort them. Send them up."

Nick instructed the Japanese sailors to board the ship and waited. After the last sailor had climbed the rope ladder, Nick asked. "What about you, coxswain?"

"We're headed back out to pick up more swimmers, sir."

"Right. Please keep a look out for three Samoans who helped stop that Japanese sub."

"Will do, sir. Cast off aft!"

On deck, Nick saluted the Stars and Stripes fluttering in the morning breeze, then the bridge. His former cabinmate, Ensign Jones, met him at the rail and handed him a blanket. "Nick, what were you thinking?"

Nick wrapped the blanket around what remained of his sodden uniform. "What do you mean, Bill?"

Two marines stepped up and stood on either side of Nick. "Hey, what's going on?"

A worried look came over Jones' face and he leaned in. "Captain said you were to be confined to your cabin until we reach the harbor. These marines will guard your door. After we dock, they will escort you to the station commander's office."

"Why? Am I under charges?"

Jones nodded. "I'm sorry, Nick. Orders." He looked away sheepishly.

Nick clenched his fists. "Why not the ship's brig, Bill. Tell me that!"

Jones lowered his voice. "Nick, the Navy doesn't put officers in the brig aboard ship."

The energy drained out of Nick and he felt as if he might collapse. Bill sized him up. "After you shower and clean up, you can borrow one of my sweat suits. I'd loan you a uniform but you're way too tall to fit into my kit."

"Thanks, Bill." He glanced at the Marine lance corporal. "Lead on, McDuff."

The lance corporal tensed, "It's O'Rourke, sir."

"Of course it is." Nick sighed. "Now will you lead or shall I. I'd like to get into some dry clothes."

At the cabin, the marines took up station at each side of the door. Nick shook his head, "Is this really necessary, O'Rourke? It's not like I'm going to jump overboard."

"No offense, Mr. Grant. Orders is orders."

"Orders, huh?"

"Yes, sir. You mind telling me what you did with Cayse? Is he also out there in the bay?"

"No, Corporal O'Rourke. Cayse went back overland with a wounded Samoan. My guess is he's at the base."

"Thank you, sir. Let me know if you need anything. We'll be right outside the door."

Nick closed the door and stripped off his dripping trousers, skivvies, and socks and jumped into the shower. At first, the warm water invigorated Nick. He showered, located Bill's sweats, and flopped into his old rack. In seconds he was asleep.

He awoke to a gentle shaking. "Nick, wake up. We've made port."

Nick rolled over and saw Bill Jones. "My God, do I have a headache. Don't suppose you've got any headache powder?"

Bill opened a desk drawer and handed Nick a bottle of pills. "Here."

"What are these?"

"They're aspirin tablets. Better than headache powders and easier to take. Put two in the middle of your tongue and swallow."

Nick opened the bottle, did as instructed, and handed the bottle back to Bill.

"How long was I asleep, Bill?"

"About three hours."

"Feels more like five minutes. My head feels like it's been stuffed with cotton."

Jones handed Nick a pair of shower shoes. "I'd loan you my shoes but not with the size of those feet. Come on. The captain is waiting to escort you to the Naval Commander's Office."

On deck the morning sun stung Nick's eyes. He shaded his eyes and looked around the harbor. There, moored to the Rainmaker Hotel Jetty, was a Sikorski S-42B flying boat in Pan American Airways livery. "Wow, when did the clipper arrive, Bill?"

"Early this morning. Captain Musick and crew are staying at the Rainmaker Hotel while mechanics check out the clipper. They're off to New Zealand tomorrow."

Nick looked longingly at the flying boat. He had qualified as a flight engineer last spring and knew the airplane inside and out. "I know Captain Musick and I'd love to get a chance to speak with him."

At the gangplank, Captain Hutson stood with two marines. "There you are Grant. Good heavens man, you can't go before a captain's mast dressed in a sweat suit."

"Sorry, Captain, my uniforms are at the BOQ. The one I wore last night is torn to ribbons. That is, what's left of it."

Hutson eyed Jones. "Ensign, take Mr. Grant to the BOQ and make sure he's properly dressed for the occasion. Can't have a man up on charges appear dressed as a scallywag."

Bill saluted, "Aye-aye, sir."

Hutson eyed Nick and shook his head, "And take the marines with you."

*   *   *

196

1244 hours, 31 December 1936
United States Naval Station Tutuila,
American Samoa

Dressed in khakis and sporting a tie, Nick sat in the sweltering hall outside the commander's conference room. Two armed marines stood at parade rest across from him. Commander Hutson and the *Farragut's* XO had entered the room 40 minutes ago. Nick wondered what was taking so long when the door opened.

A petty officer looked at Nick, "Midshipman Grant, please come in and report to the board of inquiry."

Nick stood, straightened his uniform, and entered the room. Instead of a long table surrounded by chairs at the center of the room, there was a table at the far end. Behind it, and in the center, sat Captain Milne. To his left sat Lieutenant Walker, and on Walker's left sat Lieutenant Harris. Off to the right of Milne sat two other officers Nick did not recognize. One, an ensign, wore the gold wings of a naval aviator on his uniform. The ensign noticed Nick's glance and nodded, one aviator to another.

Nick stopped in front of Milne, saluted, and said, "Midshipman Grant reporting, sir."

Milne picked up a gavel and banged on the table. "At ease, Grant. The board of inquiry on the actions of Midshipman Nicholas P. Grant, on temporary assignment to United States Naval Station Tutuila, is convened. Lieutenant Walker will now read the charges."

Walker stood, paper in hand. He glanced briefly at Nick before he began. "Midshipman Grant, you are charged with deserting your post without leave, disobeying direct verbal and written orders, endangering the lives of American Samoan residents, and endangering the life of a member of the United States Marine Corps. Finally, you are charged with endangering the lives of government contractors who are also United States citizens."

Walker looked up at Nick and asked. "Do you understand the charges against you?"

"Yes but — "

Milne banged the gavel. "Defendant will answer the questions succinctly and speak only when directed."

Nick bowed his head. "Yes, sir."

"Defendant may be seated."

Nick sat in the hardbacked wooden chair that faced the board officers.

197

Milne referred to papers on his desk. "Lieutenant Walker will now take the stand."

Harris and Walker moved from behind the table and stood in front of the chair next to Nick's. Walker raised his right hand and placed his left on a Bible in Harris' hand.

Harris said. "Lieutenant Walker, do you swear to tell the truth, the whole truth, and nothing but the truth, so help you God?"

"I do." Walker lowered his hand.

Captain Milne said, "You may be seated." Then he said, "Please relay to the board your exact orders to Midshipman Grant on Sunday, the 27th of December."

"Yes, Captain. I told Grant to observe and report back any contact with Commander Miyazaki."

Milne looked over the top of his reading glasses. "And did he?"

"Yes, sir, he did."

"What else did he do on the night in question?"

Walker rubbed his chin, "We got word that Midshipman Grant had spotted the Japanese agent, Toshio Miyazaki. He then followed Miyazaki and his local companion."

Growing visibly agitated, Milne probed, "Did Mister Grant receive any orders to pursue the agent?"

"Yes, sir. I gave him those orders, Captain Milne."

"And how was it that Lance Corporal Cayse accompanied him?"

"I ordered Cayse to accompany him. I believed that Cayse might help keep Mr. Grant out of trouble."

Milne slammed his hand down on the table. "That did not turn out well, did it?"

Walker opened his mouth to reply but Milne cut him off. "Don't answer that. Now, we have an international incident. A Japanese sub landed men onto Tutuila Island, shelled a village, and attempted to kidnap an American Naval Officer! We have six Japanese sailors, and I don't know if I should treat them as prisoners or guests."

When Milne's tirade ended, Walker continued, "Yes, that is true, sir. But Nick disrupted a Japanese attempt to incite a revolution on American Samoa. With the help of three locals, he stopped the sub from inflicting further damage to the village of Vatia. And his actions aboard the submarine hastened their departure."

The Lieutenant, junior grade, seated at Milne's right spoke up. "Captain Milne, had Grant not attacked the heavy machine gun mount there was a pretty good chance that the sub would have shot the Seagull from the sky."

Milne turned to the young man. "That will be enough out of you, Lieutenant Johnson."

Johnson seemed to shrink in his seat. "Yes, sir."

Milne pointed his pencil at Nick. "Grant, what on Earth were you thinking. Your actions were rash and endangered many people." Milne glanced at Harris, "Swear in Mr. Grant, if you please, Mr. Harris."

Once that was done, Milne asked Nick, "What do you have to say for yourself, Mr. Grant?"

Standing, Nick cleared his throat. "Captain Milne, I understood my orders. But my Naval ROTC instructors stressed that Naval officers must always show initiative. When Miyazaki identified me in the crowd, he bolted. I had a choice, remain behind, and lose him or give chase. I reasoned that if I stayed on him, he might not be able to complete his assignment. So, I took the initiative and gave chase with Lance Corporal Cayse."

After Nick finished his tale, Captain Milne shook his head in disbelief. "It's a wonder you didn't get yourself killed."

"At times, I wondered that myself, sir. Miyazaki is a vicious killer, and I didn't want him loose on Tutuila." Nick lowered his eyes. "He has killed far too many so far."

Milne sat back in his chair, his fingers steepled. After a few minutes of thought he asked, "Does the board have any further questions?"

The officers replied no. Milne picked up his gavel. "Court is in recess for deliberations. Midshipman Grant is confined to the building pending my ruling." He slammed the gavel down. "Adjourned!"

Chapter Thirty-Seven

1435 hours, 31 December 1936
United States Naval Station Tutuila,
American Samoa

Nick paced the corridor, unable to sit still. The ceiling fans provided some movement to the stifling air, but his sweat had soaked through his uniform shirt. The marine guards had been dismissed and Nick was free to wander the building. Not that there was much to see. He glanced at his watch. The board had been deliberating for over an hour.

The conference room door opened, and the petty officer that had ushered him inside stepped out. As he passed, Nick asked, "Any word, Petty Officer?"

The petty officer stopped, looked up and down the corridor, then seeing no one else, spoke, "It's been pretty lively in there. Commander Hutson and the *Farragut's* XO argued for conviction on all counts, while Lieutenants Walker and Harris, and Lieutenant Johnson argue that you should be cleared and commended."

Nick nodded his thanks, "I figured a fellow aviator would be on my side, but Walker and Harris surprise me." Nick heard footsteps approaching from behind.

The petty officer glanced over Nick's shoulder and stiffened. "If that will be all, Mr. Grant, I must be on my way."

"Thanks, Petty Officer."

The petty officer winked and whispered, "Even the jarheads are rooting for you. Good luck." Then he turned and walked away.

Nick turned and saw Joe Cayse headed his way. "Hey, Lance Corporal Cayse. What are you doing here?"

"Hello, Mr. Grant." Cayse looked down, "Got to testify."

"Oh."

"Not my choice."

"Joe, tell it like it happened. No need to think twice. I'd do it again without hesitation. If the Navy thinks that was wrong, then I'm ready to accept the consequences."

"Even getting tossed out, sir?"

"Well, " Nick considered, "not that willing."

The conference room opened, and Lieutenant Walker stuck his head out. "There you are Lance Corporal. The board is waiting."

Cayse eyed Nick. "I'm sorry, Mr. Grant. But I'm betting on you. Got five-to-one odds with the marines."

Nick sighed and wondered if there was anyone on the island who didn't know about his predicament. Nick resumed his restless pacing.

After a while he sat down on the bench and closed his eyes. He awoke to a commotion in the hall. Rubbing the sleep from his eyes, he saw three locals walking toward him. Each wore a ceremonial sash hanging from their shoulders and crossing their bare chests. The most amazing thing Nick noted was the ornate head dress each wore. Two feet tall and festooned with red, blue, and white bird feathers, the head band was studded with highly polished seashells.

When they stopped in front of Nick, he recognized Loto. Loto stood in the middle flanked by two considerably older men. Loto grinned and embraced Nick. "We have come to give evidence at your trial."

Nick stepped back and eyed Loto. "Thank you, Loto. But it's not a trial. It's a board of review."

Loto's brow furrowed. "Does that mean that you are not in trouble?"

"Well, no…"

"Then let us proceed." Loto raised his heavy staff and banged on the door to the hearing room. When Walker opened the door, Loto said, "The three chiefs of the windward shore are here to give testimony."

Walker stepped back to allow them inside and closed the door. Nick stood and resumed his pacing. A few minutes later Cayse stepped out of the room. He called out, "Sorry, Mr. Grant, I'm not allowed to speak to you." Then he winked. "But I think I'm about to make a lot of money from my fellow jarheads." He turned on his heel and walked down the hall whistling a popular tune.

Nick's stomach growled and he wondered how much longer the board would meet. He was hungry and exhausted. He sat back on the bench and hung his head in his hands. Sometime later the petty officer acting as scribe shook his shoulder. "Mr. Grant, wake up, sir. The board has reconvened, and you are wanted inside."

Nick's eyes popped open, and he stood, glancing at his watch. He'd been out for thirty-five minutes.

The petty officer gestured, "This way, sir."

Inside the room, someone had provided chairs for the three chiefs who sat regally to one side of the board of inquiry. Nick stopped before Captain Milne and stood at attention.

Captain Milne said, "Lieutenant Walker, please read the board's findings."

Walker stood. "Midshipman Grant, US Naval Reserve, on temporary active duty, the board finds you not guilty on all counts due to extenuating circumstances." Walker sat down.

Captain Milne pointed a finger at Nick. "Grant, your actions were ill advised and foolhardy. I appreciate that you took the initiative and according to these fine gentlemen," he gestured at the three Samoan Chiefs, "your actions resulted in many lives saved. But let me give you a word of advice. This type of rogue behavior will not suit in the United States Navy. Discipline and following orders are essential to good order and winning against any foe. Do you understand, Midshipman Grant?"

A thousand thoughts flooded Nick's mind as he listened to Milne's words. But in the end, Nick decided to let it go. From his perspective, he was neither a hero nor guilty of any infractions.

Milne tapped the table. "Well, Mr. Grant? Do you understand what I've said?"

"Yes, sir. But I can't help but wonder what you would have done in my place?"

Milne glared at Nick as his face turned from a pasty white to a bright red. Nick was afraid that he was headed for a stroke. Walker stood, "Captain Milne is not before a board of review. You are." Walker turned to Captain Milne. "Sir, if we're done here, with your permission, I'll escort Midshipman Grant to his quarters."

His face a deep shade of red, Milne nodded, seemingly unable to find the words.

Outside, Walker stopped Nick. "What is wrong with you? Harris, Lieutenant Johnson and I stuck our necks out for you and then you are asking impertinent questions of the board president."

Nick frowned. "Impertinent? No sir, I genuinely wanted to know what Captain Milne would have done."

Walker put his head in his hands, then looked at Nick. "Didn't anybody ever tell you that there's a time and a place for things?"

Nick nodded, "Yes, sir. And what better place, with all the assembled knowledge in one room."

"Come on, Grant. Let's get you to your room. You must be beat."

"Now there's something we can both agree on."

At the doorway to the BOQ, Nick saw Cayse standing outside in the shade of the awning. Seeing Walker, he snapped to attention and executed a near perfect salute. Walker returned the salute and said, "As you were, Lance Corporal."

Clearly excited, Cayse asked, "Gentlemen, what was the verdict?"

Walker took a pack of cigarettes out of his shirt pocket, withdrew one and lighted it. He offered the pack around but both Cayse and Nick declined. Walker took a long drag and exhaled a cloud of smoke at the awning over their heads. "Grant got off on all counts. Your testimony combined with three windward side chiefs made the others realize how dangerous the situation was. After that Captain Milne wavered and then threw in with Lieutenant Harris, Lieutenant Johnson, and me."

Walker turned to Nick, "You did well, Nick, despite what Milne or anybody thought." He turned back to Cayse. "As did you, Cayse. I've recommended you to Commander Hutson for a promotion to Corporal and Captain Milne concurred. It's Commander Hutson's call, but I doubt he'll cross the Captain."

Cayse's goofy grin telegraphed his emotion. "Thanks, sir. I was expecting to wait another couple of years to even be considered."

Walker snubbed out his cigarette. "I'll leave you boys now. Grant, get some rest. Cayse, your excused until PT with the marines tomorrow at 0530."

Cayse snapped out a salute barely concealing a grin. "Yes, sir!"

After Walker had left, Nick said to Cayse, "I'm going to catch some zzs. What will you do with your free time?"

"First I'm going to collect my winnings. You made me a bundle, Mr. Grant. Five-to-one odds makes me flush."

Nick rubbed his tired eyes. The lids felt like sandpaper. "Maybe you should take the jarheads out for drinks at the enlisted men's club? Those boys might be pretty sore about your winnings."

Cayse rubbed his chin, "You know sir, for an almost officer, you're pretty smart. Gives a man confidence in our future leaders."

Were it not for the sardonic tone, Nick might have considered Cayse's words a compliment. But he knew better. "Yeah, right. Get out of here before I accuse you of being facetious."

"Facetious, sir? That's one of those college words, isn't it?"

Laughing, Nick replied, "Go get your blood money and watch your back. You know how marines can be…"

"Aye-aye, sir. See ya around." Cayse stood to attention and saluted. "It's been an honor, sir. Hope we can serve together again sometime."

Nick stood to attention and returned the salute. "The honor was mine, Corporal. I would very much like that. Goodbye."

Cayse lowered his hand, "Goodbye, sir." He turned and walked toward the marine barracks, once again whistling.

Chapter Thirty-Eight

1830 hours, 31 December 1936
BOQ, United States Naval Station Tutuila,
American Samoa,

Nick woke with a start. The desk fan creaked back and forth, blowing the hot humid air around his stuffy BOQ room. He glanced at his watch and realized that he had been sleeping for almost four hours. Then his stomach growled. He sat up, slipped on his shoes, and reached for his shirt, knotted his tie, and combed his disheveled hair. He took a quick look in the mirror, making sure that his gig line was straight. Satisfied, he grabbed his khaki garrison cap and walked out of the room.

The dining facility had closed at 1800 hours, so he decided to go to the officer's club and catch something to eat there. It was New Year's Eve and the club was hopping. It seemed as if every officer on base was in attendance. Over at a corner table, he noticed four men sitting in what had to be Pan American Airways uniforms. As he watched, Captain Ed Musick looked up and waved him over. "Grant, come join us."

A man Nick recognized as First Officer Fred Briggs grabbed a chair from another table and made room for Nick. Musick asked, "What will you have?"

"Dinner, I'm starved. It's good to see you, Captain Musick. You guys off on the survey flight to New Zealand?"

"Yes, we are. We plan to leave tomorrow morning — that is if the mechanics can get the ship back together again."

Nick picked up a menu just as the waitress arrived at the table. "I'll have a hamburger, french-fries and a salad."

The waitress wrote down his order then asked, "What do you want to drink, Hun?"

"I'll have a coke, thanks."

The four other men at the table chuckled and made rude comments. Briggs jabbed Nick playfully and said, "What? No beer for the conquering hero?"

Feeling a little self-conscious Nick replied, "I'm no hero, but no thanks. I don't drink alcohol."

Captain Musick's lips curled into a slight smile. "I understand Nick had a bout with some extraordinarily strong jungle juice back when he was working on Wake Island. That right, Nick?"

"Yes, and I don't think I'll ever live that story down."

The men around the table chuckled. Nick asked, "How's the S-42 doing? I understand it's been modified with huge fuel tanks where the passenger compartment should be."

Briggs replied, "It's more like a flying gas tank then an S-42. Sikorsky installed more powerful engines, or we'd never get the ship into the air fully fueled."

Nick nodded. "Once you're in the air, how does she handle?"

"She handles pretty good," Musick replied. "She wallows a bit for about the first two hours then settles down. Added baffles to the fuel tanks. Now the fuel doesn't slosh around too much."

Nick had an idea, "When will you be heading back to Hawaii?"

Musick continued, "We should be back in three days. Why?"

"Thought maybe I might be able to catch a ride with you boys back to Honolulu."

Musick thought for a moment. "It's okay with me if it's okay with the Navy. You are a Pan American Employee after all."

"Great, I'm guessing the Navy will be glad to be rid of me."

The waitress arrived with Nick's order, and he dug in.

*   *   *

After dinner, Nick said goodnight to the *Samoa Clipper* crew and headed out the gate toward the taxi stand. The sidewalk just outside the gate was crowded with local Samoans, sailors, and officers. There was a great deal of bartering occurring as street venders hawked their wares. As he walked by one stand, he noticed an older Samoan woman sitting behind a small table laid out with an assortment of gold and silver jewelry. There were rings, earrings, broaches, and pendants. The one that caught his eye was a gold crescent on a gold chain. He stopped to admire it.

The woman behind the table said, "You have good taste, young man. Go ahead, pick it up. Feel the weight of gold in that pendant."

"No thanks, I don't think I could afford it."

"You think that your girl on the mainland won't like it? I'll tell you that pendant is imbued with the mana of *Tangaroa-whakamau-ta,* the sea god of all the Polynesian peoples."

An odd feeling came over Nick. It was if he was drawn to the piece, "Well, I don't have a girl on the mainland and the one in Hawaii, I think she's had enough of me."

The old woman cocked her head, "Ah, then this is the perfect gift for her. For *Tangaroa-whakamau-ta* will heal her heart and bind you too together forever."

Nick dug for his wallet, "How much?"

With the pendant safely tucked into his pocket he approached the cab stand. Two beat-up old Model T Fords sat spewing black exhaust. One of the drivers, a Samoan man around forty, folded his paper and said, "Where to, admiral?"

Nick laughed, "I'll bet you say that to all the sailors?"

The cabbie smiled, "Hey, how'd you know?"

"Just lucky, I guess. Think this old heap will make it to the new dairy?"

"Maybe you better walk – you insult Betsy."

Nick frowned, "Who's Betsy?"

The cabby stepped out of the Model T, bowed, and opened the passenger door for Nick. "This classic automobile is Betsy. She was the first car on the island. Yes, sir. She landed with the Navy in 1918 during the Great War. But when the war ended most of the Navy pulled out. My daddy bought it as surplus. Ran real good for a while."

Nick got into the rear seat. "Then what happened?"

"Oh, nothing to Betsy. The only gasoline on the island was in the Navy Base. Gasoline didn't become available for the rest of the island until 1922. Betsy, she just sat there all patient like under a tarp for a couple of years." The cabbie engaged the gearshift and Betsy emitted a terrible grinding noise and leapt forward like a spurred horse. The cabbie shifted again, and Betsy settled into a solid fifteen miles-an-hour as it putt-putted around the bay.

When they came to the dairy, Betsy backfired a few times then seemed to settle into a low idle. The cabbie held out his hand. "That will be two dollars and fifty cents."

Nick paid the man and added a small tip, more than a little miffed at the outrageous price.

"Thanks, admiral. You gonna need a ride back?"

Nick considered walking back but decided he was too beat. "Yes, how will I contact you?"

"No problem, I'll wait right here?"

Suspicious, Nick asked, "What's the charge for waiting?"

The cabbie smiled, showing very few teeth, "For you, admiral, no charge."

Nick wondered what the cabbie would charge a local, probably a lot less than half. Wiser but a bit lighter in the wallet, he walked to the stable.

Shorty was grooming his mount when Nick entered. He looked up, "Howdy, Nick." Shorty spit tobacco juice on the stable floor. "Heard you had a run-in with the brass. Everything turnout okay?"

Nick removed his garrison cap and wiped sweat from his brow. "Where are the rest of the boys? I'd rather tell my tale of woe once to all of you."

Shorty shooed the horse back into his stall and closed the gate. "Sure thing, Nick." He spat again. "They're in the bunk house – if you could call it that. No real walls, just a roof."

Shorty led Nick out the side door and across to a large open-air building. Built in the island style, it had a pitched roof half again the height of the building itself. In the center Brian, Lesley, and Buck sat around a makeshift table of barrels and planks engrossed in a card game.

Brian frowned at his hand then looked up as Shorty and Nick ducked under the low roof line. "Nick! I thought the Navy threw you in the brig."

Nick reached out his hand. "Not this time, Brian." He smiled, "Maybe next time."

The cowboys put their cards down and gathered around Nick. Buck clapped Nick on the back. "Seems we spend a lot of time pulling your butt out of trouble. Glad you was able to do it all by yourself this time."

Brian pulled up a crate. "Have a seat, Nick, and tell us what happened."

Lesley said, "What's the matter, Brian? Lousy hand?"

"Yeah, that too."

Nick looked around at the men who had probably saved his life a time or two. He was glad to see that they were well and unharmed. "I wanted to thank you guys for helping me last night. I'm pretty sure you helped save a lot of Samoan lives. And at great personal risk. I don't know how I can ever repay you."

Shorty sat on his own crate looking at the floor. He looked up and chuckled. "Hell, Nick, that was the most fun I've had since we last saw you on Santa Clara Island." He looked around at the other cowboys. "What about you boys?"

They echoed Shorty's words and Brian asked. "What about you? Last we saw, you was headed out to the sub with those four Samoans."

Nick began his tale which lasted well into the night. Finally, when he had answered all the cowboys' questions, he got up to leave. "Not sure when I'm leaving, could be as early as a few days. Tomorrow I'm sitting in on the questioning of the Samoan you guys took to the naval infirmary. Doc says he'll make a complete recovery."

Nick frowned and bit back his emotions. "So, I'll say my goodbyes now. Don't know when we'll meet again but I look forward to it." He handed Brian an envelope. "Here's my address in Alameda and Leilani's address in Honolulu."

"You mean your island girl that was all over you on Santa Clara?"

"Well, Brian," Nick paused. He had been so wrapped up in his own concerns that he hadn't thought about her until this moment. He wondered if maybe she did deserve someone who could be there for her. He swallowed and continued. "I'm not sure she's still 'my girl'. She's having second thoughts. We're 2,000 miles apart and my life hasn't made it any easier."

Shorty clapped Nick on the back, "I'll say! Your life is way too complicated."

Buck extended his hand to Nick. "We don't say goodbye in our line of work. We say, *'adios amigo'* or, go with God my friend. And in your case, God needs to send you at least two guardian angels."

Nick could hear the cabbie snoring as he approached the ancient Model T Ford. Amazed that the cabbie had stuck around, Nick rapped on the hood. "Cabbie, wake up. Time to take me back to base."

The cabbie stretched and rubbed his bloodshot eyes. He walked to the front of the cab and hand cranked the engine. It sputtered to life, backfired twice then settled into its customary putt-putt. The cabbie took the wheel. "Well, admiral, don't just stand there. Let's go."

Chapter Thirty-Nine

1455 hours, Saturday, 2 January 1937
Aboard the Imperial Navy Submarine, I-23,
45 nautical miles west of Kiribati Island, Western Pacific

Commander Toshio Miyazaki stood on the bridge next to the submarine's XO. The wind whipping off the bow tugged at his cap. "Lieutenant, I want more speed."

The XO bowed, "Sorry, sir. We are at All-Ahead-Full now and making just over seventeen knots. But the strain on the diesels is terrific. I can't guarantee that we will be able to continue at this pace much longer."

"You will continue at full speed until I tell you different."

The XO bowed again. "Commander, if we blow an engine, we will be reduced to less than ten knots. I must advise that we reduce speed to spare the engines. And running on the surface in daylight is risky. Surely, the Americans will have search planes out looking for us?"

"Lieutenant, you are correct. But remember this, big ocean – small sub. Besides, they will be looking in the other direction. The Americans will look to the west, assuming we are running for Japan.

But our destination is to the north. We will stay on the surface, and at this speed, until I order otherwise." The XO bowed deeper this time. "Hai!" "XO, you have the con. I am going below. Steady as she goes." Miyazaki dropped through the conning tower hatch and used the ladder to reach the control room. "Chief, I will be in the wardroom. Send the communications yeoman to me there."

Miyazaki made his way aft, past the galley, to the small officer's mess, or the wardroom. There he took a seat at the cramped table and began to write out a message.

TOP SECRET
TO: IMPERIAL NAVAL INTELLIGENCE
ATTN: ADMIRAL NAOKUNI NOMORA
DTG: 0930Z02 JAN 37
SUBJECT: AMERICAN SAMOA SITREP

1. 50% OF OPERATIONAL OBJECTIVES MET.
    a. CONTACT ESTABLISHED WITH SAMOAN
    TRIBAL CHIEFS.
    b. US NAVAL BASE RECONNASONCE COMPLETE.
    c. ABLE TO EVADE CAPTURE BUT NOT
    DISCOVERY.
2. MISSION OBJECTIVES NOT MET
    a. ABILITY TO INCITE LOCAL UPRISING
    DELAYED. WHILE STILL POSSIBLE, WILL
    REQUIRE ADDITIONAL RESOURCES AND
    TIME.
    b. APPROXIMENTLY TEN SEAMAN LEFT
    BEHIND AND MAY BE AMERICAN PRISONERS.
    RECOMMEND DIPLOMATIC EFFORTS TO GAIN
    RELEASE. PLAUSIBLE DENIAL: SAILORS
    WASHED ASHORE DURING MANEUVERS.
3. CONCERNS
    a. AMERICANS ARE AWARE OF JAPAN'S
    INTEREST IN SAMOA. HOWEVER, THEY MAY
    NOT KNOW OUR INTENTIONS. ALL
    SAMOANS KNOWLEDGEABLE OF
    INSURRECTION OBJECTIVES ELIMINATED.
    b. AMERICAN OPERATIVE NICHOLAS
    GRANT WAS ON ISLAND AND MADE
    POSITIVE ID OF INJ OPERATIVE.
    COINCIDENCE?
    c. RECOMMEND REVIEW OF ALL
    INDIVIDUALS WITH KNOWLEDGE OF

OPERATION. DO WE HAVE A MOLE INSIDE
INJ INTELLIGENCE OPERATIONS?
4.   SECONDARY MISSION
  a. HEADED FOR RENDEZVOUS
  b. WILL REPORT UPON COMPLETION

FOR THE GLORY OF THE EMPEROR!

T. MIYAZAKI

There was a knock on the wardroom door frame. Miyazaki looked up. "What is it?"

A voice from behind the privacy curtain replied. "Commander, it is the yeoman. You sent for me?"

"Yes, come in."

The yeoman pulled back the curtain and stood at attention. Miyazaki handed his message to the sailor. "I want this encoded and transmitted immediately."

The yeoman took the hand-written note and read it through. "At once, sir." He turned and left Miyazaki alone with his thoughts.

Looking up at the chart hanging on the wall Miyazaki did a rough calculation. They would rendezvous with the Ruko Maru in five days off Oahu. Then he would lead the newest agents ashore and get them settled. It was too bad that Grant's path would not cross his for a while. He really needed to kill that troublesome teen.

*   *   *

4:55 p.m. January 2,1937
Porta Grounds, Manoa Heights
Oahu, Hawaii Territories

Leilani Porta put the LIFE magazine she had been reading on her lap and sighed. She glanced across the pool and then up at the tall cumulus clouds drifting overhead. She wondered where Nick was. Was he safe? Was he thinking of her?

Try as she might, the tall blond pilot, her *hoale* as she sometimes thought of Nick, kept intruding into her thoughts.

"Enough of that." She stood, adjusted her swimming suit, and dove into the blue water of the pool. She swam underwater to the far edge and surfaced. Then she pushed off and started an Australian

213

Crawl. She swam back and forth across the pool as fast as she could move her arms and legs until she was thoroughly exhausted.

Clinging on to the side in the deep end, Leilani saw Hanna appear through the French doors from the dining room. Dressed in a swimsuit she said, "Mind if I join you, dear? Or do you need more time to beat the pool into submission?"

Leilani looked up at her sister, "How long were you watching me?"

"Oh, about twenty minutes. I must ask, are you considering joining the US Olympic Team?"

Leilani aimed a splash at her sister who easily avoided the water. Hanna sat on the edge and dangled her feet into the pool. "You want to talk about it?"

Leilani shook her head.

"Since you're not going to try out for the Olympic swim team, I know that something else is eating at you. Tell me. I know you, sister, and I hate to see you like this. You've been moping around for days and that's not like you."

"Oh, Hanna, it the mainland, it's the university, it's the way many people look at me. It's as if they think I don't belong. That I'm an interloper. And they are right, I don't belong there." Leilani pulled herself out of the pool, stood under the poolside shower, then wrapped herself in a bath towel.

Hanna sat on a chaise lounge and patted the seat next to her. Leilani sat and leaned on her sister. "I love it here, Hanna, and I don't want to go back to the mainland. I've decided to transfer to the University of Hawaii."

Hanna sighed, "Have you told Nick?"

Leilani frowned "No, I'm afraid that we didn't part on good terms."

"Oh dear. Why didn't you tell me sooner?"

Leilani sat up, crossed her arms, and stared at her sister. "You're the one that said I should dump him."

"Hmm, did I? Can't say I remember."

"Back in San Diego, just before we flew to Mr. Hughes' airport."

Hanna avoided Leilani's eyes and put a finger to her chin. "Well, I might have said that dating a flyboy could be tiresome. But I think Nick's an exception. If he were a few years older I might have a go at him ..."

"Hanna! You wouldn't."

"I might …" Then Hanna began to laugh.

"What's so funny?"

Between laughs and gasping for air, Hanna replied, "You! Your reaction when I said I'd consider making a play for Nick. You still love him!"

Leilani thought for a moment, *do I?* As Hanna got herself under control, Leilani realized that she did. She was disappointed and angry at all the cancelled dates, the missed holidays, the no-notice departure on some God-forsaken errand. But deep down she still loved Nick. "I do Hanna, but I'm afraid I might have driven him off. I was really quite abrupt. God knows what he'll think when I tell him I'm not going back with him to the mainland."

Hanna smiled at her little sister. "Oh, girl, you have so much to learn about men."

"I do not," Leilani protested. Then she thought a moment and asked, "Like what?

Chapter Forty

0548 hours, 4 January 1937
Pago Pago Bay,
American Samoa,

The Pan American Airways *Samoan Clipper* swung from her mooring in the gentle breeze. Her silver sides glistened, reflecting the sun's early morning rays. Against the green backdrop of the Rainmaker Mountain, NC-16744 seemed to shimmer in the heat. Nick had a special place in his heart for the S-42 airliners. His first clipper flight had been on an S-42, the *Pan American Clipper* NR-823M. The NR denoted a research aircraft while NC denoted a commercial variant.

Nick admired her sleek lines. Unlike most contemporary air transports, most of her structural reinforcement was internal to the fuselage and the wing sitting atop the central mount. Mr. Sikorsky had told him that the parasol wing provided clearance for the four oversized propellers. Those oversized propellers, the radial engines embedded in the leading edge of the wing, and her streamlining made the S-42 Clippers fast and efficient. Only the Martin M-130 had more range than the S-42 and the Martin was much more difficult to fly.

Nick had spent a large portion of the evening pressing his very rumpled Pan Am uniform and the corresponding white shirt. It wasn't a good job, but he thought he might get by Captain Musick's preflight inspection. Flight Engineer Victor Wright walked up the jetty and stopped next to Nick. "What on earth did you do to that uniform?"

Nick sighed. "It spent the last few days smashed at the bottom of my sea bag."

Victor Wright lit a cigarette, took a drag, and then exhaled slowly, "You will be happy to know that since this is a survey flight, Captain Musick won't hold a uniform inspection this morning."

Nick sighed, "That's a relief." He looked at the assembled crew and counted seven men.

Captain Musick looked up from a sheaf of papers he was holding and nodded to Nick, "Glad you could make it, Grant."

"Thank you, Captain. I plan to work off my passage, like any good stow-a-way."

The crew chuckled at Nick's remark, then Musick said, "Okay, men, board the launch and let's get this show on the road. I want to reach Kingman Reef before dark." He held up the papers. "And there's a front moving in from the west that I don't want to tangle with."

The gray navy launch roared away from the jetty and pulled up alongside the S-42. Nick was the last to clamber aboard, somewhat inhibited by his large sea bag. Wright boarded before him, then turned back. "Hand me your sea bag, Nick."

Nick hoisted the bag up with a grunt. Wright grabbed the top of the bag and almost dropped it into the bay. "Say, what do you have in the bag, lead weights?"

Nick scrambled through the boarding hatch and retrieved his sea bag. "It's the service automatic, magazines, and web gear. Weighs a ton."

Wright stared at Nick. "What exactly did you need a pistol for?"

Nick smiled. "Would you believe me if I said that I was put in charge of hunting down a Japanese spy ring secretly landed on American Samoa?"

Wright removed his uniform hat and scratched his head. "No, can't say I would, Nick. Was it target practice or something like that?"

"Sure, Vic, of course. Who'd send a college freshman to chase down a spy ring?"

"You had me for a minute, there. Still there was that business in Pearl Harbor last year..."

"Oh, that. That was pretty stupid of me. Swimming with the sharks – I don't recommend it."

Wright clapped Nick on the shoulder. "Stow your gear in the crew rest compartment then come join me at the flight engineer station. You heard old Captain, by-the-book, Musick. Let's get this show on the road."

Nick opened a small locker under a crew rest bunk and saw it was empty. He swung the sea bag off his shoulder and placed it gently on the deck. Opening it, he took out a small velvet box and looked inside. The gold necklace was safely nestled in its velvet cradle with the gold chain wrapped around the pendant. The pendant was an open circle that remined Nick of a gentle wave. He hoped that Leilani would like it. He further hoped that she would see it as a peace offering. He loved her and couldn't think of life without her. He might have to give up his lifelong dream of a pilot's career, but he was determined to fight to keep her – no matter the cost.

"Nick!" he heard Vic Wright bellow from the flight deck. "Get your butt up here and lend a hand. Stow-a-ways have to work for their passage."

"Coming, Vic." Nick yelled back. He repacked the necklace, stowed his sea bag, and moved forward.

The engine start-up procedure was standard and only took a few minutes. Musick cast off from the buoy and taxied up and down the watery runway repeatedly. He ran the engines at maximum throttle before cutting the power, turning, and roaring back the way he came.

This struck Nick as odd. Musick was known for his cautious approach to flying and was once quoted as saying, "There are bold aviators and there are old aviators. However, there are no bold, old aviators."

Still this running up the engines repeatedly was out of character even for Musick. He turned to Wright and shouted over the engine's roar. "What's with the Captain?"

Wright leaned over and spoke into Nick's ear. "We lost an engine about two hours out on the ferry flight from Alameda to Honolulu. Musick braked the prop and continued at a reduced speed. Had we been closer to the mainland, he would have turned back."

"That must have been tense. If you'd lost another engine, you would have been in the drink."

218

"Don't you know it. Took the Honolulu maintenance crew five days to find and fix the problem. Since then, every time we get ready to take off, we go through this drill."

Nick nodded. "Better safe than sorry."

The clipper turned close to the end of the bay and Musick ordered, "Full take off power!"

Wright advanced the four throttles. "Nick, keep your eyes on number three's gauges. That's the engine that quit on us."

"Will do, Vic!"

The clipper gained speed across the smooth bay. She was heavily laden with sufficient fuel to make the 1,400-mile hop to the speck of land in the middle of the trackless Pacific Ocean known as Kingman Reef.

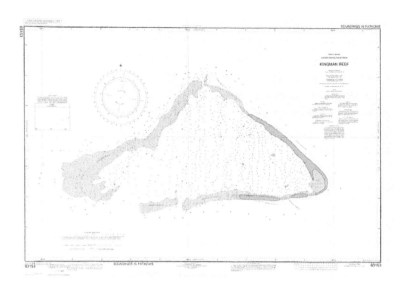

Chapter Forty-One

1423 hours, 4 January 1937
6°25′02.2″North, 162°26′43.8″West,
Pacific Ocean

Captain Musick leaned in between Nick and First Officer Briggs. "Frank, I'll relieve you for the landing. Nick, take the clipper while we change out."

Nick reached forward, placed his hands on the yoke and his feet on the rudder pedals. "I have the clipper."

Briggs unbuckled his harness and squeezed out of the left seat. Musick sat down, adjusted the seat to his liking, and buckled in. "Nick, we are about fifteen minutes out from splash down. Want to take her in?"

Nick smiled. "You bet." The thought of landing a twenty-six-ton flying boat in a tiny lagoon both thrilled and scared him. He'd brought numerous M-130s and S-42s into San Francisco Bay numerous times. He'd even rattled Captain Tilton's teeth a few times while training in *Myrtle*, the ancient, Consolidated Commodore borrowed from the South American Division. However, he had never attempted a landing in a tiny lagoon with a 6,000-ton freighter anchored in the middle. He hoped he didn't mess it up. Especially with the airline's chief pilot watching his every move.

Second Officer Harry Canaday, serving as navigator, handed Musick a three-by-five card with the new heading on it. Musick replaced the existing card. "Nick, bring the clipper to zero-nine-zero magnetic and reduce power to 60%."

Nick reached up between the seats to the cockpit ceiling and gently pulled the four engine throttles back. He watched the four tachometers mounted in the dashboard until they read 1,380 r.p.m., or 60% power. He shouted over the engine noise to the flight engineer station, "Vic, reducing to 60% power. Rich the mixture for optimum power."

Vic called back, "Done." Then he jokingly asked, "Since when do you get to give the orders?"

Musick replied. "Since I said so. Nick's going to take us in. Let's cut the crap and get serious."

Nick felt the clipper start a gentle decent and decided to set the flaps. He called out, "Airspeed ninety knots, altitude 2,500 feet and dropping. Flaps at 20%."

Stone-faced, Musick nodded then turned and spoke to Radio Officer Runnels, "Ray, signal the *North Wind* that we should be down shortly."

"On it, Captain."

Scanning the horizon, Nick searched for Kingman Reef land mass. According to the charts, it was only one hundred yards long and sixty yards wide. The land mass was less than the area of a football field. The light blue of the lagoon would be the first visible sign, then the outline of the ship. Flying the oceans as many times as he had, Nick knew that cloud shadows often appeared as islands and the true islands were extremely difficult to see with the naked eye. He hoped that Harry Canaday's navigation was up to Fred Noonan's standards. It would be a long swim to Honolulu, some 1,100 miles to the north.

Third Officer Morgan Holsenbeck was leaning over Nick's shoulder, peering out of the windshield. "Wait a minute. There! Look 15 degrees off the port bow. See it?"

Nick swept his eyes off to port. "I'm not seeing it, Morgan … Wait, wait … I see the lagoon."

Musick was looking through a pair of binoculars. "Yep, that's it – such as it is."

Nick adjusted his heading and nudged the throttles back a bit. "Setting flaps to 30%."

Again, no response from Musick.

The clipper gently lost altitude as Nick bled off speed. He decided to circle the lagoon once to get a sense of what the approach would be like. He pushed the throttles forward and leveled off at 200 feet. He banked to port and held the turn as they circled the tiny spit of land. "The water looks pretty tame. Ray, can you get a wind reading from the *North Wind*?"

A few seconds later, Ray announced. "Wind out of the east at eight knots."

"Okay," Nick said to himself. "That means a western approach." Nick ended his turn at 90 degrees magnetic and flew the clipper east on the downwind leg. At one minute out, he banked right to 270 degrees and lined up with the widest part of the lagoon. Easing back the throttles, he increased flaps to 50% and immediately felt the ship slow. Glancing at the angle-of-attack or AOA indicator, he was well within flight range and in no danger of an aerodynamic stall. "Ray, advise *North Haven* that we're on final approach."

The lagoon grew in Nick's view as he glanced at the AOA, his airspeed and altitude. Confident that he was on the glide slope, he concentrated on the view over the nose. He announced, "Airspeed 70 knots." Musick sat cross armed staring out the windscreen and occasionally checking airspeed. The lagoon rose slowly to meet the clipper and just before he touched, Nick flared into the landing.

Thump! The *Samoan Clipper* vibrated with the water's impact but soon settled into the lagoon. Nick reached up and advanced the throttles, heading the clipper toward the *North Wind* a little way in the distance.

Musick pointed off to starboard. "Head for the launch. The mooring buoy is hidden behind it."

"Aye-aye, Captain."

Musick frowned, "You can leave all that navy crap behind. A simple 'on it' or 'yes, sir' will suffice."

Nick eased engines three and four to idle and advanced one and two to 1,500 rpm. The clipper's nose swung gently to the right. "Yes, sir."

"That's better. I see you still remember how to use differential thrust."

Easing back on engines one and two Nick pointed the nose of the clipper, more-or-less, toward the approaching launch.

222

"That's good enough, Nick." Musick turned to Wright and ordered. "Finished with engines. Cut the power, Vic."

Wright bellowed back, "Aye-aye, Captain!"

Musick cracked a smile then added, "Smart ass. If you weren't such a good pilot, I'd can your ass."

Wright pulled off his headset and responded, "Does that mean I get a raise?"

The cockpit crew echoed in unison, "Not in your lifetime!"

As the launch drew near, Nick saw the unmistakable face of Dan Vucetich standing at the bow. Nick smiled, opened the side cockpit window, and waved.

Vucetich saw Nick, waved and yelled, "I haven't seen you since our time on Wake. Back then you were being hauled off the island for being underage. Now you're sitting in the First Officer's seat. Lord have mercy on us all!"

The launch bumped lightly against the fuselage and Canaday opened the forward cockpit hatch. The warm tropical air filled the cabin with the rich smell of the ocean. Flying between 8,000 and 10,000 feet AGL, the crew was wearing coats and sweaters against the high-altitude chill. Now everybody was madly pulling the heavy woolen garments off as fast as possible. One of the launch crew handed off a heavy line.

Musick eyed Nick. "Climb up on the top and secure the line to our forward cleat."

Dutifully, Nick shimmied onto the top of the fuselage and moved forward on his belly, holding the mooring line between his teeth. He secured it, crawled back, and dropped into the forward hatch.

Most of the crew was already in the launch. Briggs yelled from the bow, "Hurry up, Nick. Dinner's waiting."

Working his way through the cabin toward the crew rest compartment, he grabbed his sea bag and stepped into the launch. Vucetich engulfed Nick into a bear hug. "How's my favorite stow-a-way?"

Nick choked out, "Right now, having trouble breathing."

Chapter Forty-Two

From the fan tail, Nick watched as the *North Wind* crew secured the bow of the *Samoan Clipper* to the stern of the steamer. Musick stood next to Nick keenly watching every move. Once secured to the mooring buoy and the ship's stern, the crew began the refueling operation.

Joe Copeland, the chief mechanic on Kingman, and Vic Wright dragged heavy hoses over the fantail and down to the clipper floating below. The lagoon was as still as a duck pond, but the men were still extremely cautious. It would be easy to puncture the clipper's duraluminium skin or the rubber fuel lines.

Copeland stood and yelled. "Okay, start the pumps."

From the rear hold, Nick heard a small gasoline engine start up. The hose tensed as the fuel began to flow. Wright, sitting opposite Copeland, held the wing cap open and held a second fuel line in place. Nick turned to Musick. "How long will it take to top off the tanks?"

"Three maybe four hours. You'll get your turn out there, too."

"Great, I also have anchor watch. What time do you plan to push off tomorrow?"

"Breakfast at five-thirty – airborne by seven."

224

Nick frowned, "But that means only three hours sleep."

Musick smiled, "Welcome to the glamourous world of transoceanic airlines. You better get some food. You're on fueling duty in thirty minutes."

Below deck, the galley reminded Nick of the *North Haven's*. It was in the same location on the ship, the chow line was identical, heck even the support columns were in the same place. Nick grabbed a tray and loaded up his plate. There was steak, fresh fish, fried potatoes, and even some oranges. Over against the bulkhead Dan Vucetich sat drinking a cup of coffee. "Nick, come on over and sit a while."

An odd feeling swept over Nick. When he was young, he had a fever – his head felt stuffed and his hands felt enormous. While this feeling was not the same, it was the closest thing he'd felt since he was a child. He drifted over to the table and sat down.

Vucetich eyed him. "What is it, Nick? Don't tell me you're seasick?"

"No, it's weird. I feel like I'm reliving some part of my life. The ship, you, the clipper. It's a bit unsettling."

Vucetich put his coffee cup down. "Unsettling was watching you bring the *Samoan Clipper* into a perfect landing."

Nick picked up his fork then set it down. "It was far from perfect, or so Captain Musick says."

"Ed's a good egg. He wants everybody to fly like he does. Says it will save lives."

"That may be, Mr. Vucetich, but –"

"Hold on, Nick. You're a Pan American crewman. We're equals and it's long past time for you to call me Dan, or Dano."

Nick picked up his fork and played with the food on his plate. "Thank you, Mr. V – I mean Dano. Calling you by your first name is also kinda weird, too. It's like I'm experiencing a very lifelike dream. Yet, I know I'm awake."

Dano smiled and nodded. "I think you're experiencing *Déjà vu*."

"What the heck is day-sha-vue?"

"It's the feeling that you have lived through the present situation before."

Nodding, Nick picked up his fork. "Yeah, that's pretty much how I feel." His appetite returning, he speared a piece of fish and

225

popped into this mouth. "Wow! This fish is amazing. I've never tasted anything like it. What's it called?"

"We're calling it, Kingfish. Nobody knows for sure, even Dr. French, the site surgeon. He caught it this morning along with a whopping great tuna."

Nick speared another piece. "Well, whatever it's called. It's fantastic."

Vucetich stood, "I'm on fueling duty in ten minutes, but I'll look you up later. You can fill me in on what you've been up too since Wake."

Through a mouthful of steak, he replied, "Deal, but I also want to hear how your family is doing."

*   *   *

1421 Hours, 5 January 1937
21°05'02.2"North, 158°07'43.8"West,
Above the North Pacific Ocean

Victor Wright, sat in the first officer position and called out. "Nick, reduce power to 80% and rich mixture. We are descending."

At the flight engineer position, Nick responded, "On it, Vic." The roar of the four Pratt and Whitney Wasp engines eased a bit as Nick smoothly reduced power and increased the fuel to air mixture. "Done." It was a redundant response as Vic could easily see the four tachometers nestled in the dashboard between the two pilot positions. Still, that was the way Musick wanted it so, by the Skygod, that's the way it would be. Checking and rechecking was tedious, but Nick had to admit that it reduced mishaps. Mishaps that could lead to accidents.

He headed over the navigation table and peaked out of Canaday's porthole. In the distance he saw the unmistakable outline

226

of Dimond Head. Tracing the hill crest west, along the Ko'olau Range, located Manoa Valley. At this distance and angle, he could not make out the Porta House, but he knew it was there and soon he would face Leilani again. Cold sweat trickled down his back as he thought of what he would say to try to win her back. Funny, he thought, facing Miyazaki seemed easier by comparison.

Wright brought the *Samoan Clipper* in to a near perfect landing in the Middle Locke – even Musick said so. While taxiing to the Pearl City pier, Wright turned and eyeballed Nick, "See young whippersnapper, that's how it's done."

Never one to let a jib go unanswered, Nick shot back, "And how many times have you shot a landing in an S-42?"

Wright beamed, "This makes thirty."

Musick looked over from the left seat and stared at Wright. "Vic, does that include counting all the bounces from your earlier attempts? As I recall your third S-42 landing didn't go so well. As it was followed in quick succession with your fourth and fifth. I kept wondering when you were going to stick the landing."

The cockpit crew guffawed. Even Musick cracked a smile. "Less levity, gentlemen. More piloting if you please."

Wright maneuvered the clipper alongside the pier with an expertise born of much practice. "Finished with engines."

Dutifully Nick, cut the ignition switches to all four engines and quiet descended over the clipper. He opened the Flight Engineer Log and recorded the final entry. Since this was not a passenger or mail flight, no crowds or dignitaries awaited their arrival. Each crew member finished their assigned tasks, gathered their things, and headed for the terminal building. Finishing the log took a while and as Nick grabbed his sea bag, he realized he was the last one on board.

Mounting the rear passenger stairway, he stepped onto the boarding stairs placed by the ground crew. At the bottom of the stairs stood Leilani. The gentle breeze tousled her waist length brown hair revealing the suns highlights. Her long red muu-muu matched the red hibiscus tucked behind her ear. She saw him and smiled. "Aloha, Nick."

He flew down the stairs, dropped his sea bag, and wrapped his arms around her. Before she could object, he asked. "How's your royal highness today?"

She looked up into his eyes and smiled. "I am well, you crazy Haole. How about you? No new bullet holes in your chest?"

"No bullets holes but a big hole where my heart used to be. I couldn't stop thinking about you."

She hugged him tightly, "You'd better be thinking about me, flyboy, you'd better."

Nick opened the top of his sea bag. Reaching in, he removed the velvet box with the pendant. "Here, I got this for you in Samoa. The lady who made it said that it is imbued with the mana of *Tangaroa-whakamau-ta,* the sea god of all the Polynesian peoples."

Leilani opened the box and carefully removed the gold pendant and chain. "Nick, it's lovely. And the curve of the gold is shaped like a breaker on the beach." Then her eyes narrowed. "It must have cost the earth. Where did you get the money?"

"Leilani, it's a long story. What say I buy you dinner and I'll tell you all about it?"

"I'm not still mad at you but yes." She reached into her purse and retrieved a small oblong box wrapped in Christmas paper. "Here, this is for you, *Mele Kalikimaka.*"

Nick tore of the wrapping and opened the box and gapped open mouthed. "Leilani, it's the Hamilton Aviator! It the wristwatch every pilot dreams of owning. Thank you so much!" He eyed her, "Does this mean you're still my girl?"

"Possibly." That impish grin had returned to her face.

"Did you drive the Cord?"

"Yes. Don't even think about it. I'm driving."

Nick took her hand and walked toward the terminal building. "As long as I'm with you, Princess, I'm as happy as a clam.

The End

Learn more about Nick's world online at
www.nickgrantadventures.com

All of Nick Grant Adventure novels are available at Amazon.com and at: *www.jamiedodsonbooks.com*

List of Illustrations
Cover Art: *Pan American Clipper over Tahiti*, by Ron Cole
WWW.RONCOLE.NET.

	Description	Owner	Permission
Chapter One	JN-4 S	Public Domain	
Chapter Two	Grant House	Public Domain	
Chapter Three	IJN Intel HQ	Public Domain	
Chapter Four	S.S. Aladdin in fog	Ian Marshall Jr	Granted with acknowledgment
Chapter Five	Stevens Hall	Public Domain	
Chapter Six	Alameda Street Scene	Public Domain	
Chapter Seven	Mac's Truck	Jamie Dodson	
Chapter Eight	IJH I-23 Sub pencil	Public Domain	
Chapter Nine	UC Berkley	Public Domain	
Chapter Ten	S.S. Aladdin	Ian Marshall Jr	Granted with acknowledgment
Chapter Eleven	Alameda Clipper Base	Jamie Dodson	
Chapter Twelve	Philippine Clipper	Jamie Dodson	
Chapter Thirteen	Clipper at Pearl City	Jamie Dodson	
Chapter Fourteen	Clipper at Pearl City	Jamie Dodson	
Chapter Fifteen	Naval Security Group Activity (NSGA),		
Pearl Harbor began	Public Domain		
Chapter Sixteen	Porta's Home	Public Domain	
Chapter Seventeen	US NAVY Staff Car	Jamie Dodson	
Chapter Eighteen	USS Farragut DD 348	Public Domain	
Chapter Nineteen	DD-348 USS Faragut	Public Domain	
Chapter Twenty	Wardroom DD 348	Public Domain	
Chapter Twenty-One	HQ Building	Public Domain	
Chapter Twenty-Two	HQ Building	Public Domain	
Chapter Twenty-Three	Tutula Island Map	Public Domain	
Chapter Twenty-Four	Bay Road, Pago Pago	Public Domain	
Chapter Twenty-Five	Tutuia Bay	Public Domain	
Chapter Twenty-Six	Samoan Celebration	Public Domain	
Chapter Twenty-Seven	Rainbow Mtn Trail	Public Domain	
Chapter Twenty-Eight	Vitia Bay	Public Domain	
Chapter Twenty-Nine	IJN Rubber Boat	Public Domain	
Chapter Thirty	Cowboy	David Rogers	Granted with

			acknowledgment
Chapter Thirty- One	Seagull		Public Domain
Chapter Thirty-Two	Submarine I-23	Jamie Dodson	
Chapter Thirty-Three	Seagull	Public Domain	
Chapter Thirty-Four	Cowboy	Jamie Dodson	
Chapter Thirty-Five	USS Farragut	Public Domain	
Chapter Thirty-Six	IJN I-23	Public Domain	
Chapter Thirty-Seven	Farragut Launch	Jamie Dodson	
Chapter Thirty-Eight	HQ Building	Public Domain	
Chapter Thirty-Nine	Ford Model T	Jamie Dodson	
Chapter Forty	INJ I-21 CiC	Jamie Dodson	
Chapter Forty-One	S-42B Pago Pago	Ian Marshall Jr	Granted with acknowledgment
Chapter Forty-Two	Kingman Atoll Chart	Public Domain	
	S-42 at Pearl City	Ian Marshall Jr	Granted with acknowledgment

230

25356672R00128